HOLLYWOOD, ENDING

ALSO BY
JOHN GREEN

FICTION

Looking for Alaska

An Abundance of Katherines

Paper Towns

The Fault in Our Stars

Turtles All the Way Down

NONFICTION

The Anthropocene Reviewed:
Essays on a Human-Centered Planet

Everything Is Tuberculosis:
The History and Persistence of Our Deadliest Infection

HOLLYWOOD, ENDING

JOHN GREEN

DUTTON BOOKS

DUTTON BOOKS
An imprint of Penguin Random House LLC
1745 Broadway, New York, NY 10019
penguinrandomhouse.com

Edited by Julie Strauss-Gabel
Design by Anna Booth
Text set in Adobe Caslon Pro Regular

Library of Congress Cataloging-in-Publication Data is available.

First published by Dutton Books, 2026

Manufactured in the United States of America
LSCH

ISBN 9780525426073
1st Printing

The authorized representative in the EU for product safety and compliance is Penguin Random House Ireland, Morrison Chambers, 32 Nassau Street, Dublin D02 YH68, Ireland, https://eu-contact.penguin.ie.

To Elyse Marshall Pfeiffer

HOLLYWOOD ENDING

2019

PART 1

THE SHOOT

JUNIPER

1

When I got the news that Matthew Malone wished to make my acquaintance, I was rereading the script for *Andy Warhol Never Gets Old* in a bare-walled apartment the studio had rented for me. Matthew, I was told, wanted to meet in the lobby of his hotel. We'd all just moved to Pittsburgh, a city not known for its hotels, but Matthew had found the good one, of course. So I took an Uber there, pounding Altoids the whole way, thinking about what I'd say to the one and only Matthew Malone, who was playing Warhol in the movie. Matthew and I had exchanged phone calls and a couple of text messages, but my friends all wanted to know what he smelled like, how he walked, what kind of emotion his eyes held, whether or not he was a typical Pisces, and so on.

The first time we talked, a few months after my mother died, he called me and said, "I'm so excited to work with you on this," and I said, "Me too," and then he said, "I know you've been crossing through a hard time, and I'm sorry." What a phrase. *Crossing through a hard time.* I was indeed crossing through a hard time.

In the first weeks after Mom died, I mostly felt relief that it was over. I felt like I was coming up for air after a long time underwater. But eventually, I learned that it was not, in fact, over. The dead are not in the past, not really, because you carry them around with you.

When I got to the hotel, I walked into the lobby—absurd chandelier, abstract paintings with flashes of neon. I scanned the room for Matthew, but didn't see him. I noticed instead a beautiful boy—slight, unstyled brown hair, impish green eyes—slumped into a semicircular couch. He was writing in a Moleskine notebook. He looked—I don't know how else to say it—like a movie star. I am attractive in a way gossip blogs sometimes call *interesting* or *surprising*. I have a slight overbite. My eyes are just a bit too far apart. I have a face built for the screen: an expressive but not particularly symmetrical one. This boy, though, in his fitted black jeans and his baby-blue button-down shirt, almost seemed to have a visible aura. Plenty of people are attractive. Precious few are genuinely magnetic. I wanted to buy stock in him immediately, even having never seen his acting. I took a few steps toward him and managed to say, "You must be Kai."

He looked up from his notebook. He was chewing gum, and he smiled shyless and broadly as he removed AirPods from his ears. "Juniper," he said, as if we'd known each other for years. He stood, and offered me a hand. I shook. Stronger than I expected.

Not long before, I'd gotten out of a relationship, except I hadn't *gotten* out of it so much as I'd been cast out of it, like a fallen maiden cast out of the church's good graces. On the dude's way out, he'd told me there's a word to describe what I felt for him—that the word isn't *love* or *lust* but *limerence*, a state of involuntary obsession. I was twenty-two. He was thirty-six. He'd been the cinematographer on my last movie, which had sort of flopped, and now he was moving on to the next one.

After the movie did a paltry seven million dollars in its opening weekend, I had nothing lined up, so I enrolled in college and took a course in modernist literature and art. I kind of suspected my life as an actor could be over, but then along came Matthew Malone to save me.

If there had been room in my life for new limerence, I might have started to feel it toward Kai in that hotel lobby, but I'd learned that true love cannot coexist with true ambition. I was not looking to get laid on the set of *Andy Warhol Never Gets Old*. I was looking to do my job well enough that I became undeniable, that I ceased to be, as the phrase turns, *a former child star* and became something else.

"Is that your character notebook?" I asked.

"This? Oh, yeah, no. This is just, like, a sketch pad, I guess. I just draw. You keep one?"

Always. Even when I played the daughter of the Guy Who Didn't Do It on a network procedural, I found a way to make her worthy of a hundred pages of notes. The less serious your job, the more seriously you must take it. "Yeah," I said.

"I read you're like that," he said. "Not quite method, but pretty hardcore, right?"

"I guess," I said. Fucking hell he was handsome, especially standing now, back straight, plenty tall enough for me.

I just looked at him for a minute, let my eyes settle on his. "You're very comfortable with eye contact," he said.

"Part of the job," I answered, my eyes still on him. At last he laughed a little and glanced away.

"I'm glad one of us is fearless," he said. "I'm fucking terrified."

"Of what?"

He listed the reasons, counting them out on his long, thin fingers. "Fucking up my lines, not being able to forget about the camera, not being able to share a screen with Matthew Fucking Malone. I'm scared that I'll look scared. I only ever went on a movie set once before and that was as a PA. I got fired after one week."

About these things, I *was* without fear. I'd been on sets since I was six. Most comfortable way for me to live, really. When I wasn't shooting or promoting something, I didn't know what time to wake up or how to meet people or what to eat. On set, all of those questions are answered for you.

"You'll do great," I said. "What were you drawing?"

"Um," he said. "You, actually. Since he's trying to fathom you and everything. Jude, I mean." He opened his notebook and showed me the loveliest little line drawing of me on the red carpet for the premiere of my last movie. In his rendering, you could hardly see my face through my hair, and my dress cascaded down to my ankles.

"That's so nice, Kai. Really. Also, that's a really important picture."

"Oh yeah?"

"Yeah, I wore open-toed shoes to that premiere and someone put the pictures up on WikiFeet, so I have the great honor of a WikiFeet page all to myself."

He laughed. "What the fuck is WikiFeet?"

I heard a voice just behind me say, "A website where foot and toe enthusiasts rate celebrity feet. I'm a 4.6." It was Matthew, of course. "Out of five," he added after a beat.

Skin pale. Hair black. All shadows and angles, his eyes furiously vital. He looked more like Warhol than I expected, the thin face and pronounced cheekbones, like even before the shoot he was becoming his character. He hugged me, then Kai. He held Kai by the shoulders for a moment, then turned to me, then back to Kai. "I used to be twenty-one," he said.

He said it like being twenty-one was a debilitating illness you only sometimes survived, which had more or less been my experience.

2

Matthew brought us up to his penthouse suite in the hotel, which featured a view of Pittsburgh's skyline and the Allegheny River. Our director, Kathryn Johnson—tall but still wore heels, blond hair cut into a bob—was there, and Matthew poured everyone champagne, except he'd bought sparkling grape juice for me because he knew that I didn't drink. Of course he knew.

After a while, we sat down on a huge U-shaped couch, where Matthew and Kathryn started talking about Andy. Kai, sitting next to me, asked, "What do you know about Carly?"

I liked that Kai put it that way. Directors often ask, *What's your thought process here*, or *What's your impulse*, because they don't want to accept that you, a mere actor, might know the character in a way no one else can.

"She's self-destructive," I said, "but she's also dedicated. She knows you have to want it worse than everyone else. What do you know about him?" I asked. Kai's character, Jude, was an intern for Andy at *Interview* magazine.

"I think he would rather feel almost anything than feel alone," Kai answered. I had expected Kai to be a sort of a standard Hollywood Guy, but in that moment I knew I was dealing with something else entirely.

"Yeah," I said finally.

Next to us, Matthew Malone was talking. "Every industry is in the business of eating human time and consciousness and shitting out money, but in Hollywood, they're not using your labor to turn iron into steel or whatever; they're using your labor to turn *you* into something. They're turning you into movie tickets or Netflix subscriptions. You're not just the labor; you're also the raw material."

I pulled out the little notebook I always kept with me and wrote.

> *Not just the labor but also the raw material. Like that for Carly as well. Women are often seen as A Thing That Will Transform Him, A Thing He Must Save to Become His Full Self. How thrilling to meet someone like Andy, who wants things from you but not those things.*

Matthew was still talking, and I was enthralled. This comic book actor obviously thought so deeply about craft, about the relationship between art and the artist, and how strange that relationship becomes when your own body is both your canvas and your paint. "Warhol was fascinated and repulsed by his own humanity," he was saying. "Fascinated and repulsed by feeling *in extremis*. And that is my point of connection with him."

After Matthew ordered room service, Kathryn had us watch an old Alfred Hitchcock movie called *Vertigo*. Matthew told us all about the movie's star, Jimmy Stewart, who was already a celebrity when World War II broke out but insisted on signing up for the most dangerous form of combat duty in the European Theater—flying B-24 bombers over Nazi-controlled territory. "I've been thinking a lot about Stewart in preparing for this role," he told us. "What was it like for him being a public figure in a setting like a crowded barracks? How strange it must've been for someone like Andy Warhol to be in a hospital bed, without his wigs, without his clothing, getting gallbladder surgery. Fame is a kind of armor, and you need the armor to survive fame. What does it look like to refashion yourself into a normal person, like Stewart was willing to do but Warhol never was?"

"What does it mean to adhere to the true self?" Kathryn added.

"Warhol was making himself the whole time. That was the real art project. The constant construction of the self."

I felt lucky just to be in this sprawling hotel suite where Kathryn had pulled all the shades so we could see the movie in a manner befitting its purported greatness, a room where Matthew Malone said things like "the constant construction of the self." What a job for actors, or for anyone, to construct selves. Kai was sitting next to me, close enough that I could smell his skin. He was as silent as I was, taking in the surreality of being in Matthew Malone's suite with promising young filmmaker Kathryn Johnson. Like, what lottery had we won?

Vertigo felt, well, vertiginous. I kept thinking about the class I'd taken, Modernism at Night, which explored how modernist writers and artists captured nighttime. How do you paint night when it is essentially invisible? How do you display, or articulate, what can't be seen or heard or smelled or felt? In the class, we'd read Gertrude Stein and Jean Toomer and looked at paintings by Jean-François Millet and Anita Malfatti and J. M. W. Turner. I loved college, but I also knew that Hollywood forgets about you quickly. In my business, when your last project is *An A- in a Class at UCLA*, that's a sign of weakening demand for your face. There'd be time for school when the Industry retired me.

Kathryn kept pausing the film to point out this Jungian metaphor or that innovative shot. But I was mostly watching the actors, especially Kim Novak, who plays two different women in the film who are intended to be mirrors of each other, and whose personalities are quite different even as their appearances are obviously similar. It was fascinating to watch a film where the male protagonist is trying to destroy the individuality of a woman but never quite manages to. For Novak, it was a complicated trick to pull off, and I was disappointed to learn that she wasn't even nominated for an Oscar. Never been easy to be a Bright Young Thing in Hollywood.

It was past midnight when the party broke up. Kai and I shared an Uber back to our building. "Do you want a quiet day before rehearsals or a busy one?" he asked.

"Quiet, I think. I might try to find some art, or go to a record store to buy some album covers. I need something on the walls of my apartment. Right now it's too depressing."

He opened up his backpack, reached in, and found his notebook. He carefully tore out the page containing his sketch of me and said, "Here's a start."

3

I ended up buying a bunch of records from a three-dollar bin in a massive record shop in Squirrel Hill and got some frames to go with them. I got some posters, too, for bands I'd never even heard of—Michael and the Argonauts, The Bitter Pill—and put them up around the apartment. The walls felt slightly less oppressive afterward. I took a nap. I wrote in my notebook. My quiet afternoon reminded me of being a kid with my mom and my brother, how we'd kill time by playing this game we called "advanced charades" where you'd try to get someone to guess a movie by silently acting as one of the characters. Hero Walk just so, with your shoulders back and a slight slouch in your legs, and Mom might correctly guess *Reservoir Dogs*. I remembered once my brother extended his arm out from his face like an elephant's trunk and made himself seem so light, up on his tiptoes, like something was pulling him up into the air, and even though Mom and I both knew it was *Dumbo*, we didn't say anything, because we were so astonished by him. He's a nursing student now in Dallas.

I then scrolled Instagram for a while and posted a picture I'd taken with Kai. I tagged him and went through his posts. There were only a few pictures from the past year, all in New York City with friends. No one person was consistently with him, which made me think he either didn't have a romantic partner or didn't want Instagram to know about them.

My posts over the last year had been calibrated to counter any child-star narratives. No late-night party pics. No nostalgic looks back at the good old days, or pictures with my old costars. I got fewer likes than before, but I was building a different kind of credibility with an eye toward being a grown-up actor. Of course, after six years on a show about a child talent agency run by teenagers—once called "an insufferable cacophony of earnest cringe" by *Time Out New York*—a refined Instagram refresh didn't do much to distance me from the character I'd played for so long. But I don't mind being conflated with the girl from that show. I *am* earnest. Irony bores me. And "cringe" is what people who can't feel things call feelings.

I was still scrolling when I got a text from Kai. *How are the apartment walls?*

I sent him a picture that had his drawing in it. *Slightly less depressing. How's your place?*

He sent me back a picture of his wall. Every inch was covered with tacked-up Warhol prints. *Just staring at this wondering if they're gonna fire me tomorrow.*

You want to run lines?

Sure.

So he came over to my apartment. He lay on my couch and I sprawled across the adjacent leather love seat. We ran the first three days' worth of scenes together. He was nervous that night even without the cameras.

"It's all so pretentious," he complained at one point. I'd just taken a pizza out of the oven and he was absolutely demolishing it. "How am I supposed to sound real while also saying, 'What we need, dear, are new words for the old prayers'? Who talks like that?"

"But you don't have to sound real to life," I said. "You only have to sound real to the movie. That's what my acting coach always says. 'Don't be real. Be real to the material.' Anyway, you know this guy. Maybe you don't know his particular trauma, maybe you've never interned at a magazine or lived through 1986 or been abused by your parents, but I'd guess those sad eyes of yours have seen plenty of what Jude has seen."

"I . . . just, the only way for me to get to the really intense stuff, like that scene where he confesses everything to you about his brother's death and his parents and everything, the only way I can get into that stuff is by thinking about the worst thing that ever happened to me, which I'm not looking forward to."

"Your approach is that personal, huh?"

"Yeah," he said. "Yeah. Anyway, what was your childhood like?"

"That's abrupt."

"What you said was good. I'm not gonna be real. I'm gonna be real to the material. So we're moving on."

"To my childhood."

"Yes."

"My childhood was . . . public."

"I never saw that show you were in. The only thing I knew about you growing up is when you had to, like, fire your mother or something? That was in the news at some point. Because she stole your money or something."

"Yes, or something. She's dead now, so I got some of the money back."

"I'm not sure whether to say I'm sorry."

"And I'm not sure whether to be sorry." Deep down, acting is listening. Good actors tend to be good listeners, too, good enough—for example—to know that when someone changes a topic so abruptly, they're dodging something specific. But to act isn't to pry, only to be willing to listen more. "How was *your* childhood?"

"Private. I grew up in Indianapolis. My mom teaches English. My dad sells dental supplies and loves race cars. I turned out to be bad at reading and driving, so I was a slight disappointment."

"Look at you now. In a proper Hollywood movie at the age of just, what are you, twenty-one?"

"Yeah. I keep thinking, 'Is this the *first* time I'm gonna be in a proper movie, or is this the *only* time? Is this my *first* butterfly-stomached day before, or my *only* one?' You never know with acting." He grabbed another piece of pizza. "You want more?" he asked. I shook my head.

"You know this guy," I told him again.

He wiped grease off his mouth with the back of his hand. "I just want to disappear, you know? That's what I like about acting. I get a break from being my goddamned self."

We kept talking about acting for a while—I told him Alfred Hitchcock once said that actors are cattle and should be treated as such—and then Kai stood up to leave. He thanked me for the pizza before saying, "Okay. I'll see ya tomorrow. I love you."

"What now?"

"I love you."

"You what-in-the-hell, Kai?"

"I'm sorry if I shouldn't have said that but I like saying it if you don't mind. Love is big and reckless so I just say it whenever I feel it. You welcomed me into your apartment to run lines because I was nervous. You gave me good advice. You put my little drawing up on your wall. I love you."

"Wow. Well, thanks, Kai."

"I don't love you a lot or anything. But a little. I love you a little."

"Okay. I like you a medium amount. A socially acceptable amount."

"Great. See you tomorrow."

4

The next morning we started rehearsals with Kathryn at this warehouse that had been fitted out to be a 1986 nightclub. Kathryn led the blocking, walking us through our marks and discussing movement. Kai seemed nervous, but his actions and choices were on point. He saw his character as inward-focused, as precise and limited in his movements, almost like he was afraid to fully let go until this scene in the nightclub where Jude loses his composure and tells Carly about his extensive family trauma.

There's a saying in the Industry—*Don't waste it in rehearsal*—and I tend not to, but Kai gave so much that I felt like I had to meet him where he was, such that we were both really laughing and smiling when we talked inside Andy's house.

"Keep it innocent," Kathryn told me after one take where the camera operator was pretending to hold a camera as I grabbed Kai by the waist flirtatiously.

"She's not innocent," I said.

"Well, it's rehearsal," Kathryn demurred. "We'll figure her out as we go."

I nodded, trying not to reveal my annoyance that Kathryn thought she understood Carly better than I did.

I knew my reputation. Hard to direct. Challenging. Won't let a scene go. Obsessive.

But aren't those *good* qualities? Don't you want a collaborator who gives everything to make the best possible movie?

When we broke for lunch, I wandered off into a small stand of shrubs behind the warehouse. I sat down on an overturned five-gallon bucket to call my agent, Jamie. Hollywood is pure glamour.

"What's new?" I asked her.

"Now that you're in a movie with Matthew Malone, everyone's calling me. Studios are taking notice, Junie. I got a couple scripts to send you." Jamie was all business. If Jamie had hobbies, I was blissfully unaware of them. "One is a show in the *Star Wars* universe. Limited series. Very upscale. Only thing is you're blue."

"I'm *blue*?"

"Yeah, you're blue. So lots of time in the makeup trailer," she said.

"Is it one of those CGI things where the whole shoot happens in a warehouse in Atlanta?"

"To be fair," Jamie answered, "I believe the warehouse is in Manitoba. Budget's good, though. And they've got a great showrunner. Angela Simpson. Did that spy show for Netflix. Now she's with Disney on this *Star Wars* thing. Eight episodes. I like it for you. The other thing is an epic fantasy. New Brian Arawas project."

"As long as I'm not playing a kid." Part of the reason I'd fought so hard to book *Andy Warhol Never Gets Old* was because my character isn't in high school. The problem with being twenty-two is that you can still play seventeen, and when you're a Former Nickelodeon Star, it's hard to book anything but teen movies. I needed to prove I could be an adult.

"She's not a kid. She's a queen. Agrippah, Queen of the Realm.

Look, it's a fantasy. You're fighting orcs or whatever. But Brian Arawas has a half-billion-dollar franchise under his belt. I know you don't love fantasy, but there's real meat to this character, and you'd be the lead in a Brian Arawas movie."

"You don't love the script," I said.

"I don't love the script," Jamie agreed. "But I love Agrippah as a role. Actual nuance. Real feminine power. It's shit you don't see every day."

"I'll read them both," I said. "Send them over."

After another four hours of rehearsals, Kai and I shared a ride back to our apartment building.

"You want to get dinner?" he asked me.

"I gotta read some stuff my agent sent over. And I've got a call with my publicist at eight. I'd love to—just busy."

"I get it," he said. "I got a couple self-tapes to make."

"You want me to read with you?" I asked. "I should be free by nine."

"Sure, as long as I can return the favor someday."

I ordered out a salad bowl from some Pittsburgh knockoff Sweetgreen and wrote in my notebook for twenty minutes (a daily ritual) before downloading the scripts onto my iPad.

The *Star Wars* thing was about a Twi'lek (I had to google it) diplomat working for the Empire in the Imperial Defense Department. At the end of the pilot, the viewer learns that our mid-level diplomat is in fact a spy for the Rebel Alliance who meets up with her handler in a dive bar. We can see what the diplomat can't—that she's been trailed to the bar by a suspicious colleague.

The writing was crisp but to my tastes anyway a little joyless. I read through the first half of the second episode before switching over to the Brian Arawas movie, *Gods of Andromeda.*

Before *Gods of Andromeda* was a script, it had been a book, apparently a massive bestseller, even though I'd never heard of it. Both the screenplay and the book were written by a woman named Valentina Leavitt, who looked in the photos I found online very much like an author of fantasy novels—long salt-and-pepper hair, oversized glasses, and watery gray eyes.

In the Realm, a young noblewoman has just become Queen after the sudden and suspicious death of her mother. I liked the matriarchal society stuff, and the world-building was good. The dialogue struck me as a bit awkward—lots of "my lords" and "my ladys" and whatnot—but I could see the movie. Occasionally when I read a script, I can see myself as the character I'm reading for; I can feel my body as her body, and my voice as her voice. Even though Agrippah's lines were a bit stilted and formal, I could imagine myself saying them.

Most of all, I liked the way Agrippah interacted with her husband by an arranged marriage, Gavinth, the second lead of the movie. He was ambitious and somewhat conniving but in a charming way, and she recognized his machinations for what they were but still loved him. Or maybe she didn't quite love him but saw his usefulness. There was a fascinating tension in their marriage. Do these two people care for each other, or need each other, or both? When love is politically expedient, is it love?

I called Jamie at seven forty-five, as soon as I'd finished the script. I could hear some hubbub in the background. "Is this a bad time?" I asked.

"Never," she said. "Just at a kid's birthday party."

"Whose kid?"

"Mine. D'you get a chance to read?"

"Yeah, I like *Gods of Andromeda*. I like that character. It's a bit cheesy, but . . ."

"So is the American moviegoing public," Jamie said, finishing my thought. "I like it for you. And the studio is *really* behind it. Look, it's a long shot, but we love a long shot. They'd probably fly you out for an audition. Otherwise you can self-tape."

"I need to read the book first," I said.

"Yeah, sure. I'll send it to you."

"Already ordered it," I said.

"Of course you did. Good idea to read it. The author wants to be Very Involved. Insisted on writing the script. One of those. But it's Arawas's movie and that guy knows how to put butts in theater seats. Okay, I'll call the studio now and artfully lead them on."

"Perfect. I liked the *Star Wars* thing less."

"It's great if you want a TV show, but you don't want a TV show. You're a movie actor. You can do TV when—ALICE STOP HITTING YOUR BROTHER FOR GOD'S SAKE—you're a thirty-eight-year-old mother looking for some life stability. Like your long-suffering agent."

"I gotta go. I have a call with Katie."

"Tell her hi."

Katie and I went over the press outlets coming to visit set over the course of the shoot. All the press would be there for Matthew, of course, but Katie was trying to get me one-on-ones with the women's magazines as well as some online stuff, because online outlets trended younger. When I got off the phone with Katie, I had a few minutes, so I read a little of *The Philosophy of Andy Warhol (From A to B and Back Again)*, which I'd been using to prep. Warhol doesn't reveal much about his actual self in *Philosophy*; he's trying to be quick-witted and wise while remaining radically superficial. He doesn't talk about his childhood or his art-making or his lovers or even really his interests, but skimming through it that evening, I found one moment that struck me as deeply revealing:

> *Sometimes people let the same problem make them miserable for years when they could just say, "So what." That's one of my favorite things to say. "So what."*

> *"My mother didn't love me." So what.*
> *"My husband won't ball me." So what.*
> *"I'm a success but I'm still alone." So what.*

I'm a success but I'm still alone. So what. That struck me as real in a way very little in the book did. And I wondered whether loneliness is an inevitable by-product of success, because nobody else really knows what it's like to be you, and anyway you can't be sure whether people want to be near you because you're you or because you're a success, which is its own kind of aloneness. This must've been a place where Matthew could see himself in Warhol—they were both larger than life, performed selves.

Of course, there are worse problems. Pity poor Matthew Malone, who can't complain to his friends about all his fame and wealth. But that amplifies the loneliness. So what.

By then it was nine o'clock, so I went upstairs to Kai's apartment.

"How were the scripts?"

"I liked one. They're interested in me for Agrippah, Queen of the Realm."

"Well, I'm self-taping for Kevin the Intern, who has six lines in this workplace comedy about a video game company. So we're both crushing it."

Kai's phone was already nestled in a tripod placed atop the little table that straddled the kitchen area and the living area in his studio apartment. His place had the same floor plan as mine, and nearly identical furniture, but he had posters everywhere. The posters were all of shows at the Carnegie Museum of Art and the Warhol Museum—including a bunch of Warhol's flower paintings. I grabbed one of the two wooden chairs nestled under the table and got behind the camera. "You have the sides?" I asked.

"Yeah, prepare yourself for some High Art," he responded, and handed me a sheet of paper with the relevant dialogue on it. "You're my boss, Richter, the main guy in the movie." We read the script through once. It wasn't very good, but the job of an actor is not to judge the material so much as to give in to it, and the worse the script the more interesting that job becomes, because you've got to find a way in. That's what I tell myself, anyway. Kai hit record, said, "I'm Kai Laramie. Five eleven. Based in New York. Over eighteen. Okay."

"Kevin, we need that report." I tried to say it flatly so that Kai would look good by comparison.

"I've got it right here, sir," Kai said, miming handing over a piece of paper. "The issue, sir, is that there are a number of bugs."

"How many?"

"Over the summer I found one thousand three hundred, sir." He paused, gulped. "And twelve."

"You found one thousand three hundred bugs in the game."

"And twelve."

"Is it playable?"

"Um," he said.

"Would you pay $2.99 for it?"

"Sir, honestly I found it challenging, and I'm getting paid to play it."

"We pay our interns now? Christ, this company ain't what it used to be."

"I also get college credit," Kai said nervously, "if you could just sign this form saying I showed up all summer?" He mimed handing over a second form, then hit the stop button on his phone camera.

"All right," he said. "Thanks. I genuinely hope I don't get this, although my agent says it's a good gig for me."

"You don't want to try it again?" I asked.

He shrugged and leaned back in his chair. "Was my Kevin the Intern somehow lacking?" he asked, smiling.

"No, it was good. Just, I don't know, I always do a few takes."

"I bet you do. How many?"

"I don't know. A lot," I said. Dozens. I knew my process could exhaust my scene partners, but I also didn't know any other way of doing it right.

"I think I'm good with one," he said, and the truth is: He was. The kid was, as the saying goes, a natural.

5

That Friday was the table read. Matthew walked around, greeting everyone and making introductions. We'd already met some of them, but I didn't know the studio's publicist, Ellen Kim, or the script supervisor, or the studio executive, Todd Simons, who had fresh-cut hair and a perfectly tailored gray suit.

Kathryn began, "I'm so proud of the work we've done already and so excited for the work ahead. With this cast and crew, we have the chance to make a truly special film."

Todd from the studio said, "Kathryn, Matthew, it's such a gift to share this day with you. Any time we embark on a new project, I always think of the old joke by George Burns: 'Acting is all about honesty. If you can fake that, you've got it made.'"

We all laughed politely. "Todd and his jokes," Ellen said. "We've already got MTV and *Today* coming to set. We're going to have a great campaign lined up for this, mixing Matthew's experience with the freshness of Kai and Juniper."

I glanced over at Kai, who was seated next to me. He looked like he might throw up at any moment. I always felt that way after something was done, once you couldn't do anything about it, but before and during a shoot, I felt secure. Someone literally told you what words to say.

I leaned over and muttered to him, "Anxiety is the dizziness of freedom."

"Is that original?" he asked.

"Kierkegaard," I answered.

The idea of a table read is that everyone who's key to making the movie can hear the whole thing in one go. I looked down at the pages the whole time and tried to give a lot of myself to Carly but not everything. For everything, I had to wait until we were actually on set, in costume, and rolling. Kai, meanwhile, was giving everything. When he told me that he wanted me, sizzling with a confidence he'd found somewhere, I felt like *he* wanted *me*. He flattened out a bit in the scene where he and Carly fight at a nightclub where they've gone to party with Andy, but otherwise, he felt so much like Jude that I could hardly keep up with him.

Matthew, meanwhile, did his Andy voice—pinched and disaffected. He sounded almost dazed by reality, or drunk with ironic detachment. "Young people inspire and exhaust me," he said. "Art is what you can get away with." "People should fall in love with their eyes closed." "If you look at a thing long enough it loses all its meaning." He spoke in the parables of Warhol's diaries and his books, and indeed in the parable of his art. Andy was not the center of the movie, or at least not the center of *my* movie, but he was the beating heart of it, beating at first slowly and coldly and then with fear and fervor, and finally not at all.

When we finished, the whole room burst into applause, and I saw Ellen the Publicist wiping away an actual tear. I watched Todd from the studio most closely, because more than anyone else, he'd decide if the movie got a big push or a small one, or if it even came out in theaters at all. If he felt like it was small, or niche, he'd send it direct-to-streaming.

"That's brilliant," Todd said as the applause died down. "Brilliant. I think we've got magic on our hands here. Absolute magic."

On the Sunday before we began shooting, I visited the Andy Warhol Museum, where there was a huge collection not just of Warhol's art but also his tchotchkes and papers. An inveterate collector, Warhol kept everything and willed it all to the museum, from old copies of *Interview* magazine to underwear signed by Calvin Klein.

Our movie was about Warhol's later work, the stuff he made at the end, like his *Last Supper* series. Several of the *Last Supper* works were in the museum, but I was especially fascinated by his earlier film work. I watched multiple loops of his *Screen Tests*, four-minute movies that just show people staring at the camera, blinking occasionally, looking bashful or confident or each in turn. The camera is still, shooting the actors from the neck up, and it reminded me of auditioning, but without the words or actions—just your face. I thought about how strange acting in front of a camera is, how vulnerable it is. Warhol was the great poet of radical corporatization and the superficialization of human experience, but he also liked to capture people in their unprotected but still performed moments—Jackie Kennedy at her husband's funeral, for example. I was especially taken by Edie Sedgwick's *Screen Test*. Her oversized brown eyes, which reminded me of my own, seemed to hold all the terror and dread and wonder in the world. As an actor, you want to be as transparent as possible, but that also of course means that people can see all the way inside you.

I went home that evening and reread the last chapters of a Warhol biography, which, unlike Warhol's own books, actually did explore his private life. Andy wasn't just an artist—he was trying to spin the many plates of Andy Warhol Enterprises: He was a TV host with his own show on MTV and a spokesperson for multiple brands. He was running *Interview* magazine and also still making art. And all this while the art world he'd known and helped develop was in total upheaval. By 1986, many of Warhol's friends had died of AIDS or were sick with it. Meanwhile, contemporary art was passing him by as young artists like Cindy Sherman and Barbara Kruger started to make emotionally intimate but still conceptually dazzling work.

Warhol feared he'd become stale. He couldn't find a way forward, especially since his collaborations with the young Jean-Michel Basquiat had flamed out after a bad review in *The New York Times*. Meanwhile, a man who'd always felt that he was ugly was ever more uncomfortable with his aging body, altered by the surgeries he'd needed after being shot in the stomach in the late sixties. And his gallbladder was failing. Gallbladder surgery had killed Andy's father, and now his own gallbladder needed removing. Warhol felt certain that the procedure would kill him, too. And although it was routine and relatively safe, when he finally went into the hospital to get the surgery, he never came out. He died there alone, too embarrassed by his wiglessness and vulnerability to accept visits from even his closest friends.

I'm a success but I'm still alone. So what.

"Warhol presaged the degradation of meaning in an image," the book argued. "He showed us how we can't trust or be moved by images in the way we once could. With Warhol, everything is skin deep, but that's exactly what is so deep about his work. We live in a skin-deep era, staring at two-dimensional screens and endless images, an era funded by advertising and consumption and content creation, and Warhol was in all those businesses long before Instagram existed."

The book also talked a little about what Warhol might've made of the Internet. He was fascinated by technology—he did an ad campaign with

Apple and invented an animatronic robot. In general, he was obsessed with screens way before it was cool, and the book argued he would've embraced the aspects of the early Internet that refuged weirdos and the marginalized.

The doorman called up to my apartment, interrupting my reading. I had a package downstairs. It turned out to be some daisy earrings from Dior (retail cost $680) that they wanted me to model for Instagram. My deal with Dior, first struck when I was eighteen, had carried me through all the low points in my career, and I was grateful for it, but I still felt my soul leaking out of my body every time I did a post for them.

I got dressed (a black jumpsuit and kitten heels), slicked my hair back, and then recruited Kai to be my photographer. He took a bunch of pictures of me wearing the earrings in front of his Warhol-drenched walls, and then I posted some to Instagram.

The comments ranged from *You look so pretty* to *Fuck me step-sis* to *Sell out*.

So what.

6

It always astonishes me how many people work on a movie set. Carpenters and electricians and camera operators and the PAs who tell you where to be and when to be there, and the second assistant director who shouts at the PAs when they haven't gotten you where you're supposed to be. There's the on-set photographer and the studio publicist and the sound guys who make a point of not looking you in the eyes as they tape the microphone to your chest. Two people work the snack area, who are different from the seven people who do the catering. Then there are the producers who scrutinize the monitors a few yards away from the set, and the video guy who makes those monitors work. And on this bright April morning, all of them had made their way to a neighborhood in Pittsburgh, because our first day began with a scene outside the rowhouse that played as Warhol's childhood home. Kai's character, Jude, drives Andy there for an interview with my character, Carly. We were shooting what I guess amounted to Jude and Carly's meet-cute.

I play a young reporter—I am "early twenties" in the movie—writing a story about Andy for *Esquire*. He agrees, somewhat against type, to visit his childhood home with me. Warhol dies just before the piece goes to print, and I end up rewriting it feverishly over two nights, with Jude's help, and we share a byline and a bed. The movie is about the tension between a public and a private life, and about the dawn of celebrity culture, but for Carly it's mostly about trying to know an artist who no one ever really knew while also getting extremely high on quaaludes every chance she gets, snorting coke, and partying at any club that will have her. Carly wants to know if Warhol is really as skin-deep as he pretends to be, or if he's protecting some deeper self. But she'll ask him a question—like whether his latest fright-wig series is about aging—and he'll answer elliptically. "I don't make art about anything. I make art that is, not that's about."

That first day, I had a quick bit of dialogue in the entryway of the house, where I ask him what being in his childhood home makes him feel, and he says, "It smells different." Then I ask him what he's thinking about and he says, "This Lauren Bacall interview. Can I put her on the cover? And I'm thinking about young Carly here, and whether she is going to be a Great Writer. I don't know many writers. I'm dyslexic, you know."

But before we could get to my scene, we needed the exterior shot where Andy prattles on to Jude about a cocktail party he's planning and who needs to be on the invite list and where to throw it and whether it should be an *Interview* Magazine Party or just an Andy Party, and Jude is feverishly taking notes and trying to keep everything in order.

We'd already met the hair and makeup team during rehearsals. Belinda was on my makeup and Crystal on my hair. B and C. Easy to remember. But soon the names pile on—there's Sean the props master and Marina his assistant and Monique the costume director and Alicia the costuming assistant who'd just steamed the white miniskirt and low-cut orange blouse I was wearing. Kathryn explained to me during prep that orange was "my" color, and that turquoise (Kai's color) and orange were in battle, alternately collaborating and clashing in the film. Kathryn was all about color-blocking, as she told me. Everything a singular tone. It seemed a bit over-the-top to me, but her first movie got a Golden Globe nom and I got beat out for a Nickelodeon Kids' Choice Award by the girl from the second reboot of that show about proto-YouTubers, so what did I know?

Monique looked me over once I was dressed and pinned the back of my shirt to tighten it up a bit. Then Chris, the PA for the trailers, told me to get in a full-sized white van waiting outside my trailer, which was driven by Trish, who took me the half mile to set, whereupon I met a bespectacled PA named Alistair who offered to get me coffee. We were in a working-class Pittsburgh neighborhood set up on a street lined with rowhouses.

Video Village—a dense cluster of monitors and chairs—was set up in the driveway of a house across the street from the one that passed as Andy's. The producers were huddled with Kathryn discussing the weather forecast for Thursday and what rain might mean for the production schedule. Matthew said, "I'll just ensure it's a dry day. I have a direct line to the Big Man."

"And you use it to prevent rain delays?" asked Kathryn.

"Exclusively," Matthew answered, then laughed that brash laugh of his. "Juniper!" he said as he saw me. "Look at you. Orange as can be." He was wearing a black turtleneck and acid-washed jeans, his black hair tucked underneath a Warhol wig, spiky white hair shooting out in every direction.

"I guess this is really going to happen," I said.

Kai was sitting on the front lawn of the property across the street, all by himself, picking at grass. I walked over toward him and knelt down, not wanting to stain my white skirt.

"Actors are cattle," he said. "Ever since you quoted that, it's rumbling around my head."

"Takes the pressure off, doesn't it?" I said. "You show up on time. You stand where you're told to stand. You say what you're told to say. They herd you this way, then that way, and then you go to sleep."

"Easy job, really. Only if you forget your lines and they have to shoot for an extra day, it costs a hundred grand."

"Two hundred!" shouted Lon from over by Video Village. "I hear everything," he added. "*Every word* on this goddamned set I hear. *Two hundred* if you forget your lines. Which you won't, Kai. You're a pro. A rookie, but a pro."

"Thanks, Lon," Kai said.

"And actors aren't cattle," Lon added. "You're more like dolls. Ten or twenty years from now we'll have good animation that replaces you entirely but for now we're stuck with goddamned humans."

"As if your job can't be automated," Matthew said. "You're just a machine that turns money into movies."

"Putting that on my business card," Lon answered.

A PA came to take me inside the house. I wasn't actually in this first scene, but Carly was watching it all from an upstairs window, and so they needed me to stand in the window for the wide shot, looking down with concern because my silhouette might be visible. Andy's old house was supposed to be vacant when they visit for the interview, so the idea was that I'd already made my way inside to his furnitureless, dustbunnied, shag-carpeted childhood bedroom.

I was ninety-nine percent sure this shot wouldn't even make it into the movie, but I still tried to do the work to be in character, to forget about actors and cattle and the huge lights and the camera out on the street and Lon and Natalie watching us on the monitors. I tried to forget about Kathryn, about wearing an outfit I would never wear, about my ex and his avarice for my body, about my body more generally. Instead, I thought about Carly's body, her relationship with it, her simultaneous desire to be beautiful and horror at being objectified as beautiful, about her desire to harm the body, to drink and smoke and snort her way out of the body. And then I watched below as Kai—no, Jude—slammed a car door and scampered up to Matthew—no, Andy. Fame makes you big but it also makes you two-dimensional.

I couldn't really hear them from my vantage point, but it looked good—Jude nervously scrawling in his notebook as Andy rattled off names for the party.

"Yeah, cut!" Kathryn shouted after a minute. "Great. Great first shot. Looked beautiful." She turned to the producers in Video Village and chatted with them before saying, "Let's go again."

"Going again," a PA shouted, and then others down the line, including the PA downstairs in the house with me.

I knew Matthew would deliver, but I felt a measure of relief seeing Kai fumbling expertly with Jude's notebook, convincing me he was struggling to keep up with Andy. The problem with acting is that no one can tell you how to do it well, not really; they can only indicate the paths one walks to do it well. People talk about committing and forgetting and letting go and trusting—all those acting gerunds that point the way toward the work but aren't the work itself. Watching Kai and Matthew outside, I let myself dream that Kai wasn't just good but maybe truly special, perhaps special enough to make our movie special.

They did six more takes while I stood there in that upstairs window, looking down and not hearing much, feeling the awe that one feels in the presence of renowned individuals. In that sense, Carly looking at Andy wasn't too different from me looking at Matthew Malone. Matthew Malone—Avenger, action star, popcorn actor extraordinaire—was no Andy Warhol, of course, but the fame radiates regardless. My ex told me once that *star* is the perfect word for celebrity actors, because they burn so hot and bright that you feel warmer in their presence.

"And cut," Kathryn said, waking me from the reverie. I realized I hadn't been even remotely within Carly during that last take, but of course it didn't matter much. Insofar as I existed, I was only a silhouette in the window. "That was great," she said, after consulting with the producers. "Let's move on."

The words repeated and grew louder as they spread. "Moving on!" the PAs shouted. "Okay, moving on!" I heard the first AD shout from the street. "We're going tight on Matthew. Tight on Matthew."

During the break, the three of us caught the same van back to the trailers, so I took a couple selfies of us. Kai seemed quiet—drained, even—and Matthew was typing on his phone the whole time, so I just sat there and posted the pics as a carousel to my Instagram, and then we were at the trailers.

You can judge your career status by your trailer situation. Matthew, of course, had a full trailer. Kai and I shared the unfortunately named "double-banger," where one trailer accommodates two living spaces. I had a faux-leather couch that folded out to a bed, as well as a bathroom with a small shower. The only issue with a double-banger is that you can hear everything going on in the room next to you, so if your costar is playing video games or fucking someone, you're able to follow along. Also, the bathroom noises.

Then there's a triple-banger, at which point you've barely got enough room to get dressed, and finally for day players a so-called "honeywagon," which contains several dressing stations, each a few feet wide. I'd been in a honeywagon when I booked my first commercials and guest appearances on TV shows. On *Star Catcher*, I'd had a triple-banger at first, then a double-banger after the show's second season.

For the two teen movies I'd made after *Star Catcher*, neither of which were big hits, I'd had double-bangers, and then on my last movie I'd had a full trailer, because I was the lead. Now I was back down to a double-banger.

I'd only been in my trailer a few minutes when I heard a knock. "Hey, it's Ellen," she said, as if on day one I'd know who Ellen was. "Ellen Kim. The studio publicist," she added after a moment. Aha. I opened the door. Thin woman, shortish straight hair, wearing black jeans and a turtleneck sweater. "Hey," she said, "I'm sorry about this, but the studio is asking for you to delete your Instagram post."

"Oh," I said. "Oh, shit. I'm so sorry. That's my bad. I didn't—"

"It's not a big deal. It's just, we offered *People* the first look, and that means costumes and everything. When you're in civilian clothes, absolutely, take pictures. I hate that they're doing this actually, because your socials are so key for this movie." Another way of saying that my socials were part of the reason I'd been hired. "We *want* you to post. Just nothing with costumes if that's okay. And yes I realize that you're in costume and makeup most of the day so it's not ideal. But the studio—"

"I get it and I'm so sorry. Is there anyone I should write or call to apologize?"

"No, no. It's nothing like that, but there are some fans back at set and when y'all go back, if you could walk over and take selfies, that'd be helpful. And then you'll notice that one of the fans has a very nice camera, and if you can take some pics for her, I'd appreciate it, because she is actually a photographer for *People* magazine. We moved up the exclusive."

"Yeah, of course." I felt terrible. I'd hurt the movie before I'd even been in the movie.

Thirty minutes later, Kai and Matthew and I walked over to the security perimeter half a block down from set and signed autographs for kids in the neighborhood and took selfies. Indeed, one of the purported fans had a very nice camera and said she didn't need to be in the picture; she just wanted a picture of the three of us together. It appeared on *People*'s Twitter and Instagram that afternoon.

7

Someone told me once that when your mother is dead, you are living both lives—your life and hers. I lived my mother's life even when she was alive. We stayed each pilot season in an apartment building full of other child actors who were also there for pilot season, and whenever I booked a commercial or something, Mom would brag about me around the pool like she'd booked it. Supposedly, I loved acting. But I was six. No six-year-old dreams of labor.

And yet. I missed her. I kept thinking about her, how excited she'd feel the first day on set. I thought about how she'd leave a little early for lunch each day to make me a plate so I wouldn't have to stand in line and could eat quickly and stay focused. She'd been a constant with me until I had to kick her out the last season of *Star Catcher*. Except for when she'd abandon us on her drinking binges, we were never apart. And then we were always apart.

Now, I was living her dream. She'd always professed a crush on Matthew Malone, and I was looking up at him, saying words that had been written for me by a properly good screenwriter. I felt sick about having pissed off the studio with the Insta post, and so it was harder than usual to lock in to Carly, but after a couple takes of the wide shot I felt like I had a good rhythm. Kathryn offered the kind of abstract notes I find a bit annoying—"Can we try it with more air," or, "There was something very generous about that one that I loved"—and again she kept wanting me to play it young or innocent, which just wasn't the Carly I imagined. After we finished that shot, I was on my way back to the trailers when the producer Natalie came up to me and said, "Good first day so far?"

I didn't want to live up to my reputation for being difficult. But I also didn't want to make bad movies. "She's having me be all doe-eyed and ignorant," I said.

"Well, you're, like, twenty-two in the movie."

"I'm also twenty-two in real life, and that doesn't make an idiot."

"Sure," Natalie said. "Right. Absolutely. I'll have a word with her."

Matthew, meanwhile, was acting campy and overstated as Andy. But there was no other way to be Andy. I mean, when Carly asks him about his affection for Basquiat, he says, "Jean-Michel painted me out. Everything we did together, he painted me out of it. It was wonderful." How can you say those words without a bit of camp?

Kathryn kept trying to rein Matthew in. "Think *Vertigo*," she told him. "Imagine we're swimming in a small pond, not the ocean." But when you've spent most of the last two decades embodying literal comic book characters, it's hard to keep subtlety in your toolbox. Still, Matthew seemed down to work hard, and I appreciated that he gave a reasonably good performance during the shots that were close up on me.

A lot of times big-name actors won't stick around for your coverage at all, or else will read their lines in a monotone. Matthew stayed, and kept being Andy, which made it a lot easier to be Carly. Just before we wrapped on that first day, Kathryn found me and hugged me and said, "You're our anchor. I thought it would be Matthew, but it's you." That felt nice, even if I was being treated like a wide-eyed ingenue instead of the smart and worldly girl I'd imagined.

When I made it to the makeup trailer after we wrapped for the day, I was surprised to find Ellen the Publicist waiting for me. "Juniper," she said, "I've made a terrible mistake."

"How's that?"

"Your Instagram post got more likes in the one hour it was up than *People* magazine has received in the last seven hours. So we're shifting. Do whatever you want. Post costumes. Post conversations. Post everything. You're this movie's number one media outlet. I had no idea how *engaged* your following is."

"It's the Nickelodeon thing," I said. "This whole generation of kids who kinda grew up with me."

"Well, post everything. That's an order from the studio. You have total creative freedom."

So I posted a series of photographs of my makeup being undone with the caption "Carly to Juniper: A Journey in Five Photos." As they finished removing my makeup, I kept refreshing my Instagram page, watching the number of likes go up: 302 one minute, 487 the next, 1,645 the one after that. I was getting ten or twenty followers every time I refreshed—just from a post in the makeup chair.

I do not want to want to be loved by strangers, but I do not want to want most of what I want.

Because I took longer in the makeup trailer than Kai, I ended up getting a ride home alone in a van driven by a guy named Tony. I called Katie to check in and tell her about my Instagram disaster, which she of course minimized, saying that if anything the studio should thank me. I got a text from Matthew then, to Kai and me: *There's a raw vegan restaurant . . . in Pittsburgh? I'll be there at seven. Hope to see U 2.*

I replied immediately. *I'd love to but I've gotta read for a project tonight. Another time!*

I knew the *Gods of Andromeda* book would be waiting for me back at the apartment, and wanted to read it as soon as possible.

Ours was a small movie—a thirty-four-day shoot, only a $14,000,000 budget—but I had high hopes for it, because Kathryn's previous movie had done well, and also because sometimes comic book actors like Matthew Malone get a role like this one and shock everyone with their talent. I let myself fantasize that the movie might be big, that *I* might be big.

"Can you tell," I asked Tony, "if the movie's gonna be good? From the vibes on set or whatever?"

"No way," Tony said. "Sometimes I think, man, people are gonna watch this film in fifty years, and it's a total bomb. I'll be driving around Clooney and Pitt and everybody gets along like gangbusters and the movie comes out and nothing. Other times, I remember once I worked this teen movie, about a Very Special Gal with Very Special Powers, and everybody was fighting all the time and nobody would share a van and the whole crew was walking on eggshells for two months and I thought this movie is gonna be an absolute shitfest, but then it was good. Not just popular, but good. So I never know. Do you?"

"No, but I haven't been around as long as you."

"That's for damn sure. I think it's like baking a pie, only you don't have a recipe and a hundred thirty people are making the pie and everyone's blindfolded except the director. The movie business is a crapshoot, kid, so you gotta have fun with it."

Kai called then. "You can't just tell Matthew Fucking Malone you're unavailable for dinner."

"I have to read this book. *Gods of Andromeda*. The project could be huge for me."

"It's Matthew Malone," Kai said. "Asking us to dinner. I can't go alone. It will be awkward. I *need* you there."

"I'll ask Tony. Tony, should I be a responsible adult and go home and read for what I hope will be my next job, or should I go out to dinner with Matthew and Kai?"

"Go out to dinner, kid. This is a relationship business. You could do worse than having a relationship with Matthew. That guy got me hired. Worked with him ten years ago on a blockbuster and then he comes back to Pittsburgh for this and makes sure he hires me back. What a guy. Let him take you out to dinner."

"Listen to Tony," Kai said.

"Fine, fine." I hung up and texted Matthew, telling him we'd meet him at seven. That left me with half an hour to get home and read.

I was ten pages into *Gods of Andromeda*—not a novel to be praised for its sentences but still immensely enjoyable in its world-building—when Kai knocked on my door.

He was wearing slacks, a tucked-in button-down, and a blazer with narrow lapels. I was wearing a sweatsuit.

"Christ, I didn't know you had to dress up for Pittsburgh's dining scene. Hold on." I closed the door on him, threw on a dress, pulled my hair back, and put on some lip gloss and mascara, then opened the door again. "Ready."

"You clean up nice," he said.

"You look like you're trying hard," I said.

"I am," he answered.

I don't drink. Insofar as possible, and it's not very possible, I like being in control of my life. Also, having grown up with an alcoholic mother, I have a generally low opinion of the stuff. From what I can tell, alcohol can make you love alcohol more than you love your friends or your children or your house or anything else, and I'd rather steer clear of Life

Ruining Serum, even if it does have "floral notes" or "a hint of nutmeg on the finish."

Which is what Kai and Matthew were saying about the white wine at Unheated, the raw food restaurant. We'd been ushered into a private room across from the kitchen. But even so, Matthew's arrival could not go unnoticed. The hostess's eyes had widened slightly when he walked in, and she said, "Could I . . . I'm sure you get this all the time, but could I get a picture?" Matthew said of course, and I took the phone from the girl's shaking hands and took two horizontal and two vertical, and then she said, "Oh my God are you—are you Janie from *Star Catcher*?"

"Yeah," I said.

"Oh my God I used to love that show," she said, and then Kai offered to take a picture, and I smiled. When I was a little kid, my mom always criticized my smile. She said it looked like I was in pain, or like I was baring my teeth in anger or fear. But I didn't know how else to bare my teeth. I thought smiling *was* showing your teeth. Now, of course, I know that it's acting, that you must briefly connect yourself to the idea of joy so that your eyes and your cheeks and your body all smile together.

I thought about my mother's memorial service, how I had to think of a happy memory with her, or at any rate with someone, to smile as each person came up to hug me and express condolences. Everyone kept saying, "I'm sorry for your loss," but I'd lost so much even before she died. I'd lost the certainty that mothers are good, that love is simple, and with her death, I'd lost even the ability to hate her. Grief is a strange bedfellow.

In our private dining room, Matthew smiled and said, "One does tire of being an icon. But without them, who am I?"

"You sound like Warhol," I said.

Matthew nodded, laughed a bit to himself, then took another long pull from his wineglass.

"How was your first day?" Kai asked.

"More fun than making a Marvel movie, that's for sure," he said as our waiter arrived with "carrot fries," which seemed to be raw carrots cut into French fry shapes and sprinkled with salt. "Most days with those, you're just in a studio doing choreography. How was *your* first day? It all must be new for you."

"I was terrified until the second or third take, and then I was . . . in it."

"I love that your first scene in a movie was with me," Matthew said. "I'll never forget that, kid. Here's to Kai."

We all raised a glass—mine some kind of blackberry-infused kombucha—and cheered Kai. He was blushing. "I love you guys," he said.

"Kai is quite profligate with his I love yous," I said.

"Well, I love *that*," Matthew said. He pressed his napkin to his mouth, put it back in his lap, and then said, "You know, when we were casting this movie, I said I want real kids, real young people, not thirty-year-olds playing young, because there's an energy to these characters. They're both yearning—for acceptance, for love, for power. And we found the perfect kids. Truly. I can tell from day one, you're both—as Kai says—*in it*."

It was quiet for a moment when the waiter returned with some kind of cauliflower rice that had been soaked in brine. Matthew asked me what I was working on that I'd initially chosen over dinner.

"It's this epic fantasy my agent likes," I said. "Brian Arawas's next project. It's based on a book called *Gods of Andromeda*. So I'm reading the book now."

"Same studio as *Warhol*, right?" he asked.

"Yeah," I said. "It's set in a world where all the leaders are young women. When you turn thirty, you age out of ruling. And the men are, like, courtiers."

"Fascinating. I don't know Brian well, but I know the head of the studio. You'd really like this film?"

"It would be huge for me. I've never been in anything with that kind of budget."

"But do you like the project?" he asked.

"I really do," I said. When Matthew spoke to you, you felt like you were the only person who existed. His eyes never left yours.

"It's good of you to read the book," he said. "I tried to read Warhol's diaries, but they bored me. Even on audio. My attention span isn't what it used to be. I prepped by watching interviews on YouTube mostly."

"Juniper *prepares*," Kai said. "Like, didn't you read everything Warhol ever wrote?"

I shrugged.

"I'll call Tom," Matthew said out of nowhere. "Todd's boss at the studio. I have an iron in the fire with him anyway. This Christmas movie with Brad." He paused. "Pitt."

"Right," I said. "You call Brad Pitt 'Brad.'"

"And you call me Matthew," he said. "Everybody turns out just to be a person in the end."

8

I'd begun to see a pattern with Kathryn: She'd let us take each shot according to our own instincts several times, and then she'd slowly ask for it more her way—me as innocent and confused by the Big Boy World, Kai as expressive and entranced by me. I worried she'd cut a movie using only her takes, but at least she was letting me act from within myself a bit, which is more than can be said for many directors.

By that Friday, we were shooting from seven p.m. to seven a.m. to get some night shots. We first filmed Kai and me at Magic Hour on a rooftop talking about Andy, about his genius for not letting anyone get beneath the skin. "I am," as he once put it, "a deeply superficial person."

In interviews, I'd noticed how often Andy referred to things as "wonderful" or "excellent" without ever seeming to derive any joy from their wonder or excellence. For someone constantly surrounded by pleasure—fancy food, great parties, celebrities, art, and everything else—he seemed curiously immune to it. So that was in the back of my head as Kai and I sat on that roof.

Then we transitioned to the nightclub set, where my character is partying. I wasn't in the first scene. Andy and Kai stand outside the club and Andy tells Kai he's beautiful and Kai says, "If you want to sleep with me,

Andy, just ask," and Andy responds, "I like sleeping I think more than I like the other stuff." Which I found relatable, although sometimes I think that maybe I've just never had good sex, whereas I've definitely had good sleep.

By the time I was needed again, it was closing in on midnight. I was tired, but my mom had trained me to use the fatigue. If the fatigue makes you cranky, feel that emotion and know that you can transform it into any other emotion. In the scene we shot next, I snort coke until my nose is dripping blood and Jude screams at me for being a goddamned idiot and he confesses to me that his brother died from a drug overdose after years of them both being beaten by their father. The fatigue helped me, as feeling always does, so that by two a.m. I was a weeping mess, all my nerve endings on the outside of my body, feeling exhausted and exhilarated, fake blood all over my blouse mixing with real snot from my sobbing.

I didn't even need to think about my mother, my actual family member who died of a substance use disorder. I didn't have to think about the times I've watched people snort coke at parties, invulnerability thrumming through them. Didn't have to think about the one time I tried weed, maybe a week after Mom died. A friend gave me some gummies and I took one in the hopes that I might be able to sleep, but I just lay in bed immobilized, thinking about all the worst things that still might happen, how if my brother and dad died I'd be actually alone in the world.

I didn't need memories to be within Carly. I only needed what I already felt, to feel the fatigue in my body and transform it into fear and longing and pulsating yearning.

With each take the word *cut* was a slight surprise, and then Kathryn would talk to me, but I couldn't really listen because I was so deep in the experience of being high as hell, wanting to fuck someone just so they would look at me the way men do when you make them come. "You're doing great," Kathryn told me. "I hesitate to tell you to pull it in but we probably need a smaller version as well."

"Got it," I said. I closed my eyes. Took some slow breaths. I was high in a nightclub where the music didn't actually play while we shot, because we didn't know what would be on the soundtrack yet. Kai was yelling over silence, because he needed to be shouting above music that wasn't there. And I was screaming at him, blood dripping from my nose, trying to make "a smaller version" of my most emotional scene in the movie.

Jude was crying, too, begging me to go back to his apartment. "You're gonna die like Cam did. You're ruining your fucking life."

"MY LIFE!" I shouted back. "ALL FUCKING MINE."

"I care about you. Because you're worth caring about."

I danced sloppily toward him, then lost my balance but saved myself by grabbing hold of him. I tried to kiss him and he dodged it. "WE ARE HAVING A GREAT FUCKING NIGHT."

"I am having a terrible night."

"TAKE A LUDE AND CHILL THE FUCK OUT."

"You're bleeding."

I looked down at my shirt. Blood dripped. I wasn't crying now. I was more casually baffled. "ANDY IS HIGH TOO AND YOU'RE NOT YELLING AT HIM."

"Andy's not bleeding on his shirt. I gotta get you out of here." He sounded strangely distant as he said it, but I tried to stay in the scene.

"MY LIFE," I shouted back, pulling away from his grip. "MINE TO SPEND. MINE TO WASTE. MINE."

Jude rolled his eyes, raised his hands in surrender, and watched as I fell to the ground, then walked away.

"Cut," Kathryn said. She took Kai aside, and I could hear her whispers but not what they meant. Kai felt somehow blocked off, like he wasn't quite meeting me in the scene, as if he was worried about embarrassing himself. And maybe that was true to character, but I felt like the scene needed to properly explode, the way in a movie everything has to go fully wrong before anything can resolve.

"Let's go again," Kathryn said.

Kai tried again, hitting his marks and his lines, but there was something a little dead-eyed in it, something self-conscious. He kept looking around at the other people milling about, as if they mattered.

"Cut. Going again," Kathryn said.

We tried again, but we were getting further away, not closer now, and I could feel myself pulling away from him, trying to find a Carly that could exist separate from his slightly aloof Jude.

"Cut. We're gonna go again."

We tried again, and now there was anger in Kai, a frustration, which felt closer to the right note but still lacking in depth. "Let's just take lunch," Kathryn said after that take.

"Bit early for lunch," Jo the Line Producer responded.

"Lunch." Kathryn said it again, this time more forcefully.

As I was walking with a PA toward the van that would take me back to my trailer, Kathryn grabbed me by the shoulder. "See if you can get through to him," she said. "Your costar. See if you can unblock him."

Kai had been great to work with all week—fearless and heartbroken and ambitious and fast-talking and absolutely dripping with charisma. But I knew what Kathryn meant. Although there was nothing radically out of place about his actions or line readings, he seemed more concerned about the other people at the club than he was about me, which felt strangely wrong for an actor whose natural choices were always extremely right.

I went back to my trailer. I was exhausted. I could hear Kai playing a video game as I lay down for a minute on the little vinyl couch. It always took me a while to emerge from the character after intense scenes. I had the cathartic rush you feel after crying hard for a long time, when you're reminded that somehow, in spite of it all, you're still alive. I remembered the morning after they told me my mom had died, I took a shower, and as the water droplets hit me I kept thinking, *I am still alive*. It seemed impossible that I could exist without her. And yet.

I went outside into the crisp Pittsburgh darkness and poured myself a cup of coffee at the beverage station, then knocked on Kai's trailer door.

He opened the door. He looked down at me and at my blood-soaked blouse. The props team really had that fake blood pouring out of my nose and onto my shirt. He tilted his head, gesturing into his trailer. Kai's tight white shirt was glued to his skin, his arms still prickling sweat from the heat of the lights. "You okay?" he asked.

I nodded as I closed the door behind me and sat down on his couch. "This stuff is fun for me," I assured him, which I'd been saying for so long—on set, in interviews, to acting coaches—that it might've been true.

"You're so good," he said. "You make it easy."

"Right back at ya."

He was quiet for a while, our eyes settled on each other. "Are *you* okay?" I asked, and he shook his head a little and then started to cry. I got up to give him a hug, but I was thinking about the blood on my shirt and how I didn't want to fuck up his costume, so it was awkward. "It's a lot," I told him. "And it's your first movie. But you're doing amazing, Kai. You really are."

He extricated himself from the hug and looked down at me, silent tears falling. "I'm trying to bring my whole self to it," he said at last. "But I know I'm fucking up. After every take, Kathryn tries to tell me what to do, but I just can't do it. I can't *get* there."

"How do you get there?" I asked. "What's your process like?"

"I don't know how to do it except to make it real," he said. "I'm not like you. I can't just prepare my way into it. I have to make it real. Have to think about my own self, my own life, my own . . . history or whatever . . . and then take that and use it. But this. This scene. I knew it would be this one that cracked me. I tried to run it a thousand times in my mind, but I'm not good enough."

"You are plenty good enough."

"I keep trying. But to really embody the worst thing that ever happened to Jude, I have to embody the worst thing that ever happened to me, and I keep blocking off from that. It's too much." He was really crying now. "I can't do this, Juniper."

I let him cry for a while, and then finally said, "Listen, Kai. Whatever's happening in there is not real." I touched his head. "It's not really happening. What's really happening is that we're tired as shit stuck in a trailer in Pittsburgh."

"I need to use it but I can't," he said.

"Define *it*." I needed Kai to be ready for this, to be up for this. Getting this scene right was absolutely essential to our movie.

"I can't, Juniper. I can't. I can't define *it* and I can't use *it*. And it's blocking me."

"*It* is the worst thing that ever happened to you?"

"Yeah, I need to use it but I can't use it. I need to use it to get fully open, but I'm scared to, or I keep trying and it overwhelms me."

I was curious, of course, but knew better than to ask.

"Hey. When you felt these feelings in the past, wherever you felt them, you weren't safe. But this is safe. That's what acting is. It's going everywhere you can go . . . but safely."

"Yeah," he said. "Yeah. Thanks. Sorry, it's just intense for me."

"Don't be sorry. But the worst thing that ever happened to you, that's not happening now, Kai. Now you're with me."

"Yeah," he said. "Right."

"And if you need to use something to break everything down when we go back, use it. It has no power over you, whatever it is, because you're here and you're surrounded by people who care about you and are rooting for you."

"Yeah," he said. "Okay. I think I'm gonna play video games till they call us back. Love you."

Weirdly, I believed him.

When we got back to set, he crushed it. After two takes, Kathryn announced we were moving on. *"Don't know what you said,"* she whispered to me between set-ups, *"but keep saying it."*

9

Sunday morning, I was deep into the Realm, still in my pajamas reading *Gods of Andromeda*, when I heard a knock at the door. I got up and glimpsed Kai through the peephole wearing a Pittsburgh Pirates hat and jersey. I opened the door.

His smile was bright as morning, his hands clasped behind him. "Wanna go to a baseball game?" he asked.

"Sure," I said.

"Great," he said, "because I already got you a hat." He revealed it from behind his back, and placed it on my head. "I gotta get dressed," I said.

"You're gonna close the door on me, aren't—" he said as I closed the door on him.

We had a couple hours to kill before the game started, so after getting dressed and brushing my teeth, I invited him in and struggled to shut up about *Gods of Andromeda*. "It's actually really interesting, because the Queen must have a daughter because sons aren't very important, and there's this wooden staff, and having the staff means you have the power, so every ruler wants to hold on to it, but of course to hold the staff is also to be aware that you won't *always* have the power, you know? Like, it's almost as if you don't contain the power; the staff does. The staff is yours only in trust."

"Sounds like a banger," he said.

"On the other hand, if I'm trying to be, like, The Kind of Girl Who Wins Awards, this is not a movie I take. This movie has a zero percent chance of winning awards. Maybe Best Kiss at the MTV Movie Awards, but that's it."

"It has kissing?"

"Oh, it has kissing. She has a husband but then she also has . . . what are mistresses called when they're guys?"

"Misters," he said without missing a beat.

"She also has misters. Including a hot foreign mister who is half orc. Orcs are bad but half orcs are okay from what I can gather."

"So you'd get to hook up with a half orc if you got this part."

"Yeah."

"Sounds like a good deal."

"If I could even get it. My agent says it's a long shot."

"Do you have a dad?" he asked.

"In the book? If so, he's not mentioned."

"No, in real life. I got bored talking about work."

"Yeah, I have a dad. He's career army. He and my mom split up when I was four. I don't know him that well, but we're friendly. He calls on my birthday. Comes to my premieres. All that stuff."

"Do you blame your mom for the fact that you weren't close with him growing up?"

"Jesus Christ, can't we talk about the weather or something?"

"I'm just curious," he said.

"I blame my mom for a lot of things. She is, in general, the reason I ended up like this."

"Well, I like the way you ended up," he said.

The truth is, I feel like if I talk about my mom she will somehow reach out from beyond the grave and pull me into the afterlife with her, and that she'll be waiting for me in heaven with a disappointed look on her face because I ruined her reputation. I fear her. "No one ever told me that grief felt so like fear," C. S. Lewis wrote, and for me the feelings intertwine.

Kai—sprawled across the beige microfiber couch in my apartment, looking up at the popcorn ceiling—asked if I thought about her during hard scenes, like the one on Friday. "I try not to give her that satisfaction," I told him.

"Even though she's dead," he observed.

"She may be dead, but she's still my mother."

"And you don't want to give her that satisfaction because?"

I didn't feel like going into it further with him, so I just said what he already knew. "Because she stole my money."

"You're kind of a bad liar," he said.

"I am doubly offended," I shot back, kicking him from across the couch. "First off, I'm not lying, and second off, I'm a fucking phenomenal liar."

He just shrugged. "Are you quite single?" he asked.

I'm sure my face revealed a measure of surprise even though I tried not to. "Quite. You?"

"I am always a little in love with someone, but yes, I'm quite single."

"And who are you a little in love with these days?"

"You, I guess," he said, with no concern. "But I'm a bit like Andy. I'm a bit fucked up when it comes to that stuff. Okay, we should go to the game."

In the Uber on the way to the stadium, Jamie called. "Are you fucking Matthew Malone?"

"Am I *what*? Of course not."

"Hmm," she said. "Interesting. Well, Matthew Malone called the head of the studio and told him he'll make some Christmas movie for him if you get cast as Agrippah in *Gods of Andromeda*."

"You're shitting me."

"I am not."

"He said he'd make a call for me; he didn't say he'd make *that* call."

"But you're not fucking him."

"No."

"Pity. I was hoping you could tell me what it's like. Anyway, you're not working Thursday or Friday, so the studio wants to fly you out to audition."

I have no particular love of baseball, but it was fun to watch Kai sketch the stadium and the field as he explained to me who each player was and why we should root for or against them. We left after the seventh inning because the game was a blowout, and then walked along the Allegheny River for a while. Kai had a funny way of walking—he was kind of like a heat-seeking missile. I'd be walking in a straight line and he would draw toward me and then take a half step away and then get close to me again, until our hips were almost-but-not-quite touching, and then he'd take another half step away. I liked walking with him, though.

Something about the game had made him talk less, and I was enjoying the quiet, or at least what passed for quiet when you were in spitting distance of a highway. "You know a lot about baseball," I said finally.

"Yeah, well, I played growing up."

"Were you good?"

"I guess so. I was very good defensively. I was an okay hitter."

"Like, you could've played in college?"

"I had some offers. Not Division I or anything. But yeah, I could've played in college. It's just . . . there were a lot of other people who wanted it worse than I did."

"So you were an athlete *and* a theater kid?"

"I contain multitudes," he said.

"You were popular."

"I guess."

"And handsome."

"If you say so."

"And good at everything. Two parents, one brother . . . sounds like a pretty good life, Kai Laramie."

"Sure does," he said.

Monday morning, I was working alone with Matthew. In the scene, we walk through a Rothko show together, and Andy says, "I like Mark, but he's so warm." In between set-ups, Matthew and I sat on our cast chairs next to each other, and I thanked him for making that call about *Gods of Andromeda*.

"Who's your agent?" he asked.

I told Matthew I was with Jamie at CAA, and inquired about him.

"I have a team more than a person," he said. "Do you like her?"

"She's an agent," I said, and he laughed.

"They're snakes, but they're *my* snakes. The thing to remember, Juniper, is that they can always get another you. They can always find some starry-eyed kid who just got off the bus from Omaha. But you are your only you."

"Yeah," I said, with that thought—*I am my only me*—quivering through my body.

"You're good," he said.

"Thank you," I said.

"Kai is good, too. Real good." I tried not to take it personally that I got a good and Kai got a *real* good.

"He is," I said. "Hey, can I take a selfie of us? The studio wants . . . content."

"Gotta feed the beast," he said, and immediately snapped into Warhol. His cheeks hollowed out; his eyes emptied. He offered up a faint wan smile as I snapped three selfies in quick succession.

"Reminds me of Andy's Polaroids," Matthew said. "He would've loved the Internet, Andy. It would've devoured him, and he would've loved it anyway."

I uploaded all three pictures as a series. The people ate it up. Two thousand likes in fifteen minutes.

After work, Kai and I got dinner at a Middle Eastern restaurant a half-mile walk from our apartment building. We'd barely sat down when he brought up my mom again. "It was a complicated relationship, but I miss her," I said.

"You continue to be a hilariously bad liar," he said.

"Everything with you is a therapy session."

"I'm interested in you," he said. "I find you very interesting."

After dinner, we went back to his apartment to watch Kathryn's first feature, *Pro Patria Mori*, about a guy coming home from a war and visiting the families of the three soldiers he knew who died. Kai wanted to watch it to "see what Kathryn will make of us." The movie was dreary—all gray skies—but suitably sad and well-acted. It starred a guy I recognized but couldn't name, one of those blank-canvas, white-guy actors who manages to be in everything without ever becoming properly famous. Kai sat next to me on the couch, the same throw blanket over both of us, but we weren't quite touching except at the shoulders. My ex, the Cinematographer, kissed me the first time we were in a room alone together. I thought about how the Cinematographer always wanted me, how even on set he would look at me with undisguised yearning.

But Kai sat awkwardly on the couch, his hands folded carefully in his lap lest he accidentally touch me. It was like he was seeking another kind of intimacy. I thought of something I'd read in one of Andy's books: "Fantasy love is much better than reality love. Never doing it is very exciting." And that wasn't wrong. I could feel the fabric of Kai's shirt against my forearm, and just that nearly took my breath away. I thought about kissing him—I had the feeling that ten thousand years could pass and he'd never initiate a kiss—but I didn't want to ruin the feeling of his elbow almost against mine, our knees millimeters from touching.

As the credits rolled at the end of *Pro Patria Mori*, Kai said, "Do you miss your mom? Even though she hurt you and everything?"

I sighed. He was relentless, and so I relented. "She wasn't a bad person," I said, pulling my knees up to my chest and wrapping my arms around myself. "Not exactly. But yes, I miss my mom. I wanted to make her proud. I probably still do."

"I miss the person who hurt me the most, too," Kai said.

"You don't want to tell me about it?"

"I do, but it will change things, and I don't want to change things."

"Okay," I said. He was quiet for a while and then I said, "The thing about my mom is she didn't want to want what she wanted. She didn't want to drink. She didn't want to . . . I mean, I'd wake up and she'd be gone and I'd have to get myself to set. My mother was always there—every audition, every callback, every day on set—and so when she wasn't there, it was terrifying. I remember when I was like twelve or thirteen, I'd have to call the producers and someone in transpo would come and pick me up and take my brother to school and everything.

"She'd show up a couple days later sweating whiskey, and she didn't want that. I would eat cereal for dinner or stuff I took from set and watch TV and worry that she wasn't coming home at all. I would take care of my brother. He was even littler. I was so scared all the time. Of course she didn't *want* that for us, but it still happened, you know?"

He just nodded, inviting me to keep talking, so I did. "And then when she was home, it wasn't always better. She'd get drunk and say terrible things to us—terrible. She used to call me piggy whenever I'd eat, because she wanted to keep me skinny. One time she was shitfaced and she said she didn't love us, that she wanted to, but she couldn't. I wonder a lot if that was true. It couldn't have been. But then, she did say it.

"She would make me take my pulse—this was when I was six or seven—and she taught me to count the heartbeats through my wrist for fifteen seconds and then multiply times four to know my heart rate. She would sit me down at the kitchen table and have me take my pulse and I would tell her, 'A hundred,' and she would say, 'Get it down to eighty,' and so I'd calm myself, tell myself I was at peace. I'd act, you know? And I could do it. I could get my heart rate down to eighty. And then she'd hit me, and ask me my heart rate, and I'd say one twenty or whatever and she'd say no, no, get it down to eighty, Juniper. Keep it at eighty. Then she'd hit me again. And eventually I learned to keep it at eighty even as she hit me. She's standing above me, and I'm seated at the kitchen table, and she's hitting me, and I'm trying to keep my pulse at or under eighty."

I reached my right thumb to my left wrist and felt the life in me. "Even now," I said, "telling you about this, I can keep it right at eighty. I can take it lower if I want. Feel." I reached my arm over to him, and his soft fingers pressed to my wrist. I kept my pulse low, then sped it up, then slowed it down again. "Acting," I told him. "Just like she taught me.

"She always loved my success, though. Loved it when I booked a gig. I used to think, Someday she'll get sober. Someday we'll have a real relationship. She'll ask for my forgiveness, and she'll atone, and I'll forgive her, and we'll be able to have a real relationship. But now that's impossible, you know? Because she's dead now. You never realize how permanent death is until somebody you love dies." I only noticed then that Kai was still holding my wrist.

10

I had two days off because Kai and Matthew were filming scenes with the woman who played Warhol's friend Pat Hackett. My flight to LA for the audition wasn't until four p.m., so I spent the morning at the Carnegie Museum of Art. I don't know much about contemporary art other than what I learned researching Andy, but I like art museums. I like the cafes. I like watching couples look at art together. I think what I like about museums is the same thing I like about acting: Acting is a chance to visit rooms in my mind that I have no other way of discovering.

I was standing in front of an abstract Joan Mitchell triptych painting, for example, and out of nowhere I remembered this Donald Hall essay where he writes that his uncle kept everything, including a box labeled "String too short to be saved." Why did that painting make me think that thought? I kept looking at the painting and I thought about our scene at the nightclub, how it both was and was not Kai who was crying. I thought about kissing him, how one way or another—out of character or in it—I would kiss Kai soon enough.

I kept looking at the painting and I started seeing it in three dimensions. I sat down on a hard white bench and heard the low hum of an air conditioner somewhere. The three panels of the painting pulled me in. Blue, orange, yellow, and green swaths of color with occasional bursts of red. The painting didn't look like anything in particular, really, but I felt like I could walk into it. It seemed to me almost a landscape of the human interior, like the way it feels to remember that everyone you know is going to die.

In the cafe, I wrote in my journal.

> *Who is the you aside from the list of things you are? Abuse survivor, daughter, friend, ex-girlfriend. Is there a you outside of all the identities, or are you a collection of them? When conceiving Carly, you think about everything and everyone she went through, but isn't there a separate self, an ineluctable you? Do you know that part of her or are you just collecting her traumas?*

Right then, I got a text from Kai.

I miss and love you but spending the day with Matthew Malone is fucking magic. He just told me, "A good life fits in your car. A great life fits on your motorcycle."

I responded, *He just says this shit like it's nothing.*

Him: *He called me "a cool cat" earlier.*

Me: *You ARE a cool cat.*

Him: *Thank you. I have always wanted to be a cat.*

Me: *You being a cat person is maybe the least surprising thing about you.*

Him: *I just want to lie in the sun and be certain that I am loved. Where are you right now?*

Me: *I'm in the Carnegie Museum. Spent the morning looking at contemporary art, which I enjoy but do not really understand. Maybe I need to take a class in it or something.*

I saw the three dots appear and then eventually disappear. Time to go back to work, apparently. I walked through the nineteenth-century nature-y paintings of the museum, but they didn't really speak to me. Then on my way out of the galleries, I was stopped cold by a Kerry James Marshall painting of a young Black woman at an art gallery wearing a botanical-print skirt and a loose-fitting turtleneck. I loved the painting but didn't really understand it. I wished I knew more about art—why I liked what I liked or even if I was liking the right stuff.

I took a picture of the painting and then made my way back to my apartment. I ate a banana and some cantaloupe, and posted a carousel about my museum trip to Instagram. Scrolled through Insta liking and commenting on my friends' pictures and then went through and commented on some recent posts tagging me. I'd gained eleven thousand followers—I was near four million now—since posting that pic with Matthew. He'd crush Instagram, but of course he'd never get one. Proper celebrities didn't need Instagrams. Insta is *access*—you are making yourself available to the world in exchange for their attention. Real stars, the ones light-years away from the rest of us, don't need to strike that bargain.

As I packed for the trip, I grieved my mother. I thought about how excited she'd be for this audition, how she'd call and text me before auditions no matter how shitfaced she was. For me, grief isn't the same thing as missing someone or loving someone; it is the feeling of absence, the awareness of a void. She would always call me "*my* little girl" or "*my* brilliant actress" or "*my* special baby." Always hers. And I still was. I was still hers, still in her thrall.

My previous movie, the one shot by the Cinematographer, was a romantic dramedy in which my character is falling in love while grieving her father, a stand-up comic who was rarely home with her. Of course, I did not know when I took the movie that before it wrapped, I would be grieving a parent of my own.

Every movie romance needs an Obstacle, a reason the characters don't naturally fall into each other. In our movie, the Obstacle was that my love interest pretends to be married to please his parents, only my character thinks he is *actually* married. It's a stupid Obstacle—most movie Obstacles are—but you only have two hours to tell a story and so you need shortcuts. In real life, of course, the Obstacle is always confoundingly complex. For example, Andy Warhol's Obstacles to romance were: 1. He felt ugly, 2. He worshipped fame and beauty, 3. Sex terrified him at least as much as it titillated him, 4. He struggled to find the person amid the performance. In my relationship with the Cinematographer, the Obstacle was that he wanted me until he had me, at which point I became progressively less interesting. These are not good movie Obstacles.

In real life, sometimes the Obstacle is that someone's touch makes you bristle for reasons you do not understand. The Obstacle is that they are annoying, or immature, or radiate bad vibes, or whatever. I thought about Kai, and our Obstacle. Partly I didn't have time for romance, at least not for the kind of all-consuming romance that tended to overtake me. Partly he just seemed closed off to a romantic connection. But I liked that Kai liked me. I wanted him to like me more. I liked that he said "I love you" so much, the casualness of it, and I wanted him to love me more. I couldn't even tell if I wanted him because I was so busy wanting him to want me. I liked the way my breath caught in my throat every time we touched, the way he couldn't help but walk close to me, the way our knees grazed when we sat next to each other watching *Pro Patria Mori*.

When I arrived at LAX that afternoon, a car was waiting for me. I'd finished the *Gods of Andromeda* book on the plane. There's always so much in a book that can't fit into the movie, the wanderings and asides that make a story feel real. But although I'm obviously biased, I tend to find good movies *better* than the books they're adapted from, precisely because the movie has no room for air and every scene has to accomplish multiple goals.

Anyway, I'd enjoyed *Gods of Andromeda*, and as I rode in a black Mercedes directly from the airport to the audition, I kept going back to this one page I'd dog-eared, where Agrippah has a short monologue that isn't in the screenplay. Even though I'd never perform it in real life, I thought that if I learned that one monologue, I might really understand Agrippah from within.

I knew the casting director, Nina, a little, and she greeted me at the blacked-out door of her space in West Hollywood. She walked me back to a room where everyone was seated behind a table—Brian Arawas, two producers, Todd from the studio, and the author, Valentina Leavitt. Todd was, of course, telling a joke as I walked in. "So this parrot just won't stop cursing in the foulest ways imaginable, right? Finally the owner loses his temper and throws the parrot in the freezer. The parrot squawks for a minute, and then gets totally quiet. The owner's worried he's killed it, so he opens the freezer and the parrot hops out and squawks, 'Sir, I am deeply sorry for my bad language. It won't happen again.' And then after a moment, the parrot adds, 'By the way, what did the chicken do?'"

I laughed along with everyone else then said my hellos, careful to shake hands with the author first, who almost bowed when I said how much I loved the book. Arawas was last in line, a forty-something guy wearing jeans and a tie-dye Grateful Dead T-shirt. His small, round glasses magnified his already large eyes. After the hellos, I got set up in front of the camera.

"We'll do the scene at the start of the orc war first," Nina said, and I nodded.

As they set up the cameras, I couldn't help but think of my mom again. She took me to so many auditions. I was probably eight or nine when I realized that, being drunk day and night, she was also driving drunk when she took me around town, and I remember the discordance of knowing that drunk driving was bad while also knowing that my mom was good.

Mom didn't want to want what she wanted, but she wanted it anyway. She could not have labored under the delusion that smacking me was an effective strategy for making me a good actor.

Except, then again, I am a rather good actor.

I took a second, exorcised her from my consciousness, and said my name: Juniper Castillo. Five four. Over eighteen. "The orcs are at the door, my lady," Nina said, and I fell into Agrippah. For the next thirty minutes, we ran two scenes five or six times each, with Brian and occasionally Todd giving me notes between. I needed to prove not just that I could act, but that I was directable.

After we ran the scenes, as Nina started to walk toward the cameras to turn them off, I said, "Can I— There's a scene in the book, an Agrippah monologue, that I really love. Can I try that even though it's not in the script?"

I watched Valentina perk up. "Of course," Brian said, and I launched into it.

"If we abandon our traditions in this war, the orcs have already won. For seven lifetimes, and seven before that, this staff has been held by the women who rule the Realm. This staff matters more than who holds it. But right now, my lords and ladies, *I* hold it, and I shall not relinquish it, not for man or orc."

It went on like that for a couple minutes, and I could feel myself saying it from my stomach, like the air was pressed through my belly rather than my lungs.

"That was beautiful," Valentina said when I finished.

"My God, you are *prepared*," Brian added.

"Thanks," I said. "You want me to take it again, or—"

"No, Juniper," Brian said. "I think we have everything we need. What a joy to see your Agrippah. What a gift. We'll be in touch."

11

"Is that your character notebook?" Kathryn asked me one morning between set-ups. We were shooting outside—an interview scene with Jude and Carly.

"Yeah," I said. "I guess halfway between a character notebook and a journal."

"I used to keep a diary," she said. I hated the word *diary*. It sounded like kids' stuff.

"No more?"

"I thought it would be very important, that scholars of directing would compare my diary to my films and understand the art that way. Then I directed a Verizon commercial and realized: No one is coming for my diary."

"Just helps me stay in it," I said, feeling defensive.

"Yes, well, we all have our own process."

We spent almost an hour rehearsing the walk-and-talk where I'm interviewing Jude about Andy. I had my reporter's notebook out, so I needed to write notes while walking and listening as Kai talked to me about Andy. I only had one line of dialogue—"When Andy models, do you think he's in on the joke?"—but I had to decide how Carly would listen to his epic response. It was one of the best and punchiest sections of the script.

"There is no joke, dear. There is no joke. Andy Warhol wants to be *known*. He even wants to be known, don't take this the wrong way, by you and the likes of you. But Andy also wants to be known by other artists, by tastemakers, by the electric youth, by those who assign value to culture. He is not kidding when he becomes a model; he is modeling. He is not kidding when he becomes a businessman; he is . . . business-ing. He is not kidding. He is absolutely radioactively himself. He loves the freaks and the gays and the bold because they have what you want, what we all want, which is to be at the edge of everything. They know what you'll never know, which is how to love in a world that won't love you back."

"That's going right into the trailer," Kathryn said. "I can see it now. Cut."

We shot it again. I nailed my line each time, hit my marks, and Kai hit his. It felt like we'd found our way into the rhythm of the movie. The dialogue no longer struck us as difficult or foreign; it was now our shared language. Once you know your character, it's a joy to live with them. One of the big problems with being a human is that you spend the whole time you're here inside of one body, looking at the world through one set of eyes, unable to *really* imagine with any clarity what it would be like to be someone else. You see everyone, even the people who are closest to you, in the context of yourself. *My* mother. *My* brother. *My* friend. But doing that walk-and-talk with Kai, I didn't feel like Carly was my anything. I was, insofar as it is possible to be, outside of myself and within her. That's as close to proper magic as I've ever encountered, and while I did tire of shooting the same scene again and again (sixteen times, as it happened), the feeling of being not-myself never ceased to amaze.

Did I like acting, or did I like being good at acting? I liked being good at it, but I did also love the work itself. I enjoyed finding the right action, the right moment to flip the page of my reporter's notebook, the right way of glancing up at my scene partner. Also, the money didn't hurt. I was making $90,000 for this movie—less than most people think actors make but more than I could earn in three months doing anything else. And anyway it might lead to other opportunities, more deals like the one I had with Dior. I did not yet have Enough Money, but I had a path to it, which I understand is rare among twenty-two-year-old college drop-outs. I was a child of abuse, but I was also a child of privilege forged by my abuser.

I bought dinner for Kai that night—we had Thai food delivered to his apartment—and he showed me this TV show he liked about medieval people in a land of magic fighting for power. It was well-acted, and reminded me a bit of *Gods of Andromeda*. After the show ended, we were talking about it, then we drifted off into shared quiet. Eventually, I got up to leave.

"Love you," he said.

"Thanks, Kai." I stopped at his door and turned back to him. "Kai, do you like me or do you know it's good for the movie to like me?"

"Oh, I like you. I like you a lot. I think you're very smart and interesting. You *compel* me, if that makes sense. I always want to spend more time with you."

"Thanks."

"Well, it's true. I wouldn't tell Kathryn I like her, because I don't like her."

"What don't you like about Kathryn?"

"You are much smarter than me but you don't make me feel it. She does make me feel it."

"You're smart in a different way."

"That's what smart people say to be nice."

"You're a brilliant actor."

"It's easier for me. I know less than you do, so I have less to forget."

I laughed. "And you're funny."

"Thanks, Juniper. We have a real Mutual Appreciation Society going. I like it."

"Can I ask you something?"

"Sure."

I took a step back toward him. "You talk a lot about the worst thing that ever happened, but you don't say what it was. It's hard not to be curious."

"That's not a question."

"What was the worst thing?"

"I had to testify in a trial, basically."

"What happened?"

He sighed. "There is this thing that people do. A thing I've noticed. Where they think if they show each other their most horrible horrors or whatever, then they are close. Then they are friends. You tell me about your mother, and I tell you about the trial, and then we are bonded. But it's not really a way to know someone, just to see their goriest wounds. It's like a shortcut. I don't want to take a shortcut with you."

I wanted to say, *But you ask me about my mom all the time.* I knew he was just being defensive, and part of me wanted to break down those walls and get to the core of him. But it was his life, his story, and his choice about whether to share it. "Okay," I said. "Fair enough. I'm just saying I want to be close to you. I want to listen to you."

"Good night, Juniper. Love you."

"Good night, Kai."

12

In the pages we shot the next day, Andy is at a gallery opening in Italy—the last opening of his life, his *Last Supper* paintings. Kai and I are mostly just in the background commenting on how he looks (frail, unwell) and the overall pseudohappy vibe of the event (the gallerist who'd commissioned the work was hospitalized, dying of AIDS, but everyone was trying to pretend all was fine). There were reproductions of the paintings in our fake gallery that had been built inside a Pittsburgh warehouse, and in between set-ups I kept looking at them.

"You like this stuff, huh?" Kai asked.

"I don't understand it, but I like it."

"That's how I feel about people," Kai said, and I started to say something, but he had already walked away to talk with Lon and Natalie. I stayed in front of the painting for a while—a huge re-creation of da Vinci's *The Last Supper* but with swaths of Andy's colors. I thought about how I was looking at a reproduction of a Warhol painting, which was itself a reproduction of a *Last Supper* plaster sculpture Andy bought in Times Square, which was itself a reproduction of the da Vinci painting. Warhol would've liked that, I suspect.

Warhol was a Catholic, like me I guess, even though I don't go to

Mass. The paintings weren't jokes, but they didn't feel especially sacred either. Again I found myself wondering whether it was all just skin-deep with him. I looked up and Matthew, in his silver wig and skeletal frame, was standing next to me.

"I still don't get Andy," he told me. "Fortunately for me, Andy also didn't get Andy, so I'm safe."

We didn't wrap that week until four a.m. on Saturday. I slept until noon and then read some poetry from an anthology called *American Poetics* that had been part of my Modernism at Night curriculum. I'd been trying to disentangle myself from my phone, which rather ruled my life, and so it was past two p.m. when I finally got out of bed and found that my phone, plugged into the bathroom wall outlet, contained three missed calls and several text messages from Jamie.

I called her. "What's going on?"

"They want you for *Gods of Andromeda*. A million two up front and the back end doesn't suck, but we're gonna try to bump it up a little. You won't get first dollar rev share or anything, but if the movie makes money you'll make money. The book is hot. Brian Arawas is brilliant. I love this for you. What are you thinking?"

"One point two million dollars?"

"Correct. And if they make sequels, we'll negotiate higher from there."

I did the math: My lawyer would get $60,000 for the contract. Jamie would get $120,000. Then there's Katie's retainer, and a stylist, and taxes, and whatever whatever. I'm still walking out of that deal with half a million dollars in cash.

"Yes," I said.

"YES!" Jamie said. "Yes! I'll call the studio now and get it closed."

One thing about my mom: She was not stingy with her pride. She always told me she was proud of me. Even after a bad audition, she was proud. She'd always call me and my brother "my pride and joy," but when I was a kid, I thought she was saying "my pride *enjoy*," like she enjoyed feeling pride in us. I knew how proud she would be of me booking the lead in such a huge movie. I could picture her face—sallow and worn, one of those faces that reminds you that gravity is pulling us down—lighting up when I told her I booked it. *So what*, Andy might say.

I called Kai first. "I booked Agrippah."

"HOLY SHIT YES YOU DID! OF COURSE YOU DID!" he shouted. "Yes! I just punched the air like a character in a sports movie. You're Agrippah!"

"Queen of the Realm," I said.

"I'm gonna try to get in as an extra just to see you in your hot Agrippah outfits."

"Queens in the Realm mostly wear full-length robes, actually."

"Stop, it's getting too sexy," he said. "Oh my God! Juniper, this is amazing. We gotta celebrate. I don't have a 'we gotta celebrate' budget but I know someone who does. Hold on; I'll call you right back."

He hung up on me. I tried to go back to reading poetry, but I was buzzing with the thrill of it. One point two million. A proper lead in a properly big movie. Kai called back. "Okay we're meeting at a bar called the Pelican at three p.m. You and me and maybe a wealthy benefactor. Drinks are on me. By which I mean on him."

"I don't drink," I reminded him.

"I know. I googled 'best mocktail in Pittsburgh,' and the Pelican came up. You're going to get absolutely sloshed on virgin mojitos."

"Okay," I said after a minute. "I'll see you at three."

Matthew Malone was waiting for me outside the bar, wearing a ball cap and sunglasses. “Oh, Junie,” he said, “congratulations,” and hugged me. As we walked into the bar, I said, “Did you really tell Tom Weisman you’d make another movie with the studio if he cast me?”

“Maybe,” Matthew said. “But only because I was gonna do that movie anyway.” He smiled with half his mouth and I said, “Thank you, Matthew,” and he said, “Our business runs on favors. You’ll pay me back someday by casting me in a movie you’re producing when I’m old and decrepit. You’ve got the drive, Junie. You’re talented, but it’s the ambition that’ll get you where you’re going.”

When Matthew got to the bar, he took off his sunglasses and the bartender did a double take before saying, “Are you . . . who I think you are?”

“Indeed. Some friends and I are celebrating this afternoon and hoping to rent out your bar.”

“Well, there’s basically no one here.” There were, in fact, two people in a booth, staring mouths agape at Matthew Malone.

“We’d like to have a private event.”

“Sir, I’m, uh, I’m not sure I can just kick people out of here. I’d have to call my manager.”

“Would fifty thousand dollars be sufficient for a private party rental for a couple hours?”

The guy nodded rather furiously. “Yeah. Yeah. That would, uh, yeah, I’ll figure it out.”

“And as apology for the inconvenience, I’ll pay their bar tab,” he said, nodding toward the couple in the booth.

“Sure, of course,” the bartender said. The couple was soon gone.

Kai showed up a few minutes later and enveloped me in a hug. “You’re a proper movie star now,” he said. “Even if our movie sucks—”

“Which it doesn’t,” Matthew interrupted.

“Which of course it doesn’t but even if it does, you’re . . . I mean . . .

you're gonna be Matthew Fucking Malone, wearing sunglasses and a hat everywhere you go."

"Well," said Matthew, "let's not get out of hand. There is only one Matthew Fucking Malone."

I drank three different mocktails—one with some kind of fake gin that was called Juniper Everlasting, which we all got a kick out of. Matthew drank his standard old-fashioneds, and plenty of them. Kai had a couple beers, and we talked about the shoot so far, and how we only had two weeks left. "Kai will remember this as his first real movie," Matthew said, "but I wonder how you'll remember it."

"As my first really good movie," I told him.

"I'll remember it for the two of you," he said. "Two kids who clearly love their work and each other. You've reminded me why I do it. Why I still want it, in spite of everything."

Kai put his arm around me, and I felt really cared for in that moment. But of course I did. I can't help but associate success with being loved; I was trained to do it.

13

My favorite part of the script, the part that really made me want to do it, wasn't dialogue at all but the page describing a scene of Andy at the hospital, preparing for his gallbladder surgery.

The music swells. He hated hospitals. Depicted everything in his work—electric chairs, business executives, shoes, car accidents, wine bottles, drugs and cats and buildings and dollar bills. But only once a hospital bed. 1954. He was just starting out. It was an ink drawing, nearly abstract. Commission, of course. He was not Warhol then, not yet. He was still Andrew Warhola. Whatever we make, what we are really fabricating is the self. The quality of his line suggested promise, but promise is common, even ubiquitous, among twenty-six-year-olds. In the drawing, the hospital bed is in the background. In the foreground, hands. The hands that reached into his father, perhaps. The ones that took out the old man's gallbladder, the surgery from which Ondrej never recovered. Now the son was in a hospital bed. Same failed organ. Same surgery. Long time since he'd thought of himself as Ondrej's son, but here he was, a boy in a gown, no say in what happens. Awful to be wigless and dressed like this, more so since the nurses all knew. That's Warhol. The artist. What a thing to have become, Warhol the artist, forged in the smithy of his soullessness.

A nurse enters the room, the music stops, and Andy hears, "It's time to go, Mr. Warhol." He is alone—his longtime partner Jon having died of AIDS a year earlier. Warhol holds a crystal in his hand—he became a Crystal Guy at the end—and goes off into surgery, a surgery he will never recover from.

We never see the corpse; we see us hearing the news, and the world hearing the news. And then all his friends and colleagues gather at the Factory, because even though it no longer really exists it's the only place to go. Jude and I end up on the roof of his apartment and share our first kiss there, in what the script calls "a stubborn unwillingness to give in to despair."

The love scene was at the very end of the shoot, and before it we met with an intimacy coordinator who asked us each for our vision of the scene and what kind of coverage we wanted. I was never out of a bra, but Kai was ostensibly naked, so he had to wear a little patch around his crotch. That day we kissed and it felt like kissing, and I straddled him and it felt like straddling, and the camera raked across his naked torso and down past his hip, and it's just acting but it *is* also making out. It's a both/and drug of the strangest variety, not least because even though it was a closed set, lots of people were watching, including the guy holding the boom mic, who had to hold it above his head while Kathryn got her minutes-long shot, and when Kathryn finally shouted *cut*, he'd lower the mic and groan like he was also having sex, something Kai and I kept laughing about between shots.

This time around, Kai didn't struggle to go into the emotional depths. I felt him trusting me. I kissed him, and I kissed his tears. I stroked his hair as he heaved sobs into my shoulder. In between set-ups, he sat on his cast chair with AirPods in, and then he'd go back to crying. It was beautiful and quiet on set, like all of us were sharing in this terrible loss.

I kept thinking about when my mom died, even though I didn't want to. I'd been on set that day, making the movie shot by the Cinematographer, and in the middle of a take the director called *cut* and said, "Junie, I need to talk to you in your trailer." I hate being called Junie, but people always call me it anyway once they think they know me.

In my trailer, she said, "Your mom was found dead this morning. I'm so sorry, Junie." My first thought was *It's over*. It's over. The stress of it was over. Not knowing whether to take her calls, not knowing whether to send her money . . . over. But then, she *had* loved me. She had hurt me a lot, but she had loved me too, and holding that paradox only became more impossible after she died.

A hundred and thirty people were on set waiting for me to come back to work, so I went back to work. I finished the day. My mother, if nothing else, raised a professional.

Back in my trailer after shooting the love scene, I could hear Kai pacing across the thin wall between us.

"Do you want to be alone?" I asked him through the wall.

"Not really," he said, and so I went outside and walked up the steps to his trailer and I lay down on the couch with him and let his beautiful hair run through my fingers. It was not that different from the scene we'd just filmed, only without kissing.

"I can go there now," he said. "You made it safe for me, to go to the deepest places, the places that don't feel settled."

"When you love someone, part of their pain becomes yours, I guess."

"You basically just said you love me back," Kai said, laughing a bit.

"Basically," I admitted.

When we wrapped a couple days later, everybody clapped for me and for Kai, and I cried a little, and Matthew Malone came to set even though he wasn't working that day, and he hugged us and then Kai hugged me and told me he loved me for the thousandth time. Back at my trailer, there was a card on my couch. It read, *To my favorite sister-in-law, Happy Birthday.*

> *Dear Juniper,*
>
> *Thanks for making this movie. Thanks for being so fun to act with. The air is different when you are in a room. You change the atmosphere. Thank you for being a good friend, and for not judging me. Thank you thank you thank you. I love you.*
>
> *At six, I will be in the lobby of our building wearing my finest, because Matthew got a present that is for both of us.*
>
> *Love,*
> *Kai*

Tony drove me home one last time in his white van. "How was it, kid?" he asked.

"I just hope the movie's good."

"You gotta enjoy the process, kid. The hours suck, the pay is mediocre, but you're making movies, you know what I mean?"

"Yeah," I said. "I do like making movies."

"Well, it's been a pleasure driving y'all around. What's next for ya?"

"An epic fantasy," I said. "You?"

“There’s a Batman movie coming to town. I’ll try to get on that, but so will everyone else.”

“I hope our paths cross again,” I said.

“Oh, they will,” Tony said. “Life is long if you’re lucky, and don’t neither of us have enough to retire.”

14

I made myself look presentable—a long-sleeve minidress and knee-high boots that a stylist once paired for me somewhere along the way. I brushed my hair out and left it down. I've come to understand that I have good hair, or at least plenty of it. When I got downstairs, Kai was already there, leaning against a pillar in the lobby, wearing a black suit with a narrow black tie. "Wow," he said. "God, you're beautiful."

"Thanks, Kai. You aren't hard to look at either. What'd Matthew get us?"

"Any guesses?"

"I'm hoping it's a car. I heard he gave a motorcycle to every member of his stunt crew after his last movie."

"Oh. Well, uh, prepare to be underwhelmed."

In the SUV—all black, leather seats, driven by a suited chauffeur—I asked Kai where we were going.

"I was talking with Matthew about what I should get you as a wrap present, and he said that experiences last longer than possessions."

"What a Matthew thing to say."

"Yeah. And he was like, what does she like, and it occurred to me that even though we've talked a lot, I don't know what you like. I know you don't love baseball . . ."

"I don't."

"But I don't know if you, like, love knitting."

"I don't."

"Well, presumably you like *something* and so I could get you a pottery class or a visit with a professor of eighteenth-century French literature or whatever, but I actually don't know if you like any of that stuff either. The only thing I know you like is art, but you say you don't understand it. So I told Matthew that you liked art and maybe I could take you to a museum with a tour guide or whatever, and he said, 'I'll arrange something,' so we're going to the Carnegie to see whatever he arranged."

"That's very thoughtful, Kai. Also," I did not know how else to say it, "you're making my wrap present look really bad."

"The iPad case? With the Warhol Soup Can on it? I fucking adore my iPad case! Do not talk bad about my beloved iPad case."

When we arrived at the museum, a small woman with short bangs was standing outside, looking at her phone. "Kai and Juniper?" she asked, and we nodded, and she introduced herself as the senior curator of contemporary art at the Carnegie Museum. She was perhaps forty-five, large-eyed and serious. "I heard you like our Joan Mitchell triptych," she said to me.

"Yes, but I don't understand it."

"Oh, I'm not sure there's as much to understand as you may fear," she said as she unlocked the door to the museum and ushered us inside. We walked up a staircase into a long, narrow gallery. I stopped in front of that Kerry James Marshall painting of a woman in a gallery again, as the curator explained to me that Black skin had often been neglected and painted poorly. Artists like Marshall sought to capture skin in new ways while engaging deeply with art history, a point emphasized by placing the figure inside a gallery. Across from me, Kai was staring at a churning, energetic painting of what looked like a semi-deconstructed stadium. "Ah, Julie Mehretu," the curator said. "One of my favorites. I've always thought this maybe reflects what it's like to be an athlete in the Olympics or something—a swirl of flags and nationalism, of fear and pride."

As we walked through the next gallery, looking at Monet's *Water Lilies* and Van Gogh and Boudin, the curator said, "Art often seeks places language cannot seek, to express what cannot otherwise be expressed. Of course, art criticism is an intellectual exercise, but it's attempting to apply academic rigor to a field that is fundamentally beyond rigor. Anyway, in the next gallery you'll find our Joan Mitchell triptych."

She explained that caring for this painting, titled *Sans Neige,* or *Without Snow*, was one of the reasons she'd moved to Pittsburgh from New York for this job. "Mitchell painted many triptychs—you can see the work comprises three equal-sized canvases pressed together—but for me this one seems uniquely *alive.*

"In Renaissance paintings," the curator said as we stood before that immense and intoxicating painting, "when you wanted to paint innocence, you painted the infant Christ, and when you wanted to paint redemptive suffering, you painted the crucified Christ. But of course, these are not *images* of innocence or suffering; they are metaphors for innocence and suffering. How do you paint the thing directly—the feeling? This is the question that artists like Mitchell and Agnes Martin set for themselves. So what do you feel when you look at it?"

"Entranced," I said. "Engrossed. It's almost a world I want to step into."

"And you said you don't understand art," the curator said. "Mitchell called these paintings landscapes, even though they don't look like traditional vistas. You want to step into it because you're looking at a place."

As we walked through the halls, Kai grabbed my hand, his fingers interlaced with mine. I felt my pulse increase. Kai's hands were soft, his long fingers pressed against my knuckles. His skin felt so alive against mine.

I thought it might happen that night when he brought me back to his apartment to watch a movie. It was a rom-com and everything—one from the nineties about the president falling in love with an environmental attorney. We sat next to each other, me with my feet curled up on the couch, and I could feel his breath rising and falling as he sat with his hand around the back of the couch but not quite around me. I kept looking over at him, but he was always watching the movie, smiling faintly, his face gleaming by the changing light of the film. I couldn't quite identify our Obstacle. I wanted him so desperately in that moment, but something still invisible lay between us. We had talked so much across the weeks, but there was still something unspoken. If we could've said it, maybe that night might've been different, but instead, as the credits rolled, Kai jumped up and suggested we make our way to the roof deck of our apartment building.

Up there, I drank an iced tea while we talked about how it was almost like in the movie, how in the film they sit on a roof and talk about Andy being gone, and how all of us will be gone soon. It got quiet, and after a while he said, "I will miss this. I will miss you."

"Me too, Kai. I don't think I'll ever do a movie quite like this one again."

"Maybe we'll end up in a ton of movies together."

"That'd be fun," I said, "but probably not."

"Probably not. Thanks for getting me through it. I never understood it before now, but acting isn't really about *you*. It's about the people you're listening to. Your scene partners or whatever."

"The magic isn't in what I do or what you do, but what happens between us."

"Yeah," he said. "Exactly. I really love you, Juniper."

"Back at ya, Kai," I said at last, and I could feel his smile even though I was too shy to look over at him.

Making a movie is like going to summer camp. You feel certain the relationships are so real, so deep, that they will last a lifetime, but then the Cinematographer dumps you after the movie comes out, and your regular group chat with your costars drifts into occasional happy birthday messages, and the only reason you even know their birthday is because they post a cake on their Instagram. It turns out that the main reason you were friends is proximity, and having shared some strange intense experience together. In the rough seas of the real world, you can't get the magic back of being on a rooftop in Pittsburgh with someone you've finally accepted you love. I figured that in the night sky of my life, Kai Laramie would be one of those shooting stars that streaks across the sky but then burns up almost before you can even get excited.

PART 2

THE TEST

KAI

1

The day before I was scheduled to fly to Los Angeles to see *Andy Warhol Never Gets Old*, my publicist, Ellen, asked to meet me at a cafe for lunch. Ellen, along with Juniper and Studio Todd, was in New York for a media lunch launching the movie. I wasn't invited to the lunch because I hadn't yet gotten my media training, and apparently Hollywood does not trust an unvetted actor.

The cafe, three stops on the C train from my apartment in Brooklyn, was mostly empty except for a few people wearing AirPods and hunched over laptops. As I ordered my coffee and a croissant, I noticed Ellen was already there, seated in the back corner beneath a painting of the night sky. I pulled up a chair. "You realize I'm not *your* publicist, right?" she said by way of introduction.

I did not realize this. "Okay?" I said.

"I am your publicist for this project, but I work for the studio. Like if I were a lawyer, I wouldn't be *your* lawyer."

"Got it," I said.

"Right, so the studio is considering you for the junket," she said. "This would be a big deal. If I were your publicist, I'd be very excited about it."

"Which you are not."

"Which I am not. You'd be paired in interviews with Juniper, and you'd talk to a variety of media outlets in a variety of settings. Televised interviews with local morning shows around the country. Maybe some national talk show hits if we're lucky. And also some proper junketing, where every seven minutes for several hours, a reporter comes into a windowless hotel conference room and asks you questions on camera. It's a tedious process. No one particularly enjoys it. But you must concentrate, because any mistake can be catastrophic. You'll recall, for instance, when Charles Oldham said the R-word."

"I feel like it's pretty easy not to use slurs," I said.

"Great, that actually makes you better than most movie stars. So, right, then you'll also do roundtable interviews with reporters from print and online. Seven or eight people with tape recorders gathered at a table, and they'll ask you questions and you'll answer. And then we'll do some photo shoots and hopefully one or two big profiles, if we can get them, where a reporter spends a day or two with you and writes about what a genius you are, unless you're not careful and say something stupid or act like an asshole. So. Tell me about how you prepared for this role."

"I met with Kathryn and we talked about—"

"No. Did you even read the talking points?" I nodded unconvincingly, and Ellen rolled her eyes as she continued. "I don't know who Kathryn is. I'm not a film person. I'm a thirty-seven-year-old divorced father of two living in the suburbs of Chicago. What you did was dive headfirst into the life of Andy Warhol, beginning by reading his diaries."

"Well, I listened to the audiobook."

"That's reading, Kai. So yes, you start there. With your immense research. What's your acting process?"

"Well, someone said once that you read the script two hundred and fifty times and then give yourself over to the imagined circumstances, so that's what I did." This was something of a lie, but I did not feel like telling Ellen anything personal.

"That's good but you need to attribute it." She was on her iPad. "Anthony Hopkins said that. So attribute it."

"Got it," I said.

"How did you prepare for the role?"

"I began by reading Warhol's diaries and then reading every book about Warhol I could find so that I could fathom the characters in this film."

"Great, but don't say this film. Say *Andy Warhol Never Gets Old*." It went on like that—for an hour. Ellen would ask questions: What was it like to work with Matthew? How do you and Juniper achieve such chemistry in your on-screen time together? Why do you think this film is important? She'd analyze my stupid answers and recraft them, and then she'd circle back to other questions before throwing in something random. If you could say one thing to the president, what would it be? Your first celebrity crush? I hear you're dating Juniper; is that true?

"No, of course not," I said. "Juniper is married to the sea."

Ellen laughed, and made a note on her iPad. "That's so good I'm going to make one of these jackasses ask it."

"I mean it, though."

"Yeah, that's what makes it fucking hilarious. Is it true she's doing *Gods of Andromeda*?"

"Yeah, she got the lead."

"No no no no, Jesus, Kai. No. You say, 'I've read the book and it's great, but I don't know what Juniper's doing next.'"

"Right, but I wasn't talking to a journalist. I was talking to you."

"For the next twenty-four days, assume that literally everything you say out loud is going to be printed in a magazine that your grandparents will read."

"That's a bit dystopian."

She just shrugged. "On to personal shit that will get dug up about you. Here's the thing, Kai. If there's something—say, a vertical video of you punching a woman, a racist tweet you wrote when you were a twelve-year-old edgelord, or whatever, just tell me. It's so much easier not to be surprised."

"I don't tweet," I answered.

"Are we going to have sexual harassment or assault issues?"

"No."

"You ever been arrested?"

I shook my head.

"What's your number? Is it in the double digits? Triple digits?"

"My number?"

"Of sexual partners."

"Single digits."

"You need to get out more," she deadpanned. "So it's all smooth sailing from you. Where's the iceberg? Your dad's in a weird militia? You're a flat-earther? Everybody's got something, Kai."

"What's your something?" I asked her.

"If I wanted to discuss my somethings, I would've become an actor." I knew what she was asking about, but I couldn't tell if she knew what she was asking about. "You ever been sued?"

"No."

"Ever sued someone?"

I reached into my pocket and got a piece of gum. I like chewing gum—the old-fashioned stick kind. There's this flavor called Fresh Mint I've chewed since I was a kid, and it smells like a forest in summertime. I unwrapped the gum from its silver foil and started chewing. Ellen asked again if I'd ever sued anyone, and I said no, which was true, but I was pretty sure she knew. I could feel the electricity of it in the air. My chest felt tight.

I leaned backward, hands across my chest. Among the many things

I recommend about Fresh Mint gum is that when you're chewing it, you can't smell anything else.

"Ever been a witness in a trial?"

"I think you know the answer to that," I said, and she didn't respond. I thought about whether he'd done it *to* me or *with* me. Always hated prepositions. To me, I guess. *For* me, he would say.

"Yeah, I've been a witness in a trial," I said finally. "A teacher molested me or whatever."

This is part of you, he often said. *Part of you we need to bring out.*

"Don't say *or whatever*. Or *molested*. Say *assaulted*."

"I'm not saying any of those words, because I'm not talking about it."

"Okay," Ellen said. "You're not talking about it, and I will make it clear if someone digs it up that you're not talking about it. We can keep it out of the press. But I can't keep it from leaking if I don't know about it."

"Well, you know about it," I said.

"It's nothing to be ashamed of," Ellen said. "It's not bad for us."

"Well, it wasn't great for me."

"I mean it's not bad for the movie. Anyway, you need to tell me these things so that I won't be surprised. I know this part of it sucks, but it comes with the territory. Is there anything else I need to know?"

"I don't know. Did anything else come up when you called my friends from high school?"

"Your friends didn't say anything, if that makes you feel any better. I found out from one of your teachers. Nobody had a bad thing to say about you, Kai. They saw the same sweet, sensitive kid I see."

He always told me it was only me, that no other student had or could ever tempt him. That was a lie, of course. It turned out there were many of us. But I was chosen to testify at the trial, because I was the all-American, straight-presenting athlete. They kept my name sealed, but that doesn't mean much in a high school.

The gum was starting to lose its flavor. I could smell the coffee in the air again. "We done?" I asked.

"You can't be pissed at me for doing my job, Kai. You know how many movies have tanked in the last ten years because it came out that the actors were fuckwads? Studios have to be careful now. I'm sure you get it."

"I do get it. I'm just asking if we're done."

"If you want my advice, you should get out in front of it and put it behind you. We get you a sympathetic profiler—someone at the *Times* or maybe *The New Yorker*—and you acknowledge it and move on. You've got to remember, you're a victim here. You didn't do anything wrong. But if you hide it—"

"If that's it, I'm going to go home and pack," I said. "I hope I passed the test."

On the train home, I wondered if I should tell Juniper. In the four months since we'd wrapped on *Andy Warhol Never Gets Old*, Juniper and I had met up maybe five or six times. I was in Canada for a couple weeks playing Kevin the Intern in a spectacularly unfunny comedy, and Juniper was obsessively prepping for *Gods of Andromeda* in LA.

Telling her would feel weird, but also not telling her felt weird. I should've told her in Pittsburgh, but I was scared. I am always scared. Part of me will never not feel the fear that boiled up when the defense counsel began her cross-examination.

The hardest thing in life is to be small, to not have any say over what happens to you or who does it. To be at other people's mercy. I required mercy. I always would. And I hated that. You couldn't get out in front of that, not ever. You can't put it behind you. I was twenty-one years old and he was dead and he still had his goddamned hands all over me.

2

Juniper and I were sitting across from each other on the plane with a fold-out table and a sizable vase of flowers between us, such that Juniper's head seemed to be made of tightly bunched rosebuds. The flight attendant asked me if I wanted a glass of wine. I said I would love to try the red. She poured, the wine not splashing into the glass but swirling into it, and I took a sip as the flight attendant looked at me expectantly. "It's great," I told her, and she said, "I'm so glad you like it," and Juniper said, "When I die, bury me with this plane," and Katie the Publicist said, "If you want to own a plane like this, you better crush *Gods of Andromeda*."

After a while, Juniper said, "Will you run a scene with me?"

"From *Gods of Andromeda*?"

"Yeah," she said.

"Sure." I wanted to push the flowers out of the way. It was ridiculous to have a conversation without seeing each other. But I didn't do it for some reason. They didn't feel like my flowers.

Juniper scooched out from the table and came over to my side. Her hair was down over her face. She was wearing sweatpants and a tank top, but neither looked particularly casual or comfortable. She pulled out an extremely folded paper from her pocket and handed it to me. It reminded me of a middle school love letter. I unfolded the pages and scanned the action. "You're Agrippah, right?"

"I guess if I want this plane I am. Agrippah, Queen of the Realm."

I smirked and just went into it. "You dare disturb the lawful trial of Medivh?"

"I fear I must, for—"

"Strike this woman!"

"The orcs." There was gravel in Juniper's throat all of a sudden. "The orcs, my lord. They have laid waste to Calenbath. What is not fire is ash. Our allies are gone. Our enemies are at the gate. The future is in doubt and the past is buried in the ground, my lord. There is only time, and that time is now."

"Can it be—"

"The time for questions has passed, Gavinth. The time of speaking has passed. We fight now, all of us. No trials. No tribes. No guilds. Only human and orc. We fight for the Realm that was. AND WE FIGHT FOR THE REALM THAT SHALL BE!"

"That was good," I said.

"The newest rewrite made the script so much worse. It makes me want to die a little."

"Then maybe back out of it?"

"She's not backing out of it," said Katie the Publicist. "That movie is going to shit money."

Ellen, sitting next to her on the couch, agreed. "Everyone with a goddamned pulse is trying to get into *Gods of Andromeda* one way or another. Brilliant director. Massive budget. It's the next tentpole for the studio, and Katie is correct about it shitting money. It'll get money norovirus and shit money while it pukes money."

Juniper and I shared a look. "Any news on Garon?" she asked me.

I was in the running to play Gavinth's anxious brother, Garon, in *Gods of Andromeda*. I'd sent in a self-tape right after we wrapped on *Warhol*, and they liked it, so once they cast the leads, they wanted me to come in for a chemistry read. "Not yet," I said. "I haven't even seen the full script. But everyone says Brian Arawas is brilliant."

Juniper rolled her eyes a little but leaned in to me. I could smell her shampoo. "If he's so smart, why did he direct that *X-Men* movie?"

"That *X-Men* movie made Buy This Plane money," Katie said.

Also, I'd liked it, but I didn't say anything.

Studio Todd, squeezed onto the couch beside Ellen and Katie, said, "You ever heard the one about the moth?"

"Jesus Christ, Todd. If you tell one more joke, I'm going to jump out of this fucking plane," said Ellen.

"Okay, so a moth flies into a cardiologist's office," Todd said. He had gray hair, but it was cut fashionably, and he always wore a very trim suit. Talked a lot, so I knew a lot about him. He had girls, both in college, which you wouldn't believe the cost. He woke up every morning at five a.m. and ran for exactly five miles, and had been doing this six days a week since he was in high school. Told me that once he'd torn something in his knee and couldn't run for six months and glimpsed insanity. He told a lot of jokes. "And the cardiologist—a cardiologist is a heart doctor, works on hearts."

"We know what a cardiologist is, Todd," said Katie.

"The cardiologist says, 'What seems to be the problem, moth?' And the moth says, 'Oh, doc, if only there were one problem. My father is dead, and I miss him terribly. I'm still a young moth, and I don't know how to live in the world without him. My girlfriend—I guess she was my girlfriend, but I'm not even sure—has gone completely mad and no longer even recognizes me. And worst of all, my mother has taken up with my uncle. I feel so lost and alone, doc. I don't even know if I want to go on living.' And the cardiologist says, 'Well, those are very serious problems, moth, but it seems like you need to see a psychiatrist. I'm a cardiologist. What brought you *here* today?' And the moth says, 'Oh, the light was on.'"

Only Juniper laughed, but she *really* laughed.

3

When we landed in California, Katie the Publicist wanted to take a picture of Juniper and me in front of the plane, but I said no, because I couldn't have people in real life know that I was on a private plane. "You Insta for your fans not your friends," said Katie the Publicist.

"I Insta for my friends," I said.

Juniper laughed. She took a step toward me and grabbed my hand. "I love it. He's like the last Truffula Tree in Lorax Land. Don't cut him down, Katie. Let him live."

"Love you," I said to Juniper. She smiled.

There were two black SUVs waiting for us—Juniper and Katie and Studio Todd disappeared into one of them, and then Ellen and I got into the other. Our driver said his name was Al.

"Like Alvin?" I asked.

"No," he said.

"I'm Kai," I said.

"Like *Cobra Kai*?"

"Exactly like it," I said.

"You're coming in from New York?"

"Yeah."

"You don't sound like a New Yorker," he said. Beside me, Ellen was inside her phone. The SUV didn't smell like one thing or another so much as it smelled overwhelming.

"I'm from Indiana," I told him.

"My condolences."

Ellen handed me the phone. It was Juniper's Instagram, a picture of her and me holding hands with the plane in the background. "Juniper posted this?"

"If I had to guess, Katie posted it for Juniper."

"She said I was the last Truffula Tree in Lorax Land, and then she cut me down."

"No need to be dramatic, Kai. It's Instagram."

Katie was not a studio publicist like Ellen; she worked for Juniper. Once you get famous enough, you get your own publicist. Juniper was famous enough. But now she was about to happen. That's what Ellen said. Ellen said people like Juniper don't know what's coming, but it's coming anyway.

"Where in Indiana?" Al asked.

"Indianapolis."

"Race cars," he said. "That's all I know about Indianapolis."

"Yup. You from here?"

"No, I'm from Iran. You know Iran?"

"Sure," I said.

"You in a movie?"

"Yeah," I said.

"What movie?"

"It's called *Andy Warhol Never Gets Old.*"

"About the artist?"

"Yes," I said.

Ellen jumped in. "It's about the last year of Warhol's life. Kai is an absolute revelation in the film."

"So who do you play?" Al asked.

"I'm Andy's intern. The movie is mostly about Andy, but there's a subplot where me and this journalist who's writing about Andy kind of fall in love."

"They don't kind of fall in love. They do fall in love," Ellen said. "It's very romantic."

"But we're both kind of messed up," I said. "In the movie, I mean."

After a while, Al said, "I meet a lot of actors."

"You ever meet Matthew Malone?" Ellen asked.

"Sure, I met Matthew. Drove Matthew a few times. Nice guy. Quiet."

"Matthew's in the movie," Ellen said.

I could hear Al smile. Matthew makes everyone smile. It's his superpower. "That's great. Congratulations. What are you doing next?"

"I don't know," I said. "I don't even know what I'm doing tonight."

Al laughed. Outside, Los Angeles was tinted gray. I'd only been here a few times. Before the movie, I spent a year in New York auditioning and working, and before that I was a senior in high school.

I don't like to think too much about all that stuff, where you are in your life or in your career or where you live or whatever. It gives me a stomachache. I get the same stomachache when Ellen shows me the calendar laying out the twenty-three days before the movie's premiere, or when I look at Reddit, or when the ATM asks if I want to see my account balance. I have some kind of stomachache most of the time, and so I don't eat enough, which is part of the reason I don't look like someone who is about to happen. All the guys who are going to happen in young Hollywood are ripped.

Everyone always says Los Angeles is sunny, but it's mostly just dry. No weeds growing in the sidewalk cracks. Summer in Indianapolis looks like nature is about to take the land back from us—everything wet and humid and green and growing. In LA, even the green lawns look parched. Never enough water.

Al asked me if I liked Matthew. I told him I did, which was the truth, and I thought about one time when Matthew told me that it was easier to love than to be loved. But I wasn't thinking of Matthew Malone. I was thinking about Juniper. I hadn't seen her in a month before that flight. We'd FaceTimed, but I'd almost forgotten about her *presence*, the way air shifts when she's near you, like how people's voices change when they read poems out loud.

4

Al dropped us off at the Hotel Bel-Air. Ellen and I had to take three different elevators to get to my suite, which had a living room and a huge patio with its own miniature heated pool. It was larger than the studio apartment I'd had when we filmed *Warhol.*

I texted Juniper: *My room has a pool.*

Juniper texted back: *If you turn the TV on and walk around the room, it follows you.* Even when you live in a city, the studio will put you up when you're doing promo, and so while Juniper was an Angeleno, she still got a free hotel room.

I turned the TV on. Romantic piano music played while the screen showed information about the Hotel Bel-Air. Ellen and I walked all around the room, and the TV tilted itself to face us wherever we went. When I ducked, the TV rotated downward so that I could still see all of the information the Hotel Bel-Air wanted to share about itself.

I had a text from Bob. *Call me when you can. Arawas update.* I didn't really want to call him, though. Bob talked so much it was kind of exhausting, like the world was on fire and only his talking could put it out, and I was a little dizzy from the plane.

The living room couch looked beautiful but uncomfortable. Lots of right angles. There was champagne on the coffee table in front of it, and the bottle shifted a little as some ice melted. I turned off the TV. "Are we doing anything after we see the movie?" I asked Ellen.

"You are going with Juniper and the producers to the only vegetarian restaurant on earth with two Michelin stars. I am going to eat take-out Thai with my wife on our couch while we watch television and continue our long-standing argument about whether we can start a family when one of us travels so much for work."

I went into the bedroom and lay on the bed on my stomach. Ellen followed me in, sat in a desk chair, and said, "The movie is really good." She said it like she was sorry.

"But?" I said.

"No but. It's a great movie. And you're great in it."

"But?"

"How do you feel about Juniper?"

"I love Juniper."

"Wonderful." Ellen checked her phone, stood up, and typed while she talked. "Kai, the test scores for this movie are *insane*. Do you know what test scores are?" I nodded, even though I didn't really. "Ninety-two percent top two boxes. *Ninety-two percent.* So the scores are amazing, but it's an art movie. Nobody even knows this film exists. Nobody knows what it's called because the title has five fucking words. You know how many hit movies have five-word titles? None. Think of the movies that do well: *Transformers* is about cars that transform. *Meet the Parents* is about meeting the parents. This is a movie about an *artist* who is *dead.* You can't possibly know how rare this is, how lucky you are to get a first movie that is pure fucking gold and could be in the awards hunt. But *we have to get people to see the movie.*"

Ellen tossed me her phone and said, "You see a pattern there?"

It was Juniper's Instagram.

"A lot of pictures of her and me?"

The bed at the Hotel Bel-Air was the nicest bed I'd ever laid on. I started wondering how many nights I could stay there consecutively before I ran out of money. I'd never had a lot of money, but I'd gotten eighty thousand for the movie, and I hadn't spent any of it. I had enough from being in two Lowe's commercials to cover the rent in the apartment where I supposedly lived.

"How much do you think this room costs a night?" I asked Ellen.

"Are you listening?" she asked.

"Yeah, sorry. What?"

"Juniper transparently and authentically likes you, and you transparently and authentically like Juniper, and this transparent and authentic fondness should be regularly reinforced to your followers, which Juniper has been doing magnificently."

"Well, isn't Katie the Publicist doing the actual posting?"

"Another thing you need to understand is that Katie *is* Juniper, and that I am you, at least for the next twenty-three days."

"So I should give you my Instagram password."

"Also Facebook," she said. "You aren't dating anyone, are you?"

"Not really?"

"No."

"What?"

"If you're not really dating someone, no, you're not dating anyone. Yes, you're single. No, you're not in a relationship, and yes, you transparently and authentically like Juniper. Will they? Won't they? That's what we're going for here."

"Right, yeah," I said. "No, I'm not in a relationship." I wasn't, either. There was this girl in New York I had been out with a few times. She was a grad student at Columbia studying something called "social virology." She was smart, and interesting, and attractive, but she wasn't especially nice. On our last date, she had called me "fascinatingly undereducated," which stung because I *was* undereducated, and I felt it all the time.

Everyone knew more than me about everything—about wine and about strains of weed and about Russian literature and about social virology. I was always behind in every conversation.

"Kai. Your socials."

"Yes?"

"Are you literally not hearing the words I'm saying?"

I literally was not hearing the words she was saying.

"We've got your Insta and Facebook verified. You don't have a Twitter, correct?"

"Correct."

"Well, you do now. You won't ever have to think about it. Listen, your socials are great. We just need to up the PPD a bit. I can post for you—with your approval of course."

"PPD?"

"Posts per day. I know it's a lot. But when you see the movie, you'll understand. It's a special film, and you are a revelation in it. But we're gonna be heavily reliant on social to promote it."

"Okay," I said.

"What's your Insta pass?" I gave it to her, and my Facebook, too. She stood up, ruffled my hair like I was a little kid, and said, "I'll let you get ready. So excited for you."

While I was in the shower, Agent Bob called me and left a voicemail. I listened to it on speaker while lying in a Hotel Bel-Air robe on the Hotel Bel-Air bed. That bed was so nice it made me almost feel like I was weightless, like I wasn't even in a body.

"Kai, it's Bob. I know young people don't listen to voicemails but I gotta tell you kid I'm so proud of you and what you've achieved and so excited for the future. I got a call from the head of the studio this morning and he said he saw the movie and you're an epiphany. That's what he said. An epiphany! Don't fire me when you blow up, okay? I'm kidding but I'm not kidding. I'm setting up a meeting with Brian. He wants to talk to you about *Gods of Andromeda*. Wants you to test this week while you're in town. With Juniper already cast it'd be great for us. Same studio, same power couple. Not that you're a couple of course. Unless you are. None of my business! Enjoy this, Kai! This is as good as it gets. You're going to absolutely explode."

5

It's not really hot in LA, even though the sun is always shining. The air feels like nothing on your skin. Los Angeles is the opposite of weather. I went down the three elevators, got lost in the winding paths of the Hotel Bel-Air, and eventually found the entrance, where several black SUVs were lined up. Windows tinted. I wondered if they were full or empty.

I was wearing black jeans and a Mountain Goats T-shirt. Over by the valet stand, an old guy was smoking a cigarette. He was a famous actor, but I couldn't place his face or remember his name. William something. One of those guys who has been in a hundred movies, but you don't really notice him.

Ellen appeared and said, "Thanks for dressing up, Kai."

"Was I supposed to? I can chan—"

"You're fine. It's on-brand. We gotta go." She told the valet her last name and he pointed at one of the SUVs. As we approached, Al got out and opened the door for us.

"Hello again," I said.

"Cobra Kai," he said, nodding and ushering me into the car.

Al told us it would be fifteen minutes to the studio lot, so I got out my phone. I had regrammed Juniper's picture of the plane—or Ellen had, anyway. I scrolled through the comments—lots of hearts and smiles, lots of strangers saying one or both of us were so beautiful. The best comment was, "Imagine being that plane and having Kai Laramie inside of you."

I read it to Ellen and she laughed and said, "You know what's funny? I wrote that. FanGirlOfLiterally3V3RYTHING is one of my burner accounts. Glad you like my work, Kai."

Some actual friends had also commented—one of my New York roommates, Carmen, wrote, *When did you become a Jenner sister? Congrats!* with champagne poppers.

I texted Carmen. *I am no longer in control of my Instagram. It is now the property of The Studio.*

She didn't immediately reply, so I texted Juniper. *Hi.*

Her: *Hi. You nervous?*

Me: *I'm something.*

She didn't answer. I asked Ellen how many fake accounts she had. "Personally, four. But we have people who help with that stuff."

My phone buzzed. Juniper. *Sorry I feel like I'm gonna puke. Already puked at the hotel.*

Me: *Everyone says the movie is good.*

Her: *I always puke before I watch something I'm in.*
I hate it. Plus press is gonna be there.

Me: *Shit really?*

Her: *Yeah and Kathryn. And maybe Matthew.*

Me: *Now I'M gonna puke.*

Ellen looked up from her phone and said, "Apparently there's going to be a bit of press there. They won't have seen the movie, just there to meet-and-greet with you and Juniper and Matthew. You won't need to talk to them except to say hello, but just in case you *do* accidentally end up saying more than hi to anyone, we're gonna practice adjectives."

"Adjectives?"

"Yes, adjectives, Kai. I assume you attended fourth grade and remember adjectives. When press asks you about the movie or the cast, you use adjectives. Juniper is dreamy, for instance."

"Juniper isn't dreamy. She's—"

"It was an example." I could feel her nerves, and that made me feel mine.

"Okay."

"You tell me the adjectives, and I'll tell you if they're good adjectives. Matthew."

"What?"

"Matthew. Adjectives."

"Loving. Distant. Generous."

"Distant is bad."

"Loving. Generous. Mentor."

"Mentor is not an adjective but it's good. Great. Kathryn."

"Intense."

"Intense is bad."

"Bold. Confident."

"Better!"

"Dedicated. Passionate."

"Love it. Juniper."

"Um."

"Um is not great."

"I loved her?"

Ellen exhaled through clenched teeth. "Present tense, Kai. She is not deceased. You love her."

"I love her. Juniper is . . . thoughtful. Prepared. Careful."

"Careful is not great. *Caring* is great," Ellen said.

"But I don't mean caring. I mean careful."

Ellen closed her eyes. "What else?"

"Ambitious."

A slight shake of her head. "Ambitious is *terrible*."

"Hardworking."

"No," she said. Ellen was pressing her thumb and forefinger to her eyes now.

"She's a great scene partner."

"Adjectives."

"Smart."

"Meh."

"Beautiful."

"Oh, I like beautiful," she said.

I laughed. "I bet you do."

"But you don't say that. You show it with your eyes, right? You're an actor. So you say brilliant, loving, and hilarious, and the beautiful you show-don't-tell."

I didn't think Juniper was brilliant, loving, or hilarious. I thought she was thoughtful, prepared, and careful.

We turned into the studio lot, and the guard waved Al past. I could see Juniper and Katie the Publicist standing together in the parking lot, talking to Kathryn and Studio Todd.

"Three adjectives about everyone," Ellen said. "Flattering and particular. Then you expand. Matthew is kind, loving, and supportive. Insert story here about his kindness. And so on. Yeah?"

"Yeah," I said. The car had stopped. Al hustled out of the driver's seat so he could come around and open my door. Even though I knew how to open a car door, I waited for him, and let him do it.

"Kai, my love," Kathryn said as I got out of the car. She kissed me on both cheeks. Something smelled like coconut oil—her face or her lip gloss. "I can't wait for you to see our movie." She hugged me, and I closed my eyes because I always do when I hug someone. But Kathryn held on for so long that eventually I opened my eyes, and through Kathryn's ash-blond hair I could see Juniper, her face drained of color.

"Love you," I said to Juniper.

"I'm trying not to puke," she answered, not unkindly.

6

We all walked together, with Studio Todd and Ellen leading. Kathryn asked me how I was, and I said good, and she asked if I was still in New York, and I said *yes* even though I wasn't sure where I'd live after the movie came out.

Kathryn was so good at name-dropping that I couldn't even tell you how she turned the conversation to some popstar's new music video, which she had directed, and how the night before, she'd been at the popstar's house for a party that went *very* late and now she was hungover, hence the sunglasses. "You know I'm not a sunglasses person," she said, although I didn't know that.

"Have you tried the hangover IVs?" Todd asked, and Kathryn said no, she was afraid of needles, and Todd said he swore by them, that a nurse will come over to your house with a bag of saline and vitamins and thirty minutes later you feel ready for a run, no matter how much you drank. Kathryn said she'd keep it under advisement. We were walking down a fake block of New York with fake shop windows. Everything on the lot felt slightly smaller than reality—the streets were narrow, the buildings too close to the sidewalk. It felt a little like walking inside a movie, which I guess was the point. We came to a sidewalk, and I could see a miniature marquee jutting out from a stucco wall that said NOW SHOWING: ANDY WARHOL NEVER GETS OLD. I took a picture of that, then walked over to where Juniper was sitting on a bench, hands on her knees, looking down at her platform sneakers. Her face was ashen.

I sat down next to her. "Look at the marquee," I said, and she smiled a little. "You okay?" I asked.

"I think the enjoyment sector of my brain might be dysfunctional."

"Or it's just not that enjoyable," I said.

"I'm not adequately prepared for the press," she said. "Katie didn't warn me, and so I've only gone through the talking points a couple times. I don't have good answers for even the basic questions. I don't know what I want people to take away from the film. Hope, I guess? But that sounds idiotic. Maybe that the movie explores how human perseverance isn't naive but is really the glory of our species, but that sounds a bit grandiose. I hope that people realize celebrity is overrated? Too self-indulgent. What do *you* hope people take away from it?"

"I don't really go to movies like this one. I don't know why people watch sad movies."

"Well," Juniper said, "that is definitely worse than my answers."

Studio Todd's shadow arrived at the bench just before he did, and he said, "The movie is a celebration of the human spirit and the power of love." And then Ellen said, "Jesus Christ, Todd, do you write greeting cards for a living? We want people to leave the theater thinking, *That Kai Laramie deserves an Oscar.*"

"Can I get a little air?" Juniper said quietly, and everyone took a few steps back. I started to get up from the bench, but she grabbed my wrist and said, "Not you. Can you stay?" And I said, "Of course," and she looked at me and said, "I hate watching myself and not being able to change anything. Hate it. Sorry if my breath smells like puke," and I said, "It doesn't," even though it did a little bit, and she said, "Can we do this together?"

"This?"

"All of this. All of it. Just, not alone. Can we do the press and the . . . I need you. You make me feel less like barfing."

"Thanks?"

"Can we do this together?"

And I said, "Of course." When I looked up, I saw that Ellen and Katie were both taking pictures of us.

Kathryn came and sat on the other side of Juniper. She put an arm around Juniper and started half whispering to her. "Listen. I know you're nervous. But they flew you out here on the studio's plane because they love this movie. They're putting you up in the Hotel Bel-Air. They think this movie is special. And they're right." Kathryn stood up then. She is a large woman, tall and always in heels. I know the word *statuesque* means something particular, but Kathryn is actually statue-esque.

As we walked into the theater down a long, dimly lit hallway, Kathryn kept talking to us. "You are both about to just *explode* when people see our movie. Junie, I'm so excited for you to be in *Gods of Andromeda*. Brian Arawas is a genius. A true one. You know Arawas doesn't have an assistant? Never has. Answers his own phone. Isn't that amazing? The best always have time for everyone. Speaking of the best," she said, and as we turned into the theater, there was Matthew. He was wearing tight jeans, a plain gray T-shirt, and a light jacket. People were surrounding him in an awkward half circle, but they parted when he stepped toward Kathryn and hugged her.

"How *are* you?" Kathryn said. "I haven't seen you since Kim's wedding."

"I've barely seen myself since Kim's wedding," he answered, then saw us, pulled us into a hug, and told us he missed us. He smelled like cigarette smoke. He'd chewed Nicorette the whole time we were in Pittsburgh, but never fully quit. He'd told me during one all-night shoot, "The thing no one ever tells you about smoking is how great it is. The relief of giving in to it. I need a cigarette, so I have one. Needing a cigarette is the only problem in my life I know how to solve." I'd asked him for a cigarette then, and he'd laughed so hard before saying, "No way, bud."

"These are my kids," Matthew said to the people gathered about. "They're so brilliant. Can't wait for everyone to see them in this film."

Ellen grabbed me and introduced me to Jill from *The New Yorker*, who asked if I was excited to see the movie. "Mostly nervous," I said.

"Nervousness is of course a *form* of excitement," Ellen clarified.

"May God keep you innocent and honest," Jill told me, and then added, "Ellen keeps telling me how wonderful you are in the movie, and yet she won't let me see it."

"It's not locked quite yet," Ellen said.

"How does it feel, I wonder, to be on the edge of something but you don't know what exactly you're on the edge of." I opened my mouth to answer, but Ellen said, "Obviously Jill would write a brilliant profile of you. Jill, we'll be in touch."

"You are excited," Ellen mumbled to me as Jill and the rest of the reporters were ushered out. "You are in a state of perpetual excitement and good cheer for the next twenty-three days."

"Don't be afraid to share notes with us," Kathryn said after the reporters left. "We're still in edits."

The theater was small—maybe twenty-five seats. Katie the Publicist, Ellen, and Studio Todd made introductions—this is Caitlyn, the editor of the movie; this is Autumn, the music supervisor; this is Tyrell from Marketing; here is Chloe, who works with Caitlyn.

Studio Todd walked Juniper and me to a row of seats in front of everyone else. I sat down next to Juniper. Matthew sat a few seats over.

The already dim lights grew fainter. Juniper grabbed my hand, not holding it so much as clinging to it. I looked at her and smiled. I was about to see myself in a proper fucking movie.

7

When the studio's logo filled the screen, I felt a weird swell inside me. Something like happiness but not quite. Juniper was still holding my hand—hers on top of mine—and she squeezed when my name appeared in pale blue out of the darkness.

In the movie's opening scene, Matthew and I are playing a video game together—*Super Mario Brothers* on the original Nintendo. When we shot the scene, Kathryn kept wanting me to move my body and arms along with the controller, like I was trying to move Mario inside the game by moving my own body. I didn't want to do it—I felt like my character was not the sort of person to make unnecessary movements of any kind, and in general I wanted him to be very still so there would be a big shift toward the end of the movie when he gets into a fight with Juniper and is flailing everywhere.

But Kathryn really liked this idea of me trying to move my arms to move the guy inside the game, so I was trying, but it felt awkward. It was still our first week on set. I felt like the crew and producers were getting mad at me.

After a few takes, Kathryn told everyone to break for ten and brought me into this other room in the house where we were shooting. It was a kids' bedroom, and the crew had all kinds of steel rigging there, but we managed to find a corner of a twin bed to sit on, and she said, "Five slow breaths. In and out. Nice and deep." I was looking at some kid's Pittsburgh Steelers poster, wondering if he was psyched or pissed that his room was being used by a Hollywood studio, and I took five slow breaths in time with hers.

"Here's a story Bradley Cooper told me once. He's such a philosopher. He said, when a human has a fight-or-flight response, they often get stuck between fight or flight. The feeling is so new, so powerful, so overwhelming, that they just stand there. It's not the decision that kills you, Kai. It's being between decisions. Yeah?"

"Yeah," I said.

"It's like my favorite *Onion* headline: 'Road-Kill Squirrel Remembered as Frantic, Indecisive.' But today, my lovely squirrel, you will dart this way and that way, and you will survive." Kathryn stood up, and I followed her. I sat down next to Matthew, and the crew returned to the cameras and lights. The boom guy picked up the mic. Camera speeding. Sound speeding. Kathryn said, "Fight. ACTION," and I fought with the controller, moving my body in concert with the little guy on the screen. She let the scene run a little long, until Matthew and I were improvising jokes, and then called, "Cut. Great. We go again. Now flight, Kai. Flight."

And when everything was reset, she said, "Action" again, and I played the scene like I wanted to. Minimal movement. Economy in everything. Tight. Close. Interior. And when we were through the lines, she said, "Cut. Beautiful. Let's move on." Kathryn used her version in the movie, of course, me ridiculously moving the controller all around. It was still a good scene, though.

I found it hard to watch the parts of the movie I was in, because I couldn't stop thinking about my face and my voice and how I sounded like an idiot. But the stuff with Matthew was incredible. Andy Warhol, always this soulless enigma, was suddenly human—performing, sure, just like the rest of us are, but still a person, with all the frailties and insecurities of one. As he walked through his childhood home in Pittsburgh, you could see in his eyes everything he wasn't saying—how this had been the only safe space in a bullied life, and it wasn't even that safe. Your heart broke for him.

And Juniper was brilliant in it, too, raucous and unpredictable in her movements, a wound-tight cacophony of talent and self-destruction. She seemed younger than she did in real life, unready for all the adult stuff she had to go through. In the club scene where she's bleeding and I'm begging her to go home, she was so good that I started crying. I couldn't tell if I was crying for Juniper or her character, because I loved them both.

Watching the movie, I kept thinking about how the most cynical or ironic people tend to also be the most vulnerable, because they can't afford to risk sincerity. Andy was always somewhere between sincere and detached, and Matthew found that place so well.

Beside me, Juniper constantly scribbled notes into her notebook. I looked down to try to see them, but it was too dark. I hadn't even thought to bring a pen and paper. Typical.

I kept remembering what was happening on the days we shot each scene. I recalled the day Matthew invited me to his trailer to play a motorcycle racing simulator someone had sent him. I thought about how one day we had to wait for planes to pass in order to get the audio right, and Lon was shouting from behind the video monitors, "These goddamned planes have cost me twelve thousand dollars today. Do you know what twelve thousand dollars could buy?!"

During the scene where Andy and I drink beer together, I remembered laughing with Matthew about the ridiculousness of the fake beer labels. Matthew offered to pay the props master whatever it cost to get some actual Stella on set, and then I made fun of Matthew for liking shitty beer, and then Matthew said, "Can you even drink?" And I said, "Hell yeah I can," and then he tilted his head way back and looked up at the ceiling while he laughed, like God had made the joke.

I couldn't get my head into the actual movie at all, really, until the last twenty minutes or so. As Andy got sicker and we started to fall in love, the movie became so heartrending that I forgot about what had really happened and who Juniper and Matthew really were, and even who I really was. There's a scene near the end where Carly and Jude are making love and I'm sobbing into Carly's shoulder after we find out Andy died, and it had been intense to film but was somehow more intense to watch. I just felt so bad for everyone. The movie is really about what you owe the people you love, and how impossible it is to pay all those debts, and the whole thing just ripped me up until I started crying.

I glanced over at Juniper and she was dabbing her eyes, but I didn't see any tears. She looked really pretty, the light of the movie goldengray on her face.

By the time the movie ended, I was really crying. I wasn't crying about the movie, even. I was crying because even Andy Warhol was so fragile, and because everything fragile faces the same fate eventually.

8

Some people behind us clapped during the credits. The lights came up a little, and I was having a hard time stopping crying. Tyrell from Marketing walked up to me with Katie the Publicist. He asked if I was all right. I nodded and smiled. I didn't want to seem like the kind of person who cries at their own movie, but I couldn't recover from it. "I don't know why I'm crying," I said. "I mean, I knew what was going to happen." Tyrell laughed, and then said, "You must have given a lot of yourself to that performance."

I shrugged. "Yeah, thanks. Juniper's great in it, isn't she?"

"For sure, but you're a revelation. Congratulations, Kai."

Kathryn emerged from somewhere behind me, grabbed me around the waist, and said, "What'd ya think?"

"I think it's good?" I said. "The end really got me."

"It's that Lou Reed song," Kathryn said.

Everyone walked out of the theater together. The light outside was squintingly bright. Lon and Natalie were sitting in a golf cart right outside the screening room. Natalie jumped up, hugged Kathryn, and then asked Juniper, "Well?"

"It's very good," Juniper said. "I have some notes for Kathryn."

"Oh, Junie, wonderful. Of course they'll be brilliant," Kathryn said, and then Matthew walked up and she said, "But I've got to get back to the edit suite, so please share notes with Nat and Lon, okay?" She turned her back to us and hugged Matthew. "What'd you think?" she asked him.

"Even better on the third viewing." Matthew smiled.

"Let's get some dinner," Natalie said to us, "and dig into your notes."

"Nothing's locked," Lon added as he got out of the golf cart. "Absolutely want to hear your notes. Did they tell you about the test scores?"

I reached into my pocket for my phone and saw that I had a text from Agent Bob. *CALL ME.* Ellen grabbed me and turned me toward Caitlyn, the editor of the movie, who asked me what I thought.

"I think I liked it? I've never really—" Ellen tugged on my arm and said, "One moment," then pulled me aside and muttered, "You don't *think* anything."

"I am quite certain I liked it," I said to Caitlyn, who laughed.

"How did it feel, watching yourself?"

I paused. "Exposed," I said.

"I can imagine," Caitlyn said. "Most young actors mimic. They don't express fear or the terror of helplessness; they *perform* them. A kid's scream in a horror movie almost always says more about what movies they've seen than what fears they've known. But spending these three months with your performance . . . When you screamed at Carly, I mean, even now I'm saying it like it was real. But in a way it *was* real, wasn't it?"

Ellen said, "I've got to get Kai onto this golf cart for his producer meeting."

I was ushered onto the back of the golf cart, which in the end fit only Lon, Natalie, Juniper, and me. I was sitting backward, so I watched Matthew and Kathryn and everyone else recede as we pulled away.

Lon said, "We've now got release dates in eighteen territories. *Eighteen.* It's about an American artist and we have eighteen international releases. Last night—Nat says that dreams are just the brain's version of waste expulsion, but last night I dreamt I was standing on the roof of my house and a B-52 bomber flew overhead and I thought I was in a war zone but then the bomb doors opened and money flew out from the sky and fluttered down all around me, from absolutely every country on earth—dollars and euros and reals and pesos and pounds. I have seen our future, friends, and it is multinational."

"Juniper has some notes," Natalie said.

"Right. Let's talk 'em over at dinner. We want you both for the junket. Obviously one in New York a week before the premiere as I'm sure you've discussed with your teams, but with so much international buzz we're trying to capitalize. Europe looks a maybe. Could be London, could be Paris. Kai, do you have a favorite designer? Juniper, you have someone, yes?"

"Dior. Kai, do you have any notes or is it just me?" Juniper asked.

"Wait, when is the premiere?" I asked.

"The premiere is Wednesday the second," Juniper said.

"Of October?"

"Yes. Did you like the Lou Reed song at the end, or did it feel a bit on the nose?" she asked. We were getting off the golf cart now and into an SUV.

"I . . . liked it?" I ventured as I crawled into the way-back.

Juniper joined me. *"Really."*

"I mean, I'm not a music supervisor," I said.

"Indeed," Juniper said. "Nor, for that matter, is Kathryn. Natalie, do you like the Lou Reed song at the end?"

"We already paid for it," Natalie answered.

"But do you like it?"

"She likes it. We like it," Lon said. "The song isn't changing. Great song. Lou Reed wrote a song about Andy Warhol dying and we play the song over Andy Warhol dying. It's pretty simple stuff."

"But the song itself—"

"Has been purchased," Natalie finished.

"Well," said Juniper. "Yes, I see. Shall we begin discussing notes?"

"I feel like we already have," Natalie answered.

Juniper pulled out her black leatherbound notebook. "In the first scene between Andy and me, we're on my coverage when he says, "I never fall apart because I never fall together," and I look so amused and charmed by him and not at all like a real reporter, and I just think in the very first moment it undermines my seriousness as a journalist and so I wonder if at least for that line we could be on Andy's coverage and see him saying that, and then go back to a less starry-eyed version of Carly when we cut back to her." She then continued to talk like that about almost every single shot in the film. Juniper had noticed a hundred things that I hadn't, thought about a thousand angles I hadn't considered. She viewed the movie the way athletes look at film of old games.

At the restaurant, I read the menu and watched as Juniper broke down every scene of the movie and how each could be improved. While I'm sure that Lon and Natalie found that ninety minutes excruciating, I was just astounded. How could someone notice so much? Care so much? I can't remember even one percent of what she said, but, like, at one point she questioned the color correction of a scene that takes place in my bedroom because it made the windows look dark, when as she understood it the room had been lit intentionally to emphasize that all the light was coming from outside, because the house itself had become what she called a "well of metaphorical darkness."

They let her talk. Natalie took notes. I ate a quinoa bowl with grilled vegetables. Juniper had some sort of salad and a lot of water. And then as Lon placed a very sturdy-looking Amex card on top of the bill, he said, "Juniper. I adore you. You're going to make a great director someday. But you are not directing this film."

"I'm not trying to *direct* it; I'm trying to—"

"We will absolutely pass along a version of all this to Kathryn," Lon said. "Absolutely. But listen, this movie is ninety-two percent top two boxes as is. Can it be better? Sure. *Citizen Kane* could be better. But ninety-two percent top two boxes? I've been doing this a long time."

"He's been doing this a *very* long time," Natalie added.

"And this is only the second movie I've ever had that was over ninety percent top two boxes."

"The other one was *Moulin Rouge*," Natalie said.

"The studio shit the bed on the awards campaign, and it still won four Oscars."

"Should've won Best Picture," Natalie said. "They got screwed. But that's the Academy."

"I'm not going to tell Kathryn to recut the entire film when it's ninety-two percent top two boxes."

"At least the cemetery scene," Juniper said. "And the—"

"Listen, get some rest. I know it's hard to see yourself up on screen. I know this is a stressful process. It's stressful for me too."

"I'm not *stressed*," Juniper said. "I want to make the movie bet—"

"And we want to make it better, too," Lon said. "And your notes will make it better."

"We will absolutely pass on a version of this to Kathryn," Natalie said. "These are great notes. Very helpful."

"But we also want to manage your expectations," Lon said.

"The movie is basically locked," Natalie said.

"And we all need to be advocates for it. It's in everyone's best interest to love the movie."

"We're all on the same team here," Natalie added.

"Yeah," Juniper said. "Yeah. Right. I get it."

9

I almost never tell people until I have to tell them. I told my parents only after it all came out and he got arrested and the police wanted to interview me. I told the police only when they asked, and only what they asked. They kept saying, "You're not in any trouble," but they were saying it to me in a windowless, fluorescent-lit interrogation room inside a police station, which made me feel very much like I was in trouble.

I don't ever *want* to tell anyone. But for some reason, I wanted to tell Juniper. I don't know why. I just wanted to, but I couldn't find the right time. It's a difficult thing to shoehorn into a conversation.

Back at the hotel, we had some time before going out to meet up with Juniper's friends. I wanted to tell her about it, but we were talking about the movie, and she couldn't stop criticizing her performance and Kathryn's choices until finally I said, "I think the movie is good."

"Of course it's good," she said. "It's the biggest opportunity of my lifetime, and maybe of yours, too. That's why it matters so much."

"I also think you have a very analytical response to stress."

She took a breath then. "That's true," she said. "That is true. You're a good observationist."

"Maybe we should just go out with your friends and celebrate the movie being good."

And I guess I could've told her then, but it would've rather ruined the vibe.

We went to some bar in a different hotel where they poured martinis tableside and allowed you to pick from five different vermouths, each with its own flavor profile. I got a lemon twist vodka martini with cardamom-scented vermouth. The woman I was sitting next to, skinny with thick eyebrows and wide eyes, ordered the same. Juniper had a club soda.

Juniper was talking to an actor I knew a little because we often ended up in the same auditions, a guy named Casey whose glacial blue eyes made me a little jealous, not least because of the way Juniper leaned toward him as they chatted.

I talked mostly to the girl who'd ordered the same drink as me. When I meet someone new, I ask a lot of questions because I prefer listening to speaking, so we talked about where her family was from—London—and how she ended up in LA—she wanted a city where no one looks at you, and if they do, they don't care who you are—and what she did for work—"These days it feels like I'm professionally on Instagram." She said, "Speaking of which, do you mind if we get a photo together?" and I said of course as long as you tag me, and she laughed and took the photo of us cheersing with our martini glasses.

In her English accent, she said, "Juniper told me you say *I love you* to everyone, but you haven't said it to me," and I said, "I love you," and she laughed and thanked me and said she was falling in love with me, too. We ordered another round of martinis, and then another. I was starting to worry these thirty-dollar drinks were adding up, but when Juniper announced she was calling it a night, the girl I'd been talking to insisted on paying. I began to protest, but Juniper said, "Oh, let her. She's on the cover of *Vogue* this month," which was the first indication I had that maybe I'd been talking to someone quite famous all night.

Outside, we were met by a gaggle of paparazzi, some with video cameras and some taking flash photographs. I kept trying to blink away the light. I was rather drunk, and Juniper had a hand tightly around my waist, and everyone was looking behind us, shouting, "Jaya! Jaya!" They were asking if she'd broken up with Stephanie, and what caused the breakup, and whether she was now seeing Juniper. And then a few of the paparazzi saw Casey and his blue eyes and started shouting at him, but they were mostly leaving Juniper and me alone except for one guy who kept asking for Juniper's autograph. He didn't have a camera or anything, just a Sharpie and a sweaty face and an 8 x 10 photo of Juniper as a kid. The noise was getting louder because Jaya was outside now, and I saw our Uber parked across the street, so I waved it over.

I opened the rear door and Juniper slid in. Then, just as I was about to get in the car myself, the sweaty man jumped into the back seat with Juniper. "Get the fuck out," she said, kicking at him. I grabbed the man by his shirt and pulled him out of the car, throwing him onto the street and shoving him to the ground. "What the fuck is wrong with you?" I shouted, then got in the Uber and slammed the door shut. I felt the adrenaline pumping through my ears. Next to me, Juniper was shaking, her body curled up against the far edge of the car's bench seat.

"Jaya really brings out the paps. Jesus."

"Who the hell is Jaya?"

"Come on, Kai. You didn't realize you spent the whole night flirting with Jaya Hudson-Rowe, the supermodel? The, like, most famous supermodel in the world?"

"No," I said. "And I wasn't flirting."

"She's literally the most beautiful woman on earth." I found Juniper vastly more attractive, but didn't say as much.

"Have you seen that guy before?"

"No, I don't think so. I have a couple stalkers though. He could've been one of them. God, that was scary."

"Yeah," I said.

It was only ten minutes to the Hotel Bel-Air, and when we got there, I said, "Do you want me to walk you to your room?" and she said, "Yeah, but no funny business." I said, "I only engage in extremely serious business," and she offered me a wan smile.

When we got to her suite, she looked at me and said, "I know this is ridiculous, but do you mind checking? The closets and everything?" and I said sure and walked around her suite, looking under the bed and into the closet. "We're good," I said at last and only then did she enter the room. She asked if we could just watch a movie, so we turned on HBO and this strange, funny movie *Submariners* was on. We watched, my arm around her, her body fluttering next to mine, rib cage to rib cage. I wanted to kiss her but knew now wasn't the time. And anyway I can't do that stuff well; I always judge the wrong moment to kiss someone because sexually, my brain is fucked.

At last she wanted to go to sleep and I offered to sleep on the couch and she said, *No no that's fine*, so I went to my room and thought about the movie and the sweaty stranger. I couldn't sleep, so I sat outside by my ridiculous little pool and looked at the very few stars in the Los Angeles sky.

I often feel kind of empty—not necessarily in a bad way, just like my body is uninhabited. It was windy, but the air that blew in the trees seemed not to have a temperature, which only increased the weird feeling that my body wasn't really there, or I wasn't really in it. After a while, I grabbed my AirPods and listened to *Gods of Andromeda*. I'm a slow reader, so I listen to a lot of audiobooks. The story was set on a small planet in the Andromeda galaxy that only had one landmass, and the people and orcs who lived there were mostly peaceful because there was a ban on all weapons and war-making. The guy I was reading for was Garon, the lead guy's brother, who served as the civilization's chief negotiator. Garon carries this golden pen with him everywhere called the Peace Pen. When we go to war, the Peace Pen inevitably gets melted down to become a handle for my new sword. The Queen is really badass in it, and I could see how Juniper would be perfect for it.

The audiobook was interrupted by a moment of silence followed by the ringing of my phone. Agent Bob. It was past eleven o'clock, but Bob was never not working.

"Christ Kai I've been trying to get ahold of you for ten hours you have to answer your phone, okay? This generation and their phones—you're fucking obsessed with them but never use them. How are you?"

"Good?"

"How was the movie?"

"I think it's good? Juniper has some concerns."

"Sure, sure, well, I've seen it and let me tell you, kid, there's nothing to be concerned about. It's amazing. And I've been on the phone all day about you. I've got producers all over town tripping over each other to ask after your availability. You're exploding."

"Good?"

"Good? It's fucking great. We're gonna have some choices. But can I just remind you of something? I hope this won't seem rude, kid, but I just want to remind you I believed in you from Day One. Anyone calls you, you let me know, okay? I'm sure CAA will be circling you like the goddamned vultures they are, but the great thing about us is we can work with *anyone*, you get me? CAA's an incest factory. They don't make the best movies they can make; they make the best *CAA* movies they can make."

"I'm not going to fire you, Bob."

"Great. I know that. You're a loyal kid. Listen, Brian Arawas wants to have breakfast with you tomorrow. He'll come to your hotel. Brian Arawas coming to you; can you believe it? Nine thirty. Don't be late. Zoe and I will catch up with you afterward. This *Gods of Andromeda* thing could be huge. The studio's all-in on it. Sixty-eight shoot days, starts in December. If breakfast goes well, they'll do a test deal just based on your self-tape. That's how much they love you for the brother. What's his name, Zoe?"

"Garon," Zoe said. She was Bob's assistant. I guess assistants usually listen in on calls, but Bob was always calling attention to her. I liked Zoe.

"Garon. Fuck. With a book, you can't change the shitty names or the fans go fucking crazy. Anyway, Kai, test deal and then chemistry reads. You like working with Juniper, right? Judging from your socials, you like her plenty. Just don't get nervous. Brian is smart, but he's not any smarter than you. And maybe you don't even want to do a sword-swinger set in space. We'll see how the breakfast goes. You gotta ask yourself what kind of career you want. You want to be Matthew? You want to be RDJ? Or hell I don't know, maybe you want to be Will McIntire. That guy's got a good fucking life, let me tell you—famous enough to fuck hot girls but he can still go to the grocery store. Can I talk about fucking hot girls, Zoe?"

I heard the end of Zoe's sigh as she unmuted and said, "Probably best not to, Bob."

"This new Hollywood, kid. It's fucking crazy. I grow old, I grow old, I shall wear the bottoms of my trousers rolled. Can I still quote fucking T. S. Eliot, Zoe?"

Another small sigh. "Yes, Bob, you can still quote T. S. Eliot."

"Great. We'll be able to get you a good deal, and when I talked to the producer this morning—Dylan, great guy, you'll love him—he said they were beefing up the role a little, to make it fifth lead. See how the breakfast with Brian goes, then we'll put together a test deal."

"Okay," I said. And then after a second, "So what's going to happen with *Andy Warhol Never Gets Old*?"

"What do you mean?"

"I mean, like, what's going to happen with the movie? Everyone keeps saying that it's really good, but I don't know what that means."

"It means they're trying to get Matthew and Kathryn invited to the Oscars is what it means. I loved the movie, okay? It's a great fucking movie. But who wants to see a sad movie about Andy Warhol and two sad kids? This is America, Kai. Americans paid two hundred million dollars to see *Paul Blart: Mall Cop*. We are not a nation of taste or sophistication. Even with the awards, we're not talking about Nobel Prizes here. You know what got nominated for an Oscar? Fucking *Molly's Second Tooth*, kid. You see *Molly's Second Tooth*?"

"No."

"If you've ever seen a dog vomit its body weight after eating chocolate, you've seen it. Nobody has taste anymore. Maybe they never did. Can I still talk about dog vomit, Zoe?"

"Please stop doing that," I said.

"Agreed," added Zoe.

"I'm a dinosaur. But I'm a dinosaur that's going to get you a hell of a deal for *Gods of Androgyny*. You want my advice? The best time to make a deal is before anybody knows how big your movie's actually gonna get. Maybe I'm wrong and you'll be at the Oscars next year. But the world's full of great movies nobody watches and great actors nobody hires. We'll see you after breakfast."

"Andromeda," Zoe muttered.

"See you tomorrow," I said.

I kept staring up at the undark sky. I wanted to call someone, but it was too late. I scrolled through my texts. There were a lot I hadn't answered, but I didn't feel like responding to any. The thought of responding to anyone made the ache in my stomach worse, and it was already pretty bad. I tried to go back to having an empty mind and listening to *Gods of Andromeda*, but I kept thinking about Bob and Lon and Ellen and the sweaty man who got in the Uber, and how Juniper's eyes looked when she asked me to check her room. And I thought about it, of course, the pronoun that needed no further description, because it was always there, awake or asleep or in between. I thought about Ellen knowing about it, and how people are usually so kind about it, but I still don't like them knowing, because then they can't unsee me through that lens. I thought about how condescending everyone was—the cops, the lawyers—how they treated me like a kid. But of course the whole point is that I *was* a kid.

I didn't know if I really wanted to be famous. I thought about how before we watched the movie, Matthew was surrounded by those reporters, all of whom stood a step or two farther from him than you'd usually stand in conversation because he had some kind of energy that kept them at a distance. He told them that the only person who can't enjoy a Matthew Malone movie is Matthew Malone, and they all laughed. But the same energy that kept those reporters laughing made the sweaty man believe he could get into Juniper's car. I thought of something Matthew said to me once on set: "I've done a lot of drugs, but nothing hits like fame. Sometimes it's an upper; sometimes it's a downer. But it will always rock you."

10

I was woken up the next morning by a phone ringing. Not my phone. The hotel phone. "Hello?"

"Good morning, Mr. Laramie. I've got Brian Arawas here to see you."

I rolled over and looked at the clock. It was 8:12, more than an hour before our scheduled breakfast. "I'll be down in five minutes."

I brushed my teeth, put on a Mekons T-shirt and yesterday's jeans, and began the long journey down to the lobby. The sun was brighter than seemed necessary. Brian Arawas was standing outside waiting for me in the narrow shade of a palm tree. He wore Ray-Bans, a neatly trimmed beard, and a close-cropped haircut that appeared to be less than a day old. Arawas had been an actor before he'd become a director, and although his hair was graying, he still looked fit and handsome, and also aware of being fit and handsome. "Kai," he said as he approached, arms out. We hugged. There is a lot of hugging in Hollywood. "Kai, I apologize for being one hour and eighteen minutes early for our breakfast, but I am a punctual person, and an enthusiastic one, and I literally couldn't wait to meet you. Where should we eat?"

"I don't really know Los Angeles," I said.

"Amazing. Never get to know it. Stay gold, Ponyboy. You're a New Yorker, right?"

"I'm mostly from Indiana."

"Well, no one's perfect," he said, smiling out of the corner of his mouth. "We'll go to the Algernon."

In the car, a silver Audi A8 with a white leather interior, I told Brian that I'd loved his last movie, a one-off film in the *X-Men* universe about a mission to free mutants from a prison camp. "Yeah," he said, "we basically got to remake *The Great Escape* but with superheroes. We had an awesome time. The studio watered down the political message of the film, but that's Hollywood. They all love freedom and democracy until they want to sell a movie internationally, and then we have to respect that many forms of government can be legitimate. Have you read the book yet?"

"Most of it," I said. I tried to say something about how much I liked the character I'd auditioned for, but I just rambled. I said that Garon reminded me of me, which wasn't really true. He mostly reminded me of other scribes from other fantasy stories. Brian nodded, but didn't say anything in response, and I wondered if I'd ruined my shot at the part before we even got to the restaurant. We turned onto Sunset Boulevard, where traffic was crawling.

"You see that new Tarantino film, *Once Upon a Time in Hollywood*?"

"Yeah," I said.

"All of Quentin's films are about wish fulfillment, and that one imagines the most wish fulfillmenty alternate history of them all a world in which there is no traffic in Los Angeles. Is Garon really the character you most identify with in the story?"

"No," I said.

"I didn't think so. Who is?"

"Gavinth," I said. Queen Agrippah's husband.

Brian nodded. "You know, I've talked to probably forty actors about that role, and not one of them has pronounced Gavinth's name correctly, until you." I started to tell him that was only because I was listening to the book rather than reading it, but stopped myself.

"I just love how he supports his Queen, and really believes in all the rules of Andromeda, but still wants power, you know? And I like his turn. Like, I think he really loves her, but he also knows that loving her is a way to be close to her, and being close to her is a way to have a say in whether the war happens."

"Yes," Brian said. "Yes. Each character explores a human journey in the story, and Gavinth shows us how people travel from the power of love to the love of power." Brian paused as he pulled into a parking lot, and then said, "I don't want to create false expectations. I love what you're saying about Gavinth, but I see you as a Garon." I nodded, and said something to the effect that I saw myself as a Garon as well.

The Algernon was a breakfast joint, and we were immediately seated outside, on a small patio next to the restaurant's parking lot. Brian recommended I order something called Today's Harvest, so I did. It was basically sliced avocado and tomato drizzled with red wine vinegar, only it cost thirty-seven dollars. One thing that bothers me about Los Angeles is its complete lack of self-awareness. Like a baby that doesn't know there's anything weird about shitting in a diaper, Los Angeles doesn't know there's anything weird about charging thirty-seven dollars for an avocado.

Brian was waxing extremely poetic about the book. "In the film I want to make, Garon's journey charts perhaps the most important question in the movie: How does a tool become a weapon? Think about the stone axe, for instance. It was likely first used as a tool, but at some point it came to be used as a weapon. In both cases, the stone axe was powerful, but as a weapon, it became an instrument with which to enforce power, right?"

"And that's Garon's pen," I said.

"THAT IS GARON'S PEN," Brian answered, smacking the stone top of our little table. "It starts out as the tool through which laws and decrees travel from the court to the people, and then it becomes a metaphorical weapon, when Garon writes the declaration of war against the orcs, and then it becomes a literal weapon of war when it is melted into the handle of his sword. Yes. Yes. You totally get this, Kai. You get the journey. I feel like we are already on the journey together. Do you feel that?"

"Uh, yeah," I said. "Totally."

"But the real question," Brian said, "is how can the weapon journey back to being a tool. Having opened the Pandora's box of violence, how do we return to a state of peace? And that's why in the sequels, I think we will see Garon struggling with his sword, both literally and metaphorically."

"There are sequels?"

"Oh, yes, Valentina has a trilogy planned. The second one is mostly finished, and I've seen the outline for the third. I don't want to spoil Garon's journey for you, but in the end, he is once more holding a pen."

"Sounds cool," I said. "Yeah, I love that arc."

A young woman had come up to our table. "Excuse me," she said. I figured she was excited to meet the brilliant Brian Arawas, but she was looking at me. "Are you the guy who saved Juniper Castillo last night?"

"I don't know about *saved*, but—"

"Oh my God. It's so cool to meet you. I thought that was so awesome, seriously. I just wanted to say thanks."

"Yeah, sure," I said, and then she asked Brian Arawas if he could take a picture of us, which Brian did.

"I didn't know you were such a star already," Brian said, and I briefly explained that we'd just had a weird night, and then he returned to the movie. "Tell me about your familiarity with swords," he said, and I laughed a little, because I thought he was kidding, but he wasn't. Again, the baby doesn't know it's weird to shit in a diaper.

"Um, limited," I said. I remembered Matthew telling me about how when he got to the last round of auditions for a surfing movie, they asked him if he could surf, and he said, "Of course I can surf. I'm Matthew Malone," even though he'd never been surfing in his life and wasn't even a very good swimmer.

"I've got a dance background," I said, "and swordfighting is mostly dancing."

"I love it," Brian said. "I love that. I'm stealing that. The way you move in *Andy Warhol Never Gets Old* is positively spellbinding."

I swallowed a bite of avocado and said, "Thanks, yeah. That was a great part." My stomach was turning a little. "Juniper's so good in it, isn't she?"

"Ah, yes, the studio's favorite Agrippah," he said. "What was she like to work with?"

"Amazing. She's so prepared. She is just, like, incredibly competent and professional and brilliant and most of all just very, like, *ready*. You never have to worry with her."

"My only concern is that she's *too* prepared, perhaps. So studied that at times she may lack that improvisational spark, the range that comes with being open to all the moment may bring. She's more of a Bach than a Beethoven, if you catch my meaning. I tend to be most deeply attracted to Beethovens." I did not catch his meaning.

"I really like her," I said. "I think she's got spark."

"You're certainly wonderful collaborators, although of course I'm sure you understand that there are many great actors interested in Garon."

"Of course," I said. "I'm sure you'll find the right person."

"Well, hopefully this week we'll have you in for chemistry reads. The tool to the weapon, Kai. That's what I hope you'll hold in your heart."

"Right," I said. "Yeah, definitely. Thanks for breakfast; it's so cool to meet you."

"It is very cool to meet you as well," he said.

The ride back to the hotel was a little awkward; the conversation had ended, but now it had to continue for another twenty minutes. We arrived at last, and he got out of the car to hug me and told me he would love to work with me, and I said that yeah of course I would love to work with him, too, and then I was walking back to my room when I saw Bob and Zoe sitting at a table outside the Bel-Air's restaurant. "Kai!" he shouted. "Funny seeing you here."

Bob pulled me into a hug. "How was it? How was it?" He was a large man—not fat so much as large in every direction. He wore a suit, highly tailored. Nobody looks more like themselves than an agent.

"It was good, I think," I answered as I shook Zoe's hand. Zoe shook hands instead of hugging, and wore her hair pulled back into a tight ponytail, and I liked her because her face never revealed much.

"So what'd ya think of him?" Bob asked as we sat down at the table. A waiter appeared, and I asked for a cup of coffee.

"Um, I thought . . . I don't know. He's kind of pretentious."

"Well, he's a director."

"I guess."

"Brian's a genius, and like most geniuses, he knows it."

Zoe looked at her phone. "Apparently you're all over the Internet today, Kai. You beat up a paparazzo?"

"No, a guy tried to get in Juniper's car, and I . . . ensured he did not get in."

"So you're a hero."

"I don't know about that." My phone buzzed. I glanced down at it. Ellen. *Call me.*

"So Brian," Bob said.

"Yeah, I mean, I like his movies obviously. And it's a big movie, I guess."

"Speaking of which, I'm trading calls with business affairs at the studio, but it looks like around two hundred thousand up front, with a little on the back end."

"Is that good?"

"We're gonna try to get them up to two fifty, but they're always gonna lowball us. There are a thousand eager young actors they could cast, and they know that and we know that. So you want the role because it's a good role, not because it'll make you rich." Two hundred thousand dollars seemed rich to me.

"Okay," I said.

"So you want to sign the test deal," Bob said. "Assuming we can get it to two fifty."

"I guess," I said. "The book is good, but the script is pretty, uh, generic. I worry it's just another action movie, you know?"

"It's just another action movie made by the guy whose previous action movies have generated a combined billion-with-a-*b* in international box office, a guy who literally makes stars for a living. Tom Calloway can't act his way out of a fucking parking ticket, and he's the fucking face of Armani because of Brian Arawas. Kai, you pay me to give you advice, and my advice is that *Gods of Agamemnon* is going to blow up, and you can blow up with it. Honestly, with the amount of money the studio is putting behind this thing, it could be directed by a goddamned robot trained by watching *Transformers* movies and still turn a profit."

"*Andromeda,*" Zoe said.

"Right. The title is a fucking problem. You and shitty movie titles, Kai, name a better combination." He belly laughed.

"I guess I should do it."

"You should," Zoe said.

"Zoe's right," Bob said, which is when it occurred to me that Zoe had never been at any of the previous coffees or dinners or lunches I'd had with Bob. She'd always greeted me at the agency, walked me back to Bob's office, asked if I wanted anything to drink, chatted with me until he was available, and then disappeared. I wondered if she'd gotten some sort of minor promotion or if she was just here to convince me to sign the test deal.

"So if I say yes and I get the part, I have to take it, right?"

"You don't *have* to do anything. You want us to get you out of it, we'll get you out of it. But yes, broadly speaking, you're agreeing to a deal that you will take in the event that you get the part. Again, though, nothing's set in stone right now." Zoe reached into her bag and produced the contract. "This is written with you getting two fifty," Bob said, "in the hopes that they'll just be like, well, fuck, he already signed this one; we might as well give him the extra fifty grand so we don't have to bother with more paperwork."

"Seriously?"

"I'll appeal to their fear, and they'll make the deal. They always do, if they're afraid. Fear runs this town. Fear that someone else will get the thing that is so special, so unprecedented, so once-in-a-lifetime."

"And in this case, that thing is me?"

"That thing is fucking you, kid."

"Plus," Zoe said, "you're famous for saving Juniper's life last night."

"I didn't " I started, but Bob had thrust the contract at me, so I didn't say anything; I just signed it.

11

I felt like taking a nap when I got back to my room, but I made the mistake of checking in with Ellen, who informed me that she was coming by at ten to "run scenarios." It was already nine forty-five, so I took a quick shower and changed and by then she had arrived. "Gooodddddd mmoooorrrnniiiiinnngggg," she sang when I opened the door. "It's a beautiful day for my new media starlet. You are trending on Twitter, Kai. I have to know: Who set it up? Because it wasn't me. I wish I had ideas like that, but I'm not that cunning."

"Nobody set it up. Some guy got in Juniper's Uber—"

"Oh, come now. It's simply too good not to have been orchestrated. A *handsome young man* saves his *beautiful young costar* from a *sweaty old creeper*? It's all out of central casting. If anything, it's a bit *too* on the nose. I wonder if it was Katie. Katie's got a flair for the dramatic."

"There's no way it was Katie," I said. "Juniper was terrified. She was literally shaking. I don't think it was a setup."

"Well then perhaps the gods just gave us a wonderful gift. Regardless, you literally can't buy this kind of media. I'm sure it was traumatic and everything, but it's also gold. Let's have class outside, shall we?" She pulled the patio door open and sat on one of the lounge chairs with her iPad. I wondered what Ellen's life was like. I couldn't tell how old she was. Thirty? Forty?

"Do you have any pets?" I asked.

"I'm on the road too much. I used to have a cat."

"What happened?"

"It died, Kai, thanks for asking."

"I'm sorry."

"I heard you met with Brian Arawas today. Are you going to be in *Gods of Andromeda*?"

"Dunno. I signed a test deal but—"

"No. Jesus. Kai. Remember, I might as well be a reporter. *Everyone* might as well be a reporter."

"I loved meeting Brian. He's a brilliant director, but I have no idea what my next project will be. I don't even know what I'm doing this evening," I said in a monotone.

"Better. Juniper has a reputation for being difficult to direct. Did you see that on set?"

"Juniper is the best-prepared, hardest-working, and loveliest actor I've ever met," I said, holding up fingers for each of my three adjectives.

"Very nice. What do you hope people take away from this movie?"

"The feeling that love and art both have the power to truly change us."

"How did it feel watching yourself on-screen?"

"I was mostly just watching Juniper and Matthew, who made me forget that they're Juniper and Matthew. They just became Carly and Andy."

"Good. Good. We're making progress. So, listen, if anyone digs up the high school stuff, I'll make it clear that's off-limits. Is there anything else we need to avoid?"

"I don't think so?"

"Because there was something glaring you didn't tell me about before. What else don't I know about? That's my worry here. It's in your best interest to tell me everything."

"I really think that's it."

"Great," she said. "Great. You're gonna be just fine, kid."

After Ellen left, I took a nap. I dreamt about it—not about it specifically but about the courtroom. When I walked in for the first time, I remember being surprised by how small the court was, and by how few people were in the room. No press. No family. Just the jurors and the alternates and the lawyers seated at their tables and then him. I could tell he was there, but I couldn't look at him. There was just a blurry field at the edge of my vision. I felt like I was betraying him. Everyone kept saying it wasn't my fault, but I was still destroying his good name.

I woke up thinking about it, and about Ellen asking me about it. I didn't want to expose myself to more of it just to be fifth lead in some movie. It wasn't like I'd get to hang out with Juniper all the time; she'd be mostly acting with the lead guy and everyone else in the court. I called Bob.

"Flannery and Appelt," said a polite voice.

I told them who I was and got patched through to Bob immediately. It used to be that all my calls went through Zoe, who'd tell me that Bob was "in a meeting" and would call me back, but now I went straight from the operator to Bob himself, who said, "What's up, kid?"

"Say no."

"What?"

"Say no to *Gods of Andromeda*. I don't want to do the chemistry read. Sorry, but I just don't want the role."

"Can I give a reason?"

"I don't want to spend six months in Canada playing someone's little brother."

Bob didn't say anything, which was so unusual for him that I figured he'd hung up on me. But then he laughed and said, "Listen, kid. I've got a dozen more scripts to send you that came in just this week. Some you'd be auditioning for the lead. It's gonna probably be less money for you to do something else, but I'm here for your dreams, kid. I'm not like those CAA bastards. You don't want to spend six months in Canada playing someone's little brother, I'm not gonna force you. I'll let 'em know." And then he hung up.

I wanted to see Juniper, so I texted her and asked if I could drop by her room. She wrote back immediately *Ten minutes. Getting out of the shower.* I pictured Juniper in the shower. I imagined her head tilted back, her thick hair straight and waterlogged, her big eyes blinking away shampoo, her collarbone, and so on.

When I got to her room exactly ten minutes later, her hair was in a towel and she was putting on makeup in the mirror. "I know you're not as worried about this as I am, but don't you feel like the cemetery scene reads almost *satirical* with that song and the way it's currently cut?"

"Not really," I said. "I mean, honestly, Juniper, I feel like my job was during the shoot and now we just—"

"But it's our *careers*, Kai. Don't you see that? This is our *calling card.* Maybe it's different for you because—and don't take this personally—there are so many more good roles for men, but I feel like for me this is a once-in-a-lifetime opportunity and—"

"You've already booked the lead in a huge movie, Juniper. And you're good in this. You really are."

"But don't you see the inadequacy of *good*? You don't get to make this your life by being good."

"What I meant is that you're great in the movie."

"I could be better if Kathryn hadn't chosen again and again the most innocent, doe-eyed, woe-is-me take I offered her. I could be better if Lou

Reed wasn't droning on in the background of the cemetery scene. I come across as so one-note—"

"You don't. Also, I like Lou Reed."

"While you show so much range and depth of feeling," she said.

"Juniper. You *do* seem innocent in it, but that's why it's so heartbreaking. You're not ready for the shit you have to live through, but you live through it anyway. Honestly, it made me think about myself. I can give a kind of love to your character, a kind of love I can't give to myself, and watching you in the movie, I kept thinking, *I also deserve this love*."

"That's incredibly kind," she said, taking a step toward me.

"Well, it's true." I thought we might kiss but then she turned away and shook her arms out nervously.

"I can't calm down. I haven't been able to since that guy in the car last night."

"Yeah. Ellen thinks maybe someone set that up," I said. "That the sweaty guy was a plant or something. Katie wouldn't do that, would she?"

"She can be nefarious, but she always tells me. No way that was a setup."

"Right, I figured," I said.

After a minute, Juniper looked at me through the mirror and said, "Do you want to see a movie that we're not in?" She sounded shy when she said it. Innocent, even.

"Yeah," I said. "I'd like that. Can it be something terrible?"

She laughed. "Indeed, it *must* be something terrible."

Juniper and I went downstairs and got into her silver SUV. For some reason, I was surprised to learn that she could drive.

We were battling traffic, inching toward the theater. Juniper kept starting to say something critical about the movie and then stopping herself. I told her that I was gonna pass on *Gods of Andromeda*, because I just didn't think the part was big or interesting enough. She said she wished I could be the lead guy, her husband, and I said that I did too, but

I didn't look like a lead guy; I looked like the lead guy's little brother, and she laughed and said, "You underestimate yourself, Kai."

She filled the silence that followed by continuing to worry about our movie. "I just can't stop thinking about it," she told me. "I'm sorry, I know it's annoying. I just want the film to be special, to be *significant.*"

"What even makes a movie *significant*?" I asked. "Everybody keeps talking about how good the movie is, or whether the movie is good, but I don't even know what makes a movie good. Like, what is the point of making movies? Is it to make people happy? Then the movie is terrible. Is the point to make people cry? Then it's great. Is the point to, like, reveal some deep truth about the human condition? Then I think it's, like, good but not great."

"Yes, that is the problem. It could reveal something deep about the human condition if it weren't for the goddamned Lou Reed song."

I offered Juniper a stick of gum. She declined. I unwrapped it and began to chew as I looked up what was playing at the theater. "There's a Robin Hood movie that's fifteen percent fresh on Rotten Tomatoes, but forty-eight percent of users liked it," I said.

"Much too high."

"Agreed. Wait, I think I've got it. If you don't mind waiting until two fifty, we can see *Norse Redemption.* Eight percent fresh. *The Guardian* says, 'One grows accustomed in this line of work to uninspired films, but *Norse Redemption* is truly extraordinary in its failures. Although presumably it is cold in Norway or Sweden or wherever this ninety-seven minutes of ridiculousness is set, the men are always shirtless and slathered in sweat, which is the sole blessing of the film. The performances of the actors' pectoral muscles are far more compelling than those of their faces.'"

"Well," said Juniper. "Doesn't that seem literally perfect?"

And it was. We were alone in the movie theater, and so we got to shout at the screen all through *Norse Redemption*, which was much funnier than any comedy could have been. At one point, the main bad guy says, "No gods, no kings, only Odin," and Juniper said, "I'm pretty sure Odin *is* a god?" And then I said, "No gods, no kings, only certain gods."

"No gods, no kings, only one queen, Agrippah," Juniper added.

"Well, that certainly improved my opinion of *Andy Warhol Never Gets Old*," Juniper said as we walked out of the theater.

"Right?" I said.

"Was there a woman in that film?"

"Sure," I said. "The maiden. At the beginning."

"Oh, yeah, the sexualized object that was dragged away by the villain so that we could internalize the villain's true villainy."

"Also, the mother."

"Right, of course, the thing that provided food and blankets to the human characters."

"I think between them they had at least eight lines," I said.

"I guess that's the good thing about *Andromeda*," Juniper said. "Agrippah has some depth. Carries some action. And I think the love story between her and Gavinth is actually kind of sweet. They've got a good Obstacle. It's a structurally sound film, really. It's just about . . ."

"Orcs," I said.

"Yes. Quite."

I stopped at the edge of the parking lot and said, "It would be fun to be in Vancouver with you. But you'd be spending all your time with whatever meathead they get to play Gavinth."

She looked over at me, smiling. "Probably someone from the movie we just watched." Right then, I saw someone in the parking lot with a large camera taking our picture. The camera made a loud snapping sound, and the bearded guy behind it said, "What movie did you see?" We didn't say anything.

"How long have you been dating?" asked the man.

I was just frozen there until Juniper grabbed my hand and pulled me toward the car. We got in and drove away. "That was weird," she said.

"Did you tell anyone you'd be here?"

"I told Katie I was going to a movie with you. I'm supposed to keep her informed of where I go. Whatever, it's just a photographer."

I looked at Juniper, at her sundress, at her makeup. "Did you dress up for him?"

"For who?"

"For the fucking photographer." I knew as I said it that I was angrier than I ought to be, but I didn't know why. "Did you know about last night? Was that all . . . acting?"

"Christ, Kai, no. No. Shit like that happens all the time. I don't need to *arrange* for creepy fans. Now, did Katie send *that* photographer to *this* movie theater? Probably. But that's totally different from arranging an . . . assault or whatever."

"Did you dress up for him?"

"Calm down," she said. I asked a third time. Finally, after a long pause she said, "I am not dressed up. If I want to dress up, you'll know that I'm dressed up. And if I thought about anyone when I chose this particular dress, it was you. So thanks for noticing, I guess."

"Sorry," I said after a second. "I feel like I can't tell what is real right now."

"Why aren't you testing for *Andromeda*? Don't want to spend six months with a neurotic actress?"

I took a long breath. I was thinking maybe I wasn't cut out for this, but then I also wasn't cut out for anything else. "It'd be one thing if I were with you all the time, but I don't want to be Gavinth's little brother. Honestly, right now I'm not sure I want to act at all."

"Kai, you're a brilliant actor."

"Just because you're good at something doesn't mean you have to do it," I said.

I wanted to tell her then, too, but I could tell she was a little annoyed with me, so I let her drive us back to the hotel and then asked her if she wanted to watch another movie in my room. She smiled—God I love Juniper's smile—and said, "Of course."

12

"Oh, I didn't get my *own pool*," she said when she entered my room and immediately walked outside to my little patio. She lay back on one of the lounge chairs and I lay on the one next to her, such that we were both looking up at the cloudless sky.

"I obviously don't like to talk about it," I said, "but I've been wanting to tell you something."

"Okay," she said.

"I know I can trust you because you judge the fuck out of yourself but never really judge other people."

"Is this about the worst thing?"

"Yeah," I said. "Yeah." I could feel her looking at me now, but I just kept staring at the sky. It looked like a monochromatic painting or something, like it wasn't really real.

"I guess I got abused in school, by one of my teachers. An English teacher. He was like the folk hero teacher, the one everyone loved. He had a wife and kids and grandkids and everything. Old guy. He was in his seventies. And he . . . I mean . . . he said that it was natural. It was natural for special students to fall for their teachers, that Socrates and Plato did it. And it went on for like two years, not all the time, but when he felt 'weak,' as he called it. And I knew it was fucked up but I didn't say no. I liked him.

"Anyway, there were other kids, too, even though he said there weren't, and eventually one of them said something to the principal, and the guy got arrested and they made me testify against him. Honestly, that was even worse than all the stuff that happened. It was what therapists call 'retraumatizing,' I guess. And then he went to prison and his wife divorced him and his kids had to live with it, and I had to live with it, and even though I was anonymous in the trial, everyone at school knew. He's dead now. He died in prison. Heart attack. That's it. That's the worst thing."

"I'm sorry, Kai." She reached across the space between us and wrapped her hand around my forearm, just above the wrist. "I'm so sorry that happened to you."

"Ellen found out."

"Your publicist?"

"Technically she's the studio's publicist. She says I should get in front of it, talk about it publicly and put it behind me. But there's no putting it behind me. I don't want everyone looking at me the way people look at me when they find out. The way you're probably looking at me right now. With pity."

"Hey," she said, and I finally turned from the sky to her and she was not looking at me with pity. She was looking at me with something far more complex. "I don't pity you," she said. "I'm angry for you, and I'm sorry, but I don't pity you. I . . . love you."

The way she said it hit a hell of a lot harder than I expected. It took me a while even to speak again. "Well, you're unusual," I said at last. "Most people look at me and they either feel pity or they think, *Why didn't he say something earlier, why did he let it happen.*"

"Nobody thinks that." We were still looking at each other, and I just flicked my eyebrows at her, and she said, "Well, nobody *should* think that."

"I was fourteen when it started. Old enough to know better."

"Remember what you told me before, that you can love the girl in our movie in a way you can't love yourself? If someone else said what you just said, it would break your heart. Kai, you were a kid. He was an adult. You trusted him. You looked up to him. That's appropriate for a kid. What he did with that admiration . . . was awful."

"Yeah," I said. "Okay."

"Ellen's right," she said. "You should get out in front of it. It's better. And most people are nice. People tell me all the time that me talking about my mom helped them feel less alone."

"It will feel like testifying felt, only every day."

She still had her hand wrapped around my forearm. Her hands were beautiful. Her touch changed my blood pressure. "I get that it's a shitty choice," she said.

We talked for a long time—about why I didn't want to play Gavinth's brother, about whether I wanted to act at all. Her hand never left my arm.

13

After she left that evening, I ordered room service alone. I tried watching TV, but I couldn't find anything good. I didn't know what to do. I probably should've called my parents or a friend or something, but I was feeling the kind of lonely that other people can't fix. I walked into the suite's living room, pulled the bottle of champagne from its bath of room-temperature water, unwrapped the foil, and popped the cork. I went outside, stripped to my underwear, got in the pool, and tried to drink the champagne. It was too warm, and so bubbly that it went up my nose a little. I wondered why I was drinking it, why I was sitting in this plunge pool in my underwear at the Hotel Bel-Air drinking straight from a bottle of warm champagne, and I realized it was a kind of performance. I was doing it because it looked cool, even though I was the only person who could see how cool it looked.

So I took a picture of myself and posted it online. I looked good in the picture—collarbones visible, hair messy, bottle of champagne just visible. I remembered something my roommate had said to me once, that there should be a word for the distance between your actual life and your Instagram Life. She had proposed *fictance*.

My phone started buzzing. Bob again.

"I told the studio you didn't want to play someone's little brother, and they got it. Then immediately—five minutes later—I get a call back from Tom Fucking Weisman himself, and he asks me what *do* you want? Says they need somebody for the new *Jurassic World*, and they always need new *X-Men*. And then he says, get this, he says, 'I understand a talent like Kai not wanting to play somebody's brother. But what if he auditioned for the Somebody?'"

"Wait, what?"

"They want you to read for . . . I can't remember the fuckwad's name, Gavin?"

"Gavinth? The lead?"

"Gavinth, yeah. Technically second lead, behind the girl. Seven hundred thousand guaranteed, and the back end could be worse, Kai. This movie makes money, you make money. And I'm not a psychic, but this movie is gonna piss money. Money comes out of everywhere. Action figures. Sequels. You even get a little cut of the video game they're doing for the movie. Leading man."

"With Juniper as Agrippah?"

"God, these fucking names. Yeah, you'd be opposite Juniper, if you get it. Two kids who are absolutely exploding get their first blockbuster, and of course they do it together because they're so tight. So they get two breakouts with known chemistry. It's gold. It's fucking platinum. I love that you said you didn't want to be somebody's brother. Love it. And now you aren't gonna be. Let me tell them yes. Let me tell them you'll be there on Thursday totally ready to audition for Gavinth, chemistry reading with Juniper."

"I need to sleep on it."

"Kid, it doesn't get any bigger than this."

"I just want to sleep on it. We'll talk in the morning."

"Good night, Gaylord, Duke of the Manor. Am I allowed to say fucking Gaylord, Zoe?"

"I'd recommend not, Bob."

"Great. Kid, get some sleep. I'll talk to you in the morning. I'll send you the newest rewrite of the script."

I felt nauseated. Of course you take a shot at being Gavinth, consort to the Queen. Nine months ago, you were waiting tables, and not in a good restaurant. You've been in exactly one movie. It's about an artist who's been dead for thirty years. Nobody sees movies with five-word titles about dead artists. *Gods of Andromeda* is good work, and you're in the world to work.

I started to read the newest rewrite of the script. The dialogue—and there wasn't much of it—all seemed easily translatable into other languages. Minimal adjectives. Action verbs. A lot of broad observations, like, "We will destroy the enemy, or the enemy will destroy us." At one point, Gavinth literally says, "My dear Queen, the power of love is no match for the love of power." And then there were long descriptions of battle scenes, many of which I could not follow.

But I could see a lot to like in the role. Gavinth wanted to be the hero of the story, and his choices all made sense, which was a lot more than can be said for most screenplays. My drama teacher told me that theater was all about building toward a recognition, and then a reversal. It's been like that since Aristotle. And Gavinth had a hell of a recognition—two-thirds of the way through the movie, he realizes that if he backs the invading enemy over his wife, he could end the matriarchy and seize power, so he begins to undermine Agrippah. But even at the end, when he's mostly a villain, you still feel his love for his homeland, and even for his Queen. He's just convinced himself, as we all do in the end, that his interest aligns with the world's interest.

Also, the studio would presumably pay for a trainer, or whatever one does to develop larger muscles, since Gavinth was repeatedly described as *shirtless but for his golden armor*.

I took another pull on the bottle of champagne. It was dark in LA, but not really, of course, because it never got all the way dark. It got some kind of grayish orange.

Seven hundred thousand dollars. Six thirty after Bob's commission. I'd probably have to hire Ellen, or *an* Ellen. That'd be twenty-five or thirty, I figured. After taxes, I might end up with around four hundred thousand dollars cash. Four hundred thousand dollars, and all I had to do was spend six months in Vancouver and maybe one month doing promotion. Four hundred thousand dollars, cash, free and clear. I liked thinking those words, the shape of them: *Four. Hundred. Thousand. Dollars.*

I got out of the pool, grabbed my clothes, went inside, and emptied the champagne into the bathroom sink. I didn't want anyone to think I'd wasted it.

As I lay in bed and watched TV, Ellen invited me to a place in Bel Air for a drink. For some reason, I felt like a drink—a cold one. Plus, it was only five minutes away. At the bar, it took a second to find Ellen, because even though there were a lot of lights, I couldn't see anybody's face. I eventually found her, along with Lon, Natalie, Studio Todd, and Katie, all crowded around a small cocktail table.

A waiter dressed in all white was hovering nearby, and I could see his uniform clearly but not the person wearing it. Across the table, Studio Todd was telling a joke. I could tell he was drunk, because his consonants kept slipping out from under him. "I want you to close your eyes and imagine a family living in abject poverty. Absolute poverty. The only thing they own is a small hut with a thatched roof. Two adults and two kids inside this tiny home. Now imagine that it catches fire. Their home. It's burning to the ground. Are you imagining it?"

"Yes, I'm imagining it," Ellen said.

"Why are you imagining that? Why are you doing that to their home?"

"Wait, is that the entire fucking joke?"

"That's the joke."

"That's not a joke," Ellen said. "It's a shitty morality play. Kai, welcome. Todd is ruining our evening with his humor."

Studio Todd waved the criticism away with one hand and took a drink of his beer with the other. The waiter brought me a glass of white wine I hadn't ordered.

"Kai, no shit you are incredible in the movie," Todd said.

"Thanks." The pianist playing behind Todd finished a song, and I applauded quietly but no one else did. "I really appreciate your support."

"Well, it's a special film," he said. "You don't get 'em that often. You gotta make a lot of *Alvin and the Chipmunks* to get an *Andy Warhol Never Gets Old*. Or I did, anyway. You hit a grand slam in your first at bat."

"I'm not much for baseball," Lon said, "but I like that metaphor. So you're going to get behind it then."

"We're all the way behind it," Todd said. "We're going to spend twice as much promoting the movie as you spent making it."

"Only because we made it for fourteen," Natalie piped in. "With the most bankable star in Hollywood."

Kathryn showed up then and hugged her way around the table, ending with me. "Kai," she said, "Brian called me today and told me you're taking him on a journey from Garon to Gavinth."

"He loves a journey," I said.

"He does. X to Y, and Y to Z. But you'll adore him. Really. And honestly, it's perfect synergy, because it's great for *our* movie to have you and Junie in *his* movie. And by the time you're done making that, I'll steal you back to be in whatever I do next. We'll just trade you back and forth for the rest of our careers. I love it. I am so thrilled for you. Of course, you'll have to win them over in the room, but you will. You will. There's never been anyone quite like you." Kathryn grabbed a glass of wine and raised it. "Here's to *Andy Warhol* and *Gods of Andromeda* and the mighty future of our young actors."

Everyone toasted, and then Natalie said, "Why are we toasting a movie that Lon and I aren't making?"

"Because Kai's reading for the lead," Kathryn said.

Studio Todd looked at me and said, "I like you for it, kid."

"Thanks," I said.

Todd motioned to the omnipresent waiter for another.

"He shouldn't do it," Lon said to Ellen.

"Who shouldn't what what, Lon?"

"Kai shouldn't take that Brian Arawas movie."

"Fuck off. Of course he should."

Lon took a sip of his drink.

"Why shouldn't I?" I asked after a minute.

Lon leaned forward, his elbows on the tiny table. "It used to be. There used to be a saying in town: *But can he hold a gun?* You'd see somebody in something, and they'd look good. Handsome. Good actor. Natural. Big talent. And the execs would say, *But can he hold a gun?* Because the weird thing about Hollywood is that for all its liberal hippie kombucha peacenikking, you can't get far if you can't hold a gun. Think about every big actor. Tom Cruise—great at holding a gun. Arguably his biggest talent. Denzel Washington—what a fucking gun holder. Paul Giamatti? Great actor. Really. Brilliant. Can't hold a gun, though. Just doesn't look right. The, uh, fucking *Twilight* guy. Rob Pattinson. What an actor. Can't hold a gun."

"Lon," Ellen said.

"There's no guns in *Gods of Andromeda*," I said. "It's all swords and spells."

"It's a saying. There's a certain kind of person who just looks all wrong with a gun, or a sword, or a magic wand, or whatever the fuck. You're a good actor. But you try to play some barrel-chested sword-toting swashbuckler, you're fucked. You can't hold a gun."

"Lon," Ellen said again. "No career mentorship after eight p.m. Also you just want him for your next project."

"I do have a script you'd be perfect for," Lon said, "but that's not it. The kid's going to the graveyard where all the other dumb twenty-year-old fucks go if he takes that movie. We all know forty of 'em who aren't working anymore."

"Shut the fuck up, Lon," Ellen said.

"Am I wrong?" he asked.

"What you are is drunk," Ellen said.

I took a sip of my wine.

The funny thing was, I knew a fair amount about holding a gun. I owned a gun, somewhere. My grandfather had given it to me on my thirteenth birthday. A double-barreled .410 made in Italy. It was probably still at my parents' house. We'd shot skeet a few times, but I'd only killed something with it once. My Pawpaw came to town for Thanksgiving and we ended up quail hunting in southern Indiana. We had hunting dogs with us and I wore a bright orange vest. I was a freshman, and terrified of killing anything. It had just started happening.

The gun felt like a lot of responsibility, which of course it was. I kept thinking that if I turned and shot, I could kill my father, or my grandfather. It felt weird to hold all that killing in one hand, barrel pointed down.

I wondered if Lon had ever shot anything. He didn't look like it.

Ellen leaned in toward me and said, "Seriously, Kai. No one at this bar including the pianist knows less about twenty-first-century Hollywood than Lon, okay? That's why he has Natalie. Todd likes you for it, and he's the executive on the movie, so his opinion actually counts."

I nodded, but I was thinking about hunting in southern Indiana with my grandfather. He only had a year to live, as it turned out, but he was healthy then. I remember telling Pawpaw that I'd been cast as Hamlet, and he said, "'The devil hath power / To assume a pleasing shape.'" I was surprised my Pawpaw knew the play. "You must keep reading," he told me. "You'll never be alone in this world so long as you have a library card."

In my memory, the dogs flushed out a covey of quail moments later. I raised my gun to my shoulder and carefully took aim a little bit away from the quail. I wanted to look like I was trying without risking an actual kill. But I was scared of the gun's kick against my shoulder, and so as I squeezed the trigger my arm jerked a little, and I watched in stunned horror as a quail fell in a descending spiral out of the sky.

I felt my grandfather clapping me on the back. My dad shouted that I was a natural as one of the dogs came running toward us with the dead quail in its mouth.

14

Ellen called me the next morning. "Three things, very quick. One, I am going to call Jill from *The New Yorker* and pitch a profile, but I need your permission."

"Okay," I said.

"She won't know about it. It will not be an issue."

"Okay," I said again. It's amazing how people always refer to it as *it*. They look at me, and I know they're thinking about it, which makes me think about it, and then the room is supersaturated with it, and it is the only noun in the room. *Why did he let it happen? Why didn't he tell anyone about it? How long did it go on? Who else knew about it? What did it involve exactly? I heard it was even happening at school.*

It overwhelmed me. In a way, it made me the it.

She told me that I was naturally good with the press, and that *The New Yorker* almost never profiled new actors. She said we could maybe even be at the beginning of an awards push, and that Jill was perfect for the job, provided I liked her. "Yeah, she seemed fine," I said.

"Jill's great. Such a writer. I'll send you her profile of Michelle Obama. I'll get working on that. I just don't want you to worry, okay,

Kai? This is literally why I'm here. Second thing, when are you reading for *Andromeda*?"

"Tomorrow, I think. I don't know; Bob hasn't called me."

"Great. Third thing, are you planning on going home? You're here today obviously, and tomorrow, and then I don't think I need you for the next eight days, so you would be welcome to go home. That is also my subtle way of saying that your stay here ends on Friday."

"And it's currently Wednesday?"

"It's currently Wednesday."

"Yeah, okay, I guess I'll go home."

"Great. I'll book you a flight for Friday morning . . . to . . . ?"

"New York, I guess. Or Indianapolis. I'll get back with you on that."

"Great. It'll be commercial, sorry to say. First class though. I have to go now to attend an *Andy Warhol Never Gets Old* marketing meeting. It's all you all the time, Kai. You can call into the meeting if you want, by the way. God knows Juniper will."

"I'm gonna pass."

"I love it. Beautiful. Speak soon."

I finally called my dad that morning, sitting in what I had come to think of as my tiny pool. It was really just an oversized bathtub, but it was mine, for two more days anyway. My dad picked up on the first ring. "Kai, where are you right now?"

"I'm in a hotel in California."

"I'm fishing on the goddamned White River with Mike Curless. You remember Mike?"

"Sure, of course," I said. "Tell Mike I said hi."

"My son the famous actor says hi, Mike. How's Hollywood?"

"I saw the movie, and I think it's good."

"Can't wait to watch it. We've got our tickets to New York booked and everything, me and your mom and Emma and your brother. Your brother's here, too. You want to say hello?"

"Yeah," I said, although I didn't, really. "Hey, Alex."

"How's Hollywood?"

"Good, I guess."

"I can't believe I get updates on your love life from my google alerts."

"You do?"

"Just this morning. You're dating that girl from the movie. June?"

I sighed. "Don't believe everything you read."

"She's a cutie."

"Yeah," I said.

"I'd hit it," he said.

"Good to know," I answered.

"Christ, you don't have to get defensive. I thought she wasn't your girlfriend."

"She's not," I said. "How's Emma?" His wife.

"Great. We're excited for the premiere. Emma got an outfit and everything. Hot as hell."

"Cool, yeah, I hope you like the movie."

"Honestly, Kai, a night out with no kids at this point and I don't give a shit how terrible the movie is."

"Thanks, I guess," I said, and then he must have handed the phone back to my dad, who asked me about the weather and if I was staying at the same hotel as him in New York. "I might come home for a few days this weekend if that's okay," I told him.

"Home like here?"

"Home like there."

"Well, you're always welcome."

I texted Ellen that I wanted to fly to Indianapolis, and then sat in my room for a while scrolling through Instagram. Juniper texted and asked if I wanted to go to lunch. I asked if we could just order room service, because I didn't feel like being photographed. She wrote back, *My place or yours?* with one of those ambiguous smiling emojis I couldn't quite translate. Emojis exist to clarify language, but the real problem is that no one actually wants to be clear.

The first time I asked the social virologist if she wanted to stay over, she said, "Either way is fine, to be honest," and I thought she meant that it was fine if we hooked up and fine if we didn't, but what she meant was that it was fine if she stayed over after we had sex and fine if she didn't stay over after we had sex. And then I said, "Maybe we should wait," and she said, "For what, marriage?" And I laughed it off, and we had sex, and she stayed over.

After she fell asleep, I got up and took a shower and barfed in the toilet for reasons that weren't entirely clear to me. It wasn't like I was thinking about him so much as I knew that he was in the room, that indeed he was in every room. And then when I finished showering and got back into bed, the social virologist rolled over and put one arm over me and said, "You smell nice."

I got up to crack the door open for Juniper and then went back to the bed, on top of the covers, pillows scrunched up behind me so I was mostly sitting. I was scrolling through the absurdly expensive on-demand movies when she walked in without knocking and said, "Hiya." Juniper was wearing faintly pink sweatpants and an Ariana Grande T-shirt.

"Say anything bad about Ariana Grande and I'll fucking cut you," she said as she leapt onto the bed and then sat down, legs crossed. She was barefoot. Her hair pulled back tight. She wasn't wearing any makeup. "I feel very looked at," she said.

"Sorry."

"It's okay. You can look at me. I'm looking at you." I didn't know what to say to that, so I just kept looking. "Can I tell you what I see?"

"Sure," I said.

"I see my Gavinth." I laughed and rolled my eyes. She launched forward into a hug that was also kind of a wrestling move, and I laughed and hugged her back. "We are going to have so much fun making war together."

"Also the money," I said.

"Also the money! So much money! Just to wear armor and pronounce place names correctly."

"Altar of Har'koa," I said.

"Dazar'alor," she answered.

"Am I correct in guessing that you've not just read the book but also listened to all the fan podcasts and everything?"

"I have joined the official fan Discord. I was placed in a guild."

"A guild?"

"Yes, a fan group within the fan group. It's a lovely community. A bit overwhelming, though."

"Awesome," I said. "You can get me up to speed in the makeup trailer on the first day of the shoot." Juniper smirked at me, and I thought about that emoji again.

She lay down on the bed, pulled me toward her, and raised up her phone. As she played with angles and facial expressions, I shrank away and said, "Must we?"

"It's just for Instagram," she said. "I mean, we are in bed together; what's wrong with taking a picture of us in bed together?"

"Because we aren't *in bed* together." She raised her phone again, and I rolled away again.

"Can we just get the terrible part of the day over?"

I rolled back toward her and put my arm around Juniper, then smiled for the camera. Juniper took a few pictures, chose one, filtered it very subtly, then showed it to me for my approval.

"Caption?" I asked.

"I was thinking, 'cud with my bud.' All lowercase. 'Cud' as in *cuddle*, of course."

"Of course," I said.

"You think you are very special for dismissing the immense power of Instagram," she said as she posted the picture.

"I do."

"Let's watch a movie."

"Okay, but are you going to check to see how many likes the picture has every five minutes and then try to use that information to guess the approximate opening weekend numbers for *Andy Warhol Never Gets Old* and then tell me that I should be happy and/or sad about how well and/or poorly our movie is going to do?"

"Uggggg, Kai. First off, it's not *our* movie. It's my movie featuring you."

"It's Matthew's movie featuring both of us," I said, laughing.

"It's Kathryn's movie, starring Matthew, featuring me, and introducing you. Secondly, yes, I am going to check how many likes my stupid picture got, and how many new follows it got you because I tagged you you're welcome. This is how I quantify my value to society, Kai. I am trying to help our movie."

"Matthew's movie," I said.

"Matthew's movie. What are we going to watch?"

"I've been wanting to see *John Wick 2*," I said.

"People say it's the Thinking Man's *John Wick 1*," she answered.

15

As we watched the movie, I kept looking over at Juniper. She had full lips and improbably large brown eyes. "I look like a cartoon that became a real girl," she told me once. Her hair fell extremely straight from her head, a rich brown, naturally highlighted red. I liked the way Juniper sat—her legs curled up together, one hand across her stomach. I liked the way she glanced at me during the most violent bits and made an exaggerated barfing face. I liked the way she laughed at the jokes in the movie, abruptly and generously. If you were onstage doing improv, you'd want Juniper in the audience, and I appreciate people like that.

And I loved how hard she worked, how much she wanted to be great. What other people found annoying about Juniper—she's too overbearing, too ambitious, too committed—were to me the coolest things about her. So I *was* attracted to her. I wanted her. In a world where I knew so little about what I wanted, I knew I wanted her. I didn't just love her; I also *liked* her. I liked being with her. But I also felt bad about loving and liking her, and especially about wanting her. Maybe wanting someone is wrong. This is the fucked-up shit my brain does when I get within a mile of human sexuality. I can't trust myself. I recoil.

About halfway into the movie, Juniper leaned over into me, and I put my arm around her, and I could feel the strangeness of her breaths rising and falling toward and away from me.

Sexuality always stressed me out, even before. I guess that's part of what made me a good target or whatever. He told me once, "You know I know what you like," which is one of those very complicated sentences made entirely of simple words. I thought of Juniper seeing me naked, what she'd say or do. When I'd been with the social virologist I definitely wasn't dating, she'd told me she liked this part of me just above the hip, and he'd said that, too. He'd said that boys and girls both had that little arc of muscle that stretched from the pelvis to the hip, and that's why he liked both boys and girls. And I sat there and let him stroke it and it felt good, or at least something adjacent to good. And then the social virologist said the same thing and I felt like I was going to throw up but we had sex anyway and if she noticed anything off she didn't mention it.

"Are you ill?" Juniper asked.

"Well, I just saw a guy get his face shot off," I allowed.

"No, seriously, you look terrified."

"I'm good, let's watch the movie."

She grabbed the remote and paused it. "What?" she asked.

"Really, nothing."

"Is it me? My proximity? The leaning?"

"No."

"Because I can sit up very straight. I have excellent posture. I didn't mean to—"

"I'm just worried about the test," I lied. "I really want to get it."

"Andromeda," she said.

"Yeah," I said after a second.

Something about her eyes calmed me down. I felt my breath back in my body. Juniper kept looking at me a long time, quiet. I did love her. I knew that much.

She seemed to swallow a breath. She sat up straight—she did have excellent posture—and unpaused the movie, and then she mumbled, "Look at me that way tomorrow and you'll get it."

The next morning I woke up early and made my way down to the lobby of the hotel and called an Uber. It was hazy and cool with a whipping wind. I turned my back to the wind and hunched over. The valet standing nearby said, "Fire weather."

"I hope not," I said.

"On the news this morning, they said it's not a question of whether, just a question of where," he said.

"Scary," I said vaguely. I was only thinking about the test, about my lines, about the way Gavinth would stand, how I needed to pull back my shoulders and make myself big in the room.

"New normal," he said, and then my Uber showed up. The driver was a little older than me. He was burly and pockmarked. "How are you today?" he asked, in a slight Eastern European accent.

"Nervous," I said. "Going to an audition."

"I am also an actor," he said. "I am tough guy, you know? I just do this between."

"Yeah," I said. "How's work lately?"

"It comes and goes. I get a day or two on this, a day or two on that. I was mobster on *NCIS* few months ago. That was good. I died. I died in over forty movies and shows. I am expert in dying now. How about you?"

"I've only booked a few things."

"Good few if you're staying at Hotel Bel-Air."

"Yes, a good few."

"Sometimes," he said, "I think Hollywood is just actors paying other actors to drive to auditions. Today, I drive Uber and you take Uber. Tomorrow, maybe you drive Uber and I take Uber."

"Yeah, maybe," I said.

"Only thing doesn't change? Uber gets money no matter who is driving. Agents get money no matter who is working."

"Yeah," I said.

"Good luck anyway," he said.

I'd done a focus exercise at drama camp one summer that stuck with me: You bring yourself into sensorial awareness. The car smells musty. We're pulling up to a stoplight and I can hear the rhythmic thud of warped brake rotors. Feel the weave of the fabric of this back seat. Breathe the air into your lungs. It tastes a little like something somewhere is burning.

"Here's good," I told him when we were a few blocks away. I wanted to walk, get my blood moving, get my posture settled. It was warmer than it had been half an hour ago. A little sun on my skin. It occurred to me that Gavinth lives in a world where his own legs are his second-fastest method of transportation, after only a horse. That smell of distant fire was undeniable now—not a matter of whether but where.

The casting director's office was a blacked-out storefront half a block off Santa Monica Boulevard, no sign or anything. I was twelve minutes early, so I walked around the block. Halfway around, I saw Juniper on the other side of the street walking in my direction, her earbuds in, her eyes cast downward. I didn't know if I would ruin her vibe, or if it would look bad if we arrived together, so I turned around and walked quickly back to the storefront. My armpits were sweating. Maybe that was okay. Gavinth sweats. Of course he does. *You've got this—if you even want it. You might not want it, remember.*

The receptionist looked up as I entered but didn't say anything. The light was low, the furniture modern. I sat down next to Callum Golding. I knew him a little bit. He and I had been up for a couple of the same things. "Kai, right?" he said, and I shook his hand, and then we made awkward conversation about work. Callum was so goddamned beautiful it hurt to look at him, with his pouty lips, square jaw, and sapphire eyes.

Juniper came in a few seconds later, nodded to us, and sat off on her own, earbuds still in, until the casting director, Nina, appeared from behind a wall and said, "Juniper and Callum?"

I waited. The sensorial awareness that I'd had in the car was gone and I couldn't get it back. Tried to feel myself sitting on this couch, but couldn't. Tried to smell the fire in the air, but it tasted like nothing. I hated casting rooms. I was so much better when I could just self-tape. I pulled out my phone after a while and went on Reddit.

There was a fire, near the Getty. Part of the 405 was closed because firefighters were working to keep it from jumping the freeway. Some famous YouTuber had posted, *How am I supposed to get to brunch with the 405 closed*, and everyone was saying that person was canceled, and isn't it amazing how celebrities can make even forest fires about themselves, and then other people were saying it's not a *forest* fire actually but more of a *brush* fire, and then other people were saying that LA was getting what it deserved, and others were saying that there aren't even supposed to be humans in large concentrations in places with so little rainfall, and other people were saying there aren't even supposed to be humans in large concentrations.

None of which much helped with the fire, or for that matter my Gavinth preparation, but it did give me something to look at while I waited for Callum and Juniper to finish. At some point another guy came in and sat down next to me, Charles Oldham. He was properly famous—he'd been the most recent Mimic in *X-Men*—and he was the guy Bob was most worried about. We talked about the fire a little, and then finally Callum came out, and Juniper right after him. I started to say something to her but she put her earbuds back in and looked down at the floor, walking in tight little figure eights.

If I'm good at acting, it's because I can always connect my life to a character's life. I like to think about how people got themselves into now, and there's always some way that their series of choices and circumstances can relate to my own. Now is always a problem that started with then. And so I turned back to Gavinth, who, like me, was in love but didn't know quite how to act on it, because he wasn't *only* in love. He was also in lots of other things.

Nina reappeared after a minute or two. "Juniper and Kai?"

I stood up. Charles Oldham told me to break a leg, and I said *Yeah you too*, and I followed Juniper and Nina down a hallway lined with headshots of every famous actor you could imagine, and then into a room with black foam sound insulation lining the walls. At the table near one wall sat Brian, two women wearing all black, and a woman with long silver hair who introduced herself as the author, Valentina. I walked over and shook their hands for some reason, even though Juniper didn't. "Our creator," I said to Valentina.

"What's that?" she said.

"I'm sorry. That's stupid. I'm nervous. Why am I nervous?"

Brian stood up and walked around the table. He reached out and kneaded my arms just below the shoulders. "You're nervous because you want this," he said. "And I like that. We good, Nina?"

"Just formatting a card, hold on," Nina said. Brian nodded to me, and squeezed me one last time before letting go. Juniper took out her earbuds, and walked over to me. She gave me a hug, and as she did, I heard her whisper, *"Give me that* John Wick 2 *look right now,"* and as we parted I looked at her, and I watched a blush spread across her face, and then Nina said, "All right, I think we're good to go," and Brian said, "I think we're already going."

After that it was easy. I was Gavinth, and she was Agrippah, and my lines felt mine, and I wanted her, and I wanted what she had, and she wanted me and wanted to keep me from getting what she had. When Brian said, "Cut, that was great," I was genuinely surprised to learn that I was in a dingy room with laminate floors surrounded by strangers.

"How did that feel?" Brian asked.

"Wonderful," I said. You're always chasing that high as an actor, feeling like you aren't stuck inside your mind, that you actually can leave your consciousness. I'd never had the experience in an audition before, not like that. Only when Juniper turned toward Brian did I realize I was still looking at her.

"I think we can go bigger," Juniper said. "I mean, this is an epic, right?"

"I'm actually wondering if you can try a little more insular, Juniper. A little more reserved. He wants what you have."

"Sure, but he's not smart enough to get it," Juniper said. "I'm not worried about that just yet, am I?"

"You're a little worried, maybe," Brian said. "Just try it."

And she did. As she became protective, I became more conniving, more intent on unlocking Agrippah's affection. Now when I said, "Surely Her Majesty knows she is beautiful," and she said, "I surely know that men believe so," it seemed like we were jousting rather than flirting. But I still felt, as they say, *in* character.

"That was great," Brian said.

"Incredible," added Valentina.

"It didn't feel too quiet?" Juniper asked.

"Not at all," said Valentina.

"Maybe a little," said Brian. "I wonder if you can show us what she wants."

"What she wants," repeated Juniper.

"What Agrippah wants from Gavinth. If you can show us that a little more nakedly. If that makes sense?"

"That makes sense," Juniper said, although I could hear the doubt in her voice. And so we went again, and now I could feel her aggression. She stepped toward me this time as she said, "I surely know that men believe so," and I felt somehow small, only eking out my next line: "In this, if nothing else, men are wise." And she seemed only to grow as she said, "Indeed, in that, and nothing else."

"Wonderful," Brian said. "Brilliant. Kai, I love how you roll with her, and Juniper, I love how you know you're the Queen. It's great. Valentina, Nina?"

"I think we can move to the next scene," Nina said. "We've got great options." And so we moved to the other scene, later in the movie, when I'm beginning to chafe at the servile role I'd earlier accepted. I started that scene with, "Am I a handmaid to you?" and Juniper paused a long time—so long I was pulled out of it and thought she might've forgotten her line—before she said, "No, my dear, handmaids . . . are . . . *critical.* You are my husband."

"But am I not critical to the Realm?"

"Every citizen is critical to the Realm. Each has duties to fulfill. Even I have duties to fulfill."

"I do not wish to be just another citizen of the Realm," I said.

"And I do not wish to have the responsibilities of a Queen, but here we are, my love."

"Am I?"

"Are you what?" she asked, clearly done with the conversation.

"Your love," I said.

She surprised me then with a kiss, a quick one on the lips, and a little patronizing. "Of course you are my love."

"And you are my love," I said, surprising myself by kissing her back. But she pulled away quickly and smirked. "Ah, but no," she said. "I am your Queen."

"Can we try it without the kissing?" Brian asked.

"Sure," I said, and we did, but it wasn't as good. We ran it a few more times—in moments it felt like Juniper was too attached to her power, and I too smarmy in my pursuit of it. Brian could sense it, too, and he talked us through options. With Juniper and the table between us, I didn't mind Brian. He did manage to make me feel like I was doing something more than being in a dumb fantasy movie, like I was after something universal and important. By the fourth time we ran it, I wanted to keep going, just so I could stay in the world with Juniper, stepping back as she stepped forward.

But soon it was over, and I was back in the reception room, and the earbuds were back in Juniper's ears, and I was walking past Charles Oldham, who told me to have a good one bro.

Outside, I called Bob and started walking. He picked up on the second ring. "How'd it go, kid?"

"I don't know. But Juniper makes it easy."

"I'll call you the second I hear something. I'm sure they loved you, kid. I gotta go."

I walked a few more blocks before I got an Uber. I could've gone anywhere, of course—to a museum or a movie or the opera or whatever—but I just went back to the hotel and ordered room service lunch and watched TV. All the networks were covering the fire. There wasn't much to say about it—it was raging and people were trying to stop it from burning down buildings—but they managed to keep talking about it nonstop anyway, and I managed to keep watching.

It was past one when Bob called me. "It's you or Charles," he said. "I think there is some internal debate. The director loves you. Nina loves you. I think we're on a journey to make sure the studio loves you. Todd is on the fence, and his boss . . . well, Charles has experience. He has a name."

"Right, I get that."

"Did you know he has fourteen million Instagram followers?"

"I did not."

"The studio salivates over that shit. They love a number. Juniper only has four million. That's what Todd told me. *Only* four million. Christ. You are basically dead on social is what I hear."

"So it's me or Charles."

"Yeah. This one might not go our way. It's the studio that makes the decision. I'm having Kathryn call Todd's boss. That might help. And Matthew has already made a pitch for you. Juniper will have some say. You should call her."

"And say what?"

"Tell her you want to spend six months in fucking Vancouver with her. If there's one thing that's obvious, it's that she wants to fuck the living daylights out of you."

"She's an actor. It's acting."

"I'm just saying," he said. I really hated when Bob said shit like that, because it reminded me that he *thought* shit like that.

"I'll call her," I said, and then got off the phone with Bob. Whenever Bob says, "This one might not go our way," that's it. They never really fully reject you; they just ghost you and one day there's the movie poster with Charles on it. I felt a rush of failure and shame, the two horsemen of my apocalypse, and a void opened up in my abdomen, just beneath my rib cage. I remembered that I had to fly home. I didn't even know what time my flight was. I was so wholly incompetent, an idiot faking my way through the world. For some reason, something Matthew said to me once came into my mind unbidden: *You get famous by getting roles, and you get roles by getting famous.*

Right then, Ellen called. "Where are you right now?" There was tension in her voice. It almost sounded like she'd been crying.

"I'm in my hotel room. What's up?"

"Okay, don't leave. Stay in your room. I'll be there in, uh, fourteen minutes."

"What's going on?"

"I'm about to say something I never say to actors: Google yourself. I'll be there in thirteen and a half minutes."

So I googled myself. I'd only seen the first headline—*Hero Starlet Kai Laramie Put His Molester in Jail*—when a call came in from Juniper.

"Where are you right now?"

"I'm in my hotel room waiting for Ellen."

"So you know."

"I know."

Bob was calling. I sent it to voicemail.

"I'm so sorry, Kai."

I took a few breaths, but I couldn't feel the air coming in or going out. I didn't know what to say or do. Everyone would know now. The casting director would know. Brian Arawas would know. Matthew Malone would know. My phone was vibrating again. My brother. Jesus. Everyone knew. "Kai," Juniper said. "You didn't do anything wrong. There's nothing shameful about this coming out. It's just a gossip site, anyway. Nobody reads that shit."

"My brother is calling," I said.

"So maybe your brother reads it."

My phone buzzed again. Matthew. "I gotta go," I said. "Matthew's calling."

I clicked over. "Kai," he said, with the calm confidence that defined him in the public imagination. "How are you?"

I could feel the heat behind my eyes. "I feel pretty scared right now."

"Kai, you saved a lot of other young people by testifying. There are a lot of kids who'll never know what you have to know."

"Thanks, Matthew."

"We'll have your back during the junket. Me and Junie. We've got you."

Phone buzzed. Bob again.

"Listen, Matthew, I need to go. My agent won't stop calling."

"You're going to be okay. I mean, in the long run you'll be dead, and in the short run it's gonna be bumpy, but in the medium run, Kai. In the medium run, you're golden."

"Thanks, Matthew."

I clicked over to Bob. "You got the fucking part, kid."

"I what?"

"They said why buy a star when we can fucking make one."

"Congrats!" Zoe jumped in.

"You and Juniper, starring in another movie together. Great for *Warhol*. Great for the future."

"Have you seen the article?" I asked.

"Oh, about that teacher? Yeah, someone just sent it to me. If anything, kid, and don't take this the wrong way, but if anything, it helps us. You're a hero twice over—saving America's sweetheart from a creepy fan and America's children from a pedophile."

"It helps us," I repeated. My stomach hurt. I remembered him making me sit on his lap, grinding against me. He always kept his clothes on. He would say sometimes, how can it be inappropriate when you've never even seen my cock? I just like to give you pleasure. Pleasure can't be wrong.

Sometimes I thought maybe it didn't actually happen; maybe it was like he said at the trial and I imagined it all, or made it up to hurt him. But then how do you explain the others? The article, which I scanned through once and then read slowly while waiting for Ellen, made it seem like *I* had been the one to out my abuser, even though it was another kid who said something to the principal. I was picked to testify because the other kid had a drug charge and wasn't seen as reliable. It made me look like a hero I wasn't. I hadn't stopped him. Someone else had stopped him.

But how do you explain what it's like? How do you explain that he'd play the nervous game with you, asking if you were nervous when he put his hand on your thigh, and you'd say no, and then he'd put his hand farther up your thigh and say are you nervous now, and you'd say no, I'm not nervous. Why did you say that? Why didn't you say yes I am fucking nervous and freaked out and I don't feel right about this? Then eventually he'd get near your cock and you'd say yes I'm nervous and he'd grab your cock anyway. I thought about the statue in his office, this bronze statue of an emaciated cowboy riding a horse, the cowboy wearing a hat with the brim pulled down low over his forehead. It is strange what gets remembered, what refuses to be forgotten.

"We got it up to seven hundred fifty grand up front," Bob said.

"Wow," I said.

"Eight hundred for the first sequel, one million for the second, and these movies make you a fucking star. The stone-cold balls on you, to tell the studio you don't want to play someone's brother and rocket yourself into the male lead."

"Yeah," I said. "Yeah. Take the deal."

"That's what I love to hear. Enjoy this, kid. Fucking drink it in."

PART 3

THE JUNKET

KAI

1

"They're the stars of the new film *Andy Warhol Never Gets Old* starring Matthew Malone as Andy Warhol."

"*The* Matthew Malone?"

"Yes, Mel, *the* Matthew Malone, and I know you love him. Welcome to *Indiana Mornings*, Kai Laramie and Juniper Castillo."

Smile. I'm inside some conference room at the Mandarin Oriental hotel in New York City staring down the barrel of a camera. We're live, via satellite, in Indianapolis. I can't see the set, or the anchors of *Indiana Mornings*. I can only hear their voices. *"Good morning,"* Juniper says. She sounds cheery for someone I know was up till three in the morning worrying about the junket.

"I have to ask you about Matthew Malone."

"The best," I say.

"The absolute best," Juniper echoes.

Remember Ellen's prep. Matthew is genuine, funny, and wise. He really transformed himself for this role. He's such a brilliant actor. I know you all know him from the MCU, but we can't wait for you to meet him as Andy Warhol.

"I understand this is based on a true story. Juniper, you play a young journalist?"

"A VERY young journalist, I'd say, Chris."

Juniper laughs ever so slightly.

My armpits are sweating. Why am I even scared? It's only *Indiana Mornings.*

"Yes," Juniper says, "I'm a journalist following Andy Warhol in what turns out to be the final months of his life, and Kai plays one of his interns."

"Kai, you're actually from right here in Indianapolis."

"That's right, Mel. I grew up watching your show." That's a lie, but a good one.

"And while here you were abused by a teacher. You've been very public about this difficult chapter in your life."

Ellen told me this would happen now that everything's been out for over a week and I posted to Instagram acknowledging the abuse to "get out in front of it." They will say *You've been very public about your abuse*, because that gives them permission to talk about it. They're not being vultures, because you've been very public about it. She taught you how to pivot. So you pivot.

"It was a really difficult time in my life, but I poured all that—and everything else I've experienced—into this movie, *Andy Warhol Never Gets Old.*"

"Well," Mel says. "I can't wait to see it."

"Thanks so much, Mel," Juniper answers. "It's a movie that really makes you believe in the power of art, and the power of love."

"Sounds like my kind of movie," Chris says. "Plus, it's got *the* Matthew Malone."

"Swoon," says Mel. "Well, thanks so much for joining us, Kai Laramie and Juniper Castillo. *Andy Warhol Never Gets Old* opens October fourth in theaters everywhere."

"Go Jaguars!" I say. My high school mascot.

"And we're out," says a voice in our ears. Then Katie comes in: "Juniper, I could feel you wince a little when you said the movie makes you believe in the power of love."

"Yeah, well, it's aggressively cheesy."

"Remember, all morning we're talking to heartland folk. This is flyover country. They don't give a shit about Andy Warhol."

"You realize you're talking about Kai, right? He's from 'flyover country.'"

"Just doing my job. Okay, we've got Omaha up next. Very similar. Three to five minutes. You're doing great."

We do Omaha. We do Cincinnati. We do Tulsa and Philadelphia and Asheville and Pasadena. I try to hold my shoulders up, even though I'm flagging. I remember my talking points, and repeat them as if I've never said them before. Juniper squeezes my hand between each interview, which helps. Brings me back into my body. Only about a third of them mention it.

The junket is the same thing over and over again: What's it like to work with Matthew Malone? You two have remarkable chemistry in the movie; what's the key? You must be so excited to work together again on *Gods of Andromeda*. Juniper, we hear Kai saved you from an overenthusiastic fan. Matthew Malone *completely* transformed himself to become Andy Warhol. Kai, is it true you told Juniper you loved her the first time you met? What do you hope people take away from the film? Juniper, you've been very public about the neglect and abuse your mother inflicted. Kai, you've been very public about the trauma you experienced; did that go into your character?

In Colorado Springs—again, we cannot see any of these people or places; we only know it's Colorado Springs because we've been told it's Colorado Springs—the anchor says, "We hear you two are besties."

Juniper and I glance at each other. "Absolutely," I say. "I love Juniper so much I signed up to do another movie with her."

"We thought we'd give you a little bestie quiz."

"Sounds fun," Juniper says. It does not sound fun, of course. Nothing that happens in this black room with lights shining down on us, with the movie poster in the background of the shot, nothing in this room can sound fun.

"Juniper, what color is Kai's toothbrush?"

"Easy," Juniper says. "Blue."

"Kai?"

"It is blue," I say.

"Kai, what is Juniper's favorite animal?"

I turn to Juniper. "You want to say it together?" I ask.

"Sure," she says.

This is an old acting trick. "A rhi—" I start, and then Juniper jumps in so quickly that you can't tell I started first: "—noceros," we say together.

"Tell me more about that, Juniper."

"Oh, years ago one escaped from a zoo in Prague," she says. "And I just thought that was so beautiful, a rhinoceros walking the streets of Prague. I've been obsessed with them ever since."

"Amazing. Juniper, what is Kai's favorite color?"

"Yellow," Juniper answers with confidence. I do not have a favorite color.

"Almost," I say. "It's the specific yellow that ginkgo leaves turn in Indiana autumn."

"We'll give it to her," the anchors say. "What about Juniper's favorite drink?"

"Club soda," we say together.

"Oh, a teetotaler. Okay, you're batting a thousand. Last one: Kai, is Juniper single?"

"Yes," I say.

"Juniper?"

"Well, he's wrong there. I'm married to the sea."

The anchors laugh together.

"Okay, you're clearly Real-Life Besties. Congratulations on the film. We haven't gotten to see it yet, but *The New York Times* preview called it one of the most anticipated pictures of the year so far, and we can't wait to see it in theaters October fourth. Juniper and Kai, thanks, besties."

"Thank you so much," I say.

"And we're out," Ellen says. "Great job. We've got two minutes until Duluth. Three more of these and we move on to the roundtables. Y'all are doing great."

I turn to Juniper. "Nice work on rhinoceros," I say.

"There actually was a rhino that escaped the Prague Zoo," she says. "I didn't even make that up. Now that will be my favorite animal forever."

"Got it. And I guess my toothbrush is now blue," I say.

"What color is it actually?"

"No idea. Are you actually married to the sea?"

"Quite."

2

One thing I learn quickly about junkets: The reporters *want* to ask questions different from the standard ones, but they also *can't*, because then they'll lose the opportunity to interview the next set of Hollywood stars. The studio will blacklist them. This is why most interviewers don't ask me about it even though it's been all over the Internet. Ellen has encouraged them not to ask. The only places that ask are places that think it's worth the trouble (like my hometown morning news show) or outlets too naive to understand the game.

One such outlet is seated at a roundtable in the hotel meeting room where we go next, once we're done with the live hits of morning shows. The young woman from "Teen Pop Craze" has barely introduced herself when she says, "It must be hard, promoting this movie while also processing the public response to your childhood molestation."

I nod. Ellen told me to nod and say nothing when I have not actually been asked a question. "Let me rephrase that," the woman says. "Has it been hard?"

"Sure," I say. "But lots of things are hard. I mean, all things considered, I've got a pretty great life, so maybe I should shut up and enjoy my good fortune." This is too harsh an answer. It sounds defensive. Ellen will gently criticize it later, I'm sure.

"Matthew really transformed himself," says another reporter, this one from *BuzzFeed*, "for the role . . ." and then we're back on track.

Yesterday: Matthew takes us out for dinner. The restaurant is dim; he has to put on his glasses to read the menu. It's strange to think of Matthew Malone's eyes failing. He tells us that on a press junket he did for a World-War-II-Jump-Out-of-Airplanes movie (his description), he answered a question about the atomic bomb by saying, "Maybe dropping the bomb on Hiroshima ultimately saved lives."

"And even today," he tells us, "twenty years later, people give me shit about it. Perhaps those who say it revealed my anti-Asian bias are right. Maybe the people who still comment that I love war are right. I've certainly made a lot of money pretending to be in wars. I don't know. But they only say that because I wasn't careful, because I offered an opinion. If I've had success since then, it's because I don't answer questions like that. I don't offer opinions. I say, 'That's a question for the director,' or 'Hmm, I can't say that I know.' Or I answer a different question."

As I talk to the roundtable, each with their small rectangular recording devices arrayed before me, I answer the questions and feel somehow like I'm not inside my body at all, like I don't belong to me, like my self is disappearing into those recording devices. At the table behind me, Juniper is talking as she always does, in full sentences and with great enthusiasm, but I can feel myself slowing down and it's not even noon yet. I say, *Kathryn made a great film*, and someone says, *How do you get yourself into the headspace to play such an intense character?* The truth is, I get there through memory, by accessing the hardest and best moments of my life and pretending that they are happening again, which is not a good or healthy way to act, but the only way I know how to do it with any verisimilitude. But I don't say that. I say that Anthony Hopkins would read a script two hundred and fifty times and then give himself over to the imagined circumstances, and that's what I try to do, too.

We're given thirty minutes for lunch, but Ellen has some notes for me, so we go up to my room and I look out at Central Park while she talks. "Kai, when you talk about it, you need to sound confident, not hesitant or defensive. I know it's hard, but you need to sound like who you are—a hero who put a bad man in jail and saved other kids in the process."

"That's not who I am."

"Well, that's who you need to be right now, okay? It's like Juniper with her mom. She acts like she's happy to talk about it. It's acting. You're an actor. Just . . . pretend, or whatever you guys do."

"Got it," I say. I place my forehead against the glass and look down at the busy streets below. A year ago, I would've given anything to have this hotel room, this life, this role.

"Also, if I can feel your disinterest, they can, too. Look, nobody *enjoys* a press junket, including the press. They didn't dream of being journalists to sit at one-eighth of a roundtable discussion about a movie they may or may not have enjoyed, right? But if they don't feed the content monster with enthusiasm, they will die, and if you don't feed the content monster with enthusiasm, you will also die."

"You make it sound so fun," I say.

"I'm just trying to be realistic with you. I know these days are long. But if you need a Diet Coke, I will fetch you a Diet Coke. Need an Ativan, I will get you an Ativan. You have a suite at a nice hotel that you aren't paying for, but it ain't free, and the cost is doing interviews with pluck and enthusiasm."

I eat a chicken Caesar salad while Ellen continues to give me instructions, then she goes out onto my balcony to smoke a cigarette. I tell her I wasn't aware she smoked, and she says, "Respectfully, Kai, you don't know much about me." And then I tell her what I do know—that she's married to a woman named Sarah, that she used to have a cat, that she keeps mixed nuts in a Ziploc bag in her purse because she doesn't eat carbs but loves a snack, and that she is good at her job. "Well, then," she says. "You know me better than most of my coworkers. One thing about you, Kai: You do fucking listen."

I eat for a while and then ask her, "Who do you think leaked it? That teacher you talked to?"

"I had that teacher sign an NDA."

"You did? Thanks."

She shrugs. "Part of the job." After a few moments of silence, she says, "Maybe it was Juniper?"

I mull it over for a minute. "No. Juniper wouldn't do that to me."

"It's just weird that it got out. I really tried to keep it under wraps."

"Unless you're lying and you leaked it," I say.

She laughs. "Kai, unfortunately, I care about you. It's a real impediment to doing my job."

3

I spend the afternoon with Juniper, answering the same questions: What's it like to work with Matthew? How did you and Juniper achieve such incredible chemistry? How did you research the part? How well do you know Juniper? Is there anything our readers should know about your relationship? Juniper, you've been so open about your history of abuse and how it has shaped you; what would you say to young people living in similar situations?

This last question Juniper always answers brilliantly, and each time it's like she's never said the words before, as if she is only now thinking of them. "Your first obligation is to survive. As a kid, I felt so powerless and so scared all the time, and I'm sorry for anyone who feels that way now. But your first obligation is to survive if you can, to make it to the other shore."

I like this answer because it doesn't pretend that there's some easy solution, that trauma is something you get over or move past. It's just something you live with. But your first obligation is to survive.

When my mom and dad finally found out, my mom said, "Why didn't you say something sooner?" The truth is, I told them the moment I could, the moment it became possible. Before that, the words strangled me.

We make it through the afternoon. Matthew is on *Entertainment Tonight*, so Juniper and I make a date to watch together. Then she wants me to go to her friend Ophelia's birthday party. But before all that, I go back to my room and lie down on top of the covers and stare at the ceiling for a while. I scroll through Instagram, post some pictures of the day, and drink a beer out of the minibar. I decide to go for a walk, but people keep recognizing me, even though I have a ball cap on, because the movie is getting a lot of attention, so I go back to the hotel and have a drink at the bar alone, watching a baseball game.

Finally, Juniper texts me to come over for some room service dinner, so I make my way to her suite, which for some reason has a grand piano in one of its two sitting rooms.

"Today was exhausting," I say.

"Oh, yeah, pretending to look upon you with fondness for nine straight hours? The horror."

I laugh. "Last year, I could barely make rent, and I still find a way to complain about my life."

"It does get old," she acknowledges.

"Well, your first obligation is to survive," I say.

"Working with Matthew was a literal dream come true," she says.

"My favorite animal is the rhinoceros that escaped from the Prague Zoo."

"Kai's favorite color is the yellow of falling ginkgo leaves." She plops herself down on one of the living room's several chairs. "Anyway, problems of privilege are still problems."

"What do you want for dinner? I'll call it down."

I'm eating a cheeseburger and Juniper a salad when Matthew comes onscreen. He's wearing a black suit, two buttons open on his purple shirt, smiling. It's strange to think that I *know* him, that this man on television is also a man who plays motorcycle racing games and can't quit smoking.

"How are you?" asks the host and Matthew says, "I'm well. I'm well," and then they talk about Warhol and transforming oneself for the role and how Matthew lost thirty pounds in thirty days and all that stuff, and then out of nowhere the host says, "Matthew Malone, what happens to us after we die?"

"I know that love is stronger than death," Matthew says. "My father died almost ten years ago, but as long as I am alive, he will be my father, and I will be his son."

"I'm sorry for your loss," the host says.

"My old man, what a guy," Matthew says. "In all our years together, he only told me he was proud of me once, when they named the oncology wing of Children's LA after me."

"Well, you've made a hell of a movie, Matthew, even if your dad wouldn't say as much."

"I wish he could've seen this one," Matthew says. "The kids in it are great. Juniper Castillo and Kai Laramie," he says. Juniper and I start pushing each other in excitement. "When you've been in this business as long as I have, you know the special ones. And those kids are special."

Ellen is calling me. Katie is calling Juniper. We answer. "Holy shit he said your name on network television," Ellen says. "God, he's class. That shit about love being stronger than death? We're gonna push the hell out of that. That's the kind of theology even atheists can get behind."

"Yeah, Juniper and I are watching together."

"Just make out already," Ellen says.

"Can't. She's married to the sea."

After our calls, Juniper and I flip through channels until we come across an action comedy Matthew made with Kevin Hart. Juniper's analyzing the movie—she can tell what lines were recorded later in voice-over sessions, when the director wanted a long two-shot but had to cut away because something wasn't right in the performances, and so on—and I love listening to her, seeing her mind interact with a movie, even a bad one. Maybe especially a bad one. When we watch good movies, we're silent, just taking it in, but the bad ones are easier to laugh at and learn from. In bad movies, you can see the strings of the puppets better, understand the actors' choices and how, in combination with the camera and the sets, they try to create the illusion that this all might be real, or real enough anyway to bring forth genuine feeling.

We lie in bed watching this not-great movie for a while, and I think about the absurdity of having never kissed Juniper in real life, and how much Ellen and Katie and the rest of the machine would like me to kiss Juniper, and how that makes me not want to kiss her. I actually *do* want to kiss her, I think—but I know that kissing would lead to all kinds of other things, including, potentially, me throwing up in the bathroom while having a panic attack. I think about how it's harder to say *I love you* to Juniper now than when we first met.

"Matthew must've known this would be a terrible film," she says. "He couldn't have been tricked by the script, you know?"

"Maybe he just loves his costar. Why do you think I'm doing *Gods of Andromeda*?"

"Because of the money?"

"Well, and I get a free personal trainer."

"Plus you get to wear gold armor."

"And that hot girl's in it."

"Which hot girl?"

"The one who plays your sister."

Juniper laughs. "That's actually a good bit of repartee for the junket, if you want to really play up the possibilities. Romances need Obstacles."

"Nah," I say. "Even joking 'I find the girl who plays her sister hot' is a bad Obstacle."

Juniper is quiet for a minute, then we go back to watching the movie, laughing both with it and at it. Out of nowhere she says, "What *is* our Obstacle?"

"Um," I say.

"I mean, you *could* like me, right?"

"In fact, I do like you very much."

"So you could kiss me."

"And you could kiss me."

She is looking at me now, and I realize I know she's looking at me because I am looking at her. Never shy of eye contact, that Juniper Castillo, and what eyes they are—a deep, enveloping brown. "I could," she says again.

I flinch. "The thing is," I say, "you can't unkiss someone. You can't go back to before you knew what that person's kiss felt like."

"You already know what it feels like to kiss me," she says.

"My character knows what it feels like to kiss your character in front of two cameras, a boom mic, and a bunch of people. That's different."

She's silent for a while, then finally nods and says, "We should go to that party."

And so we do. It's after eleven by the time we get to Brooklyn. The party is in a third-floor apartment and everyone there is young and attractive. A girl with big, curly hair asks me if I want to go into Ophelia's bedroom to do drugs, and I say *Which drugs*, and she says *Probably cocaine if I know Ophelia*, and I say *I think I'm okay*. Juniper knows everyone and I don't know anybody so I get a plastic glass and pour myself some of the wine that's in the kitchen. A girl asks me if I know how to make a martini and I tell her that I do, so I make her a martini and then Juniper appears and kisses me on the cheek and says, *Isn't Ophelia hilarious?* I haven't actually met Ophelia yet, but I smile and say, *Yes*, and then for a while I talk to a handsome young guy who is filming a movie where he's the lone survivor of a plane crash. We talk about how the wine is warm, and the guy seems really sweet, like the kind of person who's interested in acting as acting not as a vehicle to celebrity, and then his girlfriend comes up and he introduces her as a director, and she says, *Mostly of commercials*, and I say that commercials need directors, too, and she says, *You make it sound like commercials are orphans*, which makes me think about how all of us are sort of orphans, just of the ostensibly adult variety, trying to figure out how to make martinis and friends and art together. The party is really fun, and I like being there and then Jaya Hudson-Rowe shows up and hugs me, saying, *It's the boy who loves me*. Everyone tries to be cool around her, but it's *Jaya*, and I think about how much work it must be to be Jaya Hudson-Rowe all the time, even at Ophelia's party, and how she must've enjoyed spending an evening with me drinking martinis if only because I had no idea who she was.

Jaya's new girlfriend is there with her and she tells me she's already seen the movie because she works at a studio and that I'm incredible in it and I say *thanks* and by the time I actually figure out who Ophelia is, it's only because someone brings out a little handmade cake with candles on it, twenty-two candles, and I keep thinking we are all so young. Our joints are still good. Whatever has begun to harden in us is still soft in that apartment.

4

The next morning, I wake up with a slight hangover and go downstairs to meet Jill from *The New Yorker*. I recognize her from when I met her just before seeing the movie, but don't know whether to shake her hand or hug her. She comes in firmly with a handshake and says, "How's your junket been?"

"I've had worse jobs," I tell her. "In fact, all my jobs were worse jobs."

"I find them rather dehumanizing," she says. "Honestly, never been a fan of the celebrity profile, but my editor says I'm good at them, and as you say, I've had worse jobs. Shall we start with some breakfast?"

We get in a cab. She doesn't have a recorder out, and she isn't taking notes. I ask her what she doesn't like about celebrity profiles, and she says, "You're trying to get people to buy movie tickets and I'm trying to get people to buy magazines, and those goals are sometimes in tension. But mostly, and don't take this the wrong way, but I think part of the reason I'm assigned these is because I don't find celebrities particularly interesting. What did you do before this?"

"I waited tables at a restaurant in the East Village."

"See, if I'd interviewed you then, before all the media training, we could've had a great conversation. What'd you learn from serving?"

"A lot. It was an Italian place. Mostly couples. The great thing about serving is that a lot of people don't think of you as a person, so you get up close to other people's lives. People falling in love, breaking up, trying to figure out whether to put their kid in a new school. You see it all, and it's out in public, and they never notice you noticing."

"If you like not being thought of as a person, you'll love being famous." Jill laughs. I can tell that she is trying to make me comfortable so I'll slip up, but I still like her.

At breakfast, she pulls out the recorder and asks me about the movie, about how I prepared for it. She asks me about Juniper, how we were different in our processes. She asks me if Juniper wears perfume, and I say no, and for a moment I can smell her. Jill says that she writes a lot about perfume because writing about smell is the most interesting challenge she's come across, and then she asks me how Juniper smells, and I say, "I can't describe it. Like when you're inside on a rainy day, maybe."

"You say *I love you* a lot. That's come up in several of the conversations I've had. Do you love Juniper?"

"Very much."

"Do you care to comment on the rumors?"

"I do not."

"See, the media training kills the conversation." She takes a sip of coffee. "Did the studio tell you to appear to be in love with Juniper?"

Ellen has taught me to answer the question I want to answer, not the question I am asked. "Nobody has to tell me to love Juniper. She's just so kind, thoughtful, and funny."

"A few weeks ago, a fan got into Juniper's car, and you threw him out. Do you remember that?"

"Vividly."

"That man's name was Allen Marksville."

"Okay."

"Allen Marksville is a fifty-two-year-old white male from Los Angeles.

I interviewed him. When I asked him to name his favorite episode of the show Juniper was on, he couldn't. Couldn't describe a single plotline. Didn't know the name of Juniper's character."

"Okay," I say again. I am starting to sweat.

"That surprised me. It made me wonder if Allen Marksville was actually a fan of Juniper's at all."

"How did you even find the guy?"

"I'm a good reporter. Why would a fifty-two-year-old guy who isn't a fan of Juniper's pretend to be a fan of Juniper's?"

I remember Ellen telling me it had to be a setup, that it was simply too good as press. "I don't know. That's above my pay grade."

"I want to write about you, Kai. But I also want to write about the machine that is making you a star. And I'm curious if you knew that Allen Marksville was a plant, placed there to make you look heroic when you threw him out of that car."

I wish Ellen could be here, but *The New Yorker* doesn't let publicists tag along on interviews. "You're saying I did it? I promise you I'm not nearly smart enough to do all that shit."

"You're plenty smart, but I'm not sure you're experienced enough. But the studio has people, don't they?"

"The studio wouldn't do that. They're not like that."

She just smiles. "Fair enough. Why'd you decide to do *Gods of Andromeda*?"

I talk about Brian and the journey from love to power and so on, and how I was excited to work with Juniper again. But I'm still thinking about the studio, and whether they *are*, in fact, like that. Could be the studio. Could be Bob. Could be Juniper's agents, or Matthew's, or even Ellen. Could be anyone. You can't trust anybody in Hollywood. Too many people want success too badly. And yet I've kind of lucked into it.

"Are you familiar with Max Weber?" Jill asks.

"Definitely not," I respond.

"Weber maintained that there are two kinds of charisma—charisma of personality and charisma of office. Every Pope has charisma of office; only some also have charisma of personality. What is it like to have exceptional charisma of personality? Are you aware of it?"

"I mean," I say. "I don't think of myself—"

"So the world just sort of bends to your will and you don't notice it?"

"Believe me, Jill. The world does not bend to my will. I don't even know my will."

"So you're saying you could have what you want if you only knew what you wanted."

I smile. "Maybe."

She asks if I want to go to MoMA, and so we do. We look at the Warhols, of course, and she asks me how I feel about them and I don't know what to say. The truth is, Warhol leaves me a little cold. My favorite work of his is the stuff at the end he did with Basquiat, the paintings that feel less flat and superficial, but I don't say that. I talk about visiting the Carnegie with Juniper and the curator, and I tell her everything I read about Warhol's dying year—how he partied too much and his gallbladder hurt all the time and he felt like the world had passed him by. I say it's hard work to stay in the spotlight, but work that Warhol felt compelled to do. She asks me if I like being in the spotlight, and I say that I like acting and I'm not good at anything else.

We wind our way into this room of Agnes Martin paintings from her series called *With My Back to the World*. They are just bands of pale color, but even though the room is pretty busy with people, it's utterly silent. Something about the paintings demands quiet. I stare at one of them for a long time. The painting looks the way taking a deep breath feels. I think about when we visited the museum back in Pittsburgh, how the curator said that artists like Martin and Joan Mitchell are trying to paint what interior experience *is*, not just what it's *like*.

When we leave the room, Jill tells me, "Martin didn't read a newspaper or a magazine for the last fifty years of her life."

"My kind of artist," I answer.

Later, we're back at the hotel, having a drink in the lobby. I'm drinking an espresso martini because I know I'm going to be up late tonight; Matthew's hosting a party. Jill is drinking a glass of rosé. Jill looks like she could be one of your friends' moms, the kind of person it's easy to look past.

"It's quite obvious," she tells me, "that the studio wants you and Juniper to be plausibly-but-deniably in love."

I give her a vague look in response. Ellen told me they can't quote your vague looks.

"You seem an unlikely couple, I have to say. One highly analytical person, nakedly ambitious in a way that makes some uncomfortable. And then you, a doe-eyed Hollywood newbie uninterested in the Internet and seemingly ambivalent about fame."

"I love Juniper," I say. "She is thoughtful, funny, and wise."

And then I break for a moment and tell the truth. "I admire her. She is incredibly bright and ambitious, and she wants to make great art. I'm kind of over the artist who's super cool, who's effortlessly brilliant. That's not real. What's real is that artists like Juniper work incredibly hard."

"Fair enough. Are you in love with Juniper?"

"Sometimes," I say. I'm tired, and the espresso martini has loosened my tongue. I snap back into myself.

"Do you find it hard to distinguish between your emotions and the emotions that the movie studio would like you to feel?"

I just smile for a moment, and then go back to my talking points. "Juniper is genuinely and truly one of my closest friends. When something great or terrible happens, she's the first person I want to call."

"Can we go off the record?" she asks. Ellen has told me about this. If you say something stupid and then try to say "That was off the record," the reporter can still publish it, because you can't retroactively take something off the record. But if you ask to go off the record, and the reporter agrees, whatever happens next in a conversation can't be written about. But I've never heard of a *reporter* asking to go off the record.

"Sure," I say.

"I just want to talk to you like a normal human being, and I feel your brain churning every time I ask you a question. It's got to be exhausting for you, and I know it's exhausting for me. So, off the record, what's it like?"

"This? The junket?" She nods. "It's like you're a medieval soldier stabbing at me with a sword, and I'm deflecting the sword with my shield. As long as my shield holds, I'll be okay. But it does take some concentration to keep the shield up."

"But if the shield goes down, all you tell me is the truth."

"Yeah," I say. "Exactly."

"What's so bad about that?"

"The truth belongs to me. That's my life you're talking about. My most personal, intimate feelings. My . . . whatever. My worst memories. My best memories."

"Yes, but we've made a deal. You exchange pieces of yourself for celebrity. Celebrity keeps you working, keeps you paid. Keeps me paid, too."

"Except once I've traded those little pieces of myself, I can't get them back. They're not mine anymore."

"Right," she says. "Okay, I get it. Back on the record?"

"Sure."

She never asks me about it, about the ever-present it. We eat dinner, and she asks me about my childhood in Indiana, tells me she'll be interviewing my brother and my parents. She asks me if I liked high school. She asks me if I can remember the first time I knew I was good at acting.

I tell her the truth, that I'm still not sure I'm good at acting but I can remember the first time everything fell away and I felt fully absorbed into a character. I was in high school, and we were doing *You Can't Take It with You*. It was the dress rehearsal, and I wasn't thinking about my lines or my blocking; I wasn't thinking about anything because I was too busy playing Paul. Play. That's what we call it. You're *playing* a character; the thing you're in is a *play*. But if you're really lucky, in moments it stops being play, stops being make-believe and becomes a kind of magic. You aren't Kai Laramie with his baggage and his worries. You aren't just playing; you are becoming. That dress rehearsal was the first time I ever felt that I'd *become* someone, that for a flashing moment I was not playing Paul but was, in fact, Paul. And if you've ever had that high, you'll sacrifice a lot for the chance to have it again.

"That felt honest," she says after I tell her. I don't answer. Not sure what to say. "I was never an actor," she tells me, "but there's something akin to that in writing. The feeling of losing oneself, that it isn't even you writing the words but you are instead a kind of aqueduct through which the words flow."

Jill and I part ways, and Ellen is waiting for me in the lobby.

"Well?" she asks.

With Jill gone, I feel the anger well up in me. "Did you set up the sweaty guy in Juniper's Uber?"

"No," she says, but I'm watching her eyes, and I see both fear and guilt swirling in them.

"You put that guy in the Uber. He's not even a fan. Jill *interviewed him*."

"Fuuuuuccccckkkk," she says. "Fuck." She takes a few steps away from me, then paces back toward me. "We need to get somewhere private." I follow her to the second floor, to a little conference room festooned with posters of our movie. She closes the door behind us.

"I didn't know," she says. "Just for the record. They didn't tell me until three days later."

"They?"

"The studio. Todd, specifically. It's always Todd. He plays dirty."

I hear my voice rising. "And you didn't tell me."

"No, Kai, I didn't tell you, because what good is it for you to hate Todd? You hate Todd, and you don't do *Andromeda*, even though doing *Andromeda* is great for your career. I was trying to take care of you. I was trying to . . . Fuck."

"He leaked my abuse too, didn't he?" I'm almost screaming now. I can feel the heat behind my eyes. "And you knew about that, too."

"No," she says. "No no no. I never told Todd about that. I don't trust him. No. God. I should've told you. I *knew* I should've told you. But I didn't want you to hate the studio."

"Because you don't work for me. You work for the studio."

"Yeah, not for much longer if Jill publishes the story. The studio will want someone to blame and I pitched the piece. What'd you say to her?"

"That it was above my pay grade."

"Not a bad answer," she says. "Fuck, the studio's gonna look so bad."

"Gonna *look* bad? The studio *is* bad."

"Kai, it sucks, but they're selling movie tickets. And it works, okay? It worked. You trended on Twitter. Probably got you Gavinth. Todd's the *reason* you got Gavinth. Good for our movie, good for the next movie. And it's not like Juniper got hurt."

"I have to go to a party," I say.

5

I go upstairs to change into an outfit appropriate for the party—black pants and a short-sleeve button-down from Prada. I can't believe how many clothes Prada makes, or how happy they are to send them to me. They even send me nice *socks*. Who wears Prada *socks*? Me, I guess. This is the part I didn't tell Jill from *The New Yorker*—I like nice shit. I like getting dressed in Prada to go to a Matthew Malone party at a nightclub he has rented out in its entirety.

The club is off Broadway, and I get there at nine fifteen for a nine p.m. start, so it's mostly empty, but Lon is there. "You look tired, kid," he says. "I'm so glad I don't have to do that junket shit. Worst part of movies."

"Yeah," I say. "It's a hell of a business."

"Sure is, kid. But you look good in Prada. All right, I gotta go schmooze with that guy over there. He's the fucking head of IP at Mattel. Can you believe it? They're making movies out of toys now. Hot Wheels movie. Barbie movie. American Girl dolls come to life, out on the prairie, dying of consumption. People say he's the next big thing, though."

Juniper shows up after a while wearing a whisper-light silk shift dress that does rather make it harder to swallow. "I need to talk to you," I say.

We find a quietish corner and I tell her about the sweaty guy being a studio plant.

"Pretty nasty," she says.

"I'll say."

"It was good press, though. You gotta give 'em that."

"It *traumatized* you."

"I've seen worse."

"You're not pissed?"

"I mean, they didn't put us *in danger* or anything."

I don't know what to say to her after that, so I head to the bar to order a beer and get Juniper a club soda. I think about how sometimes I used to work parties like this one for extra cash, used to carry around nibbles for people. Now I am the people.

I am so goddamned lucky, and so goddamned immune to my own luck.

"How was *The New Yorker*?" Juniper asks when I return.

"Intense. Smart lady. Probably got me to say too much. What'd you do?"

"Photo shoot, mostly, for *Marie Claire*. They had me in fifteen different looks. Then I did an easy interview with them."

"In case it's in the story, she asked me if I was in love with you."

"And you said?"

"I said sometimes."

Juniper laughs and shakes her head. "So you told her the truth," she says finally.

Juniper knows everybody at the party, so she starts circulating. Charles Oldham is there, the guy I beat out for *Gods of Andromeda*. I talk to him for a while about the new Edgar Wright movie he just booked, and he makes it sound very cool. Everybody's so good at making their lives look amazing. Even though I know Charles wants the part I have, I still feel a little jealous of the one he's ended up with.

Then, at last, Matthew shows up around ten, wearing a tan suit with a button-down shirt that is hardly buttoned. His chest hair is showing. Matthew is, if nothing else, *sculpted.* He finds me and hugs me and I ask him if he wants a drink and he says he can't because he has TV in the morning and anyway he drove his motorcycle here. I ask him where he's staying and he says he has a place in the city. "Actually," he says, "come over tomorrow after press. Bring Junie. We'll have dinner." I want to tell him about what Todd did, but Juniper has made me feel like maybe it's not a big deal.

Lon introduces me to the guy from Mattel, who tells me their Hot Wheels movie is going to be incredible, and I tell him that sounds amazing, even though a Hot Wheels movie in fact sounds to me like the end of something important, like the final breath in the long life of art itself. While the Mattel guy talks at me, I'm trying to figure out what art even is, why we make it, and indeed whether I'm making it, or whether I'm making something else. I want to talk to Juniper about this, or about anything, but she's got her arm around Charles Oldham, and they're both talking to two girls who look like models.

After a while there's no one I want to talk to and I'm a little drunk, so I leave. Juniper texts me to come to an afterparty at someone's place, but I don't much feel like going out. I think maybe I like being alone too much for this job. What I really want is for Juniper to come over to my hotel room and for us to watch a movie together, slightly-but-not-confirmedly cuddling in that way we have. Maybe I also want more than that, but I can't process the wanting more, can't allow myself to want it, because what if she doesn't want to be imagined that way? Isn't it a kind of violation to think about someone as they don't wish to be thought about? He would always tell me that he thought about me constantly, that he loved remembering what we did together and imagining what we might do, and I didn't like him thinking about me.

I don't usually look for what people are saying about me, but when I get back to my hotel room, for some reason—drunkenness, probably—I go on Twitter and search for my name. I read the first result.

> I went to school with Kai Laramie and he is not the hero everyone says. He didn't stop our pedo teacher; some other kid did. But Kai gets all the credit because he's famous. He's typical Hollywood—he doesn't reveal the pedos, he indulges them.

Only six retweets and fourteen likes, but still I feel a surge of dread. It's true, too. I didn't stop our pedo teacher.

I try to go to sleep, but can't stop thinking about that phrase. *He indulges them.* Had I indulged him? I remember once I asked to go to his house. I didn't like doing stuff at school—it felt way too dangerous. I asked to go to his house and he said sure. He only lived a few blocks away. His house was low-ceilinged and dingy and poorly lit with overhead can lights that were either burnt out or too bright, and he offered me a cup of coffee and then he played with my cock through my pants and then took it out and told me we didn't have to rush for once, and I let all of that happen. Was that indulgence or survival?

6

The next day includes a long photo shoot with Juniper, and then another round of interviews in the afternoon. They're all normal and predictable and not too stressful except for one guy who comes in and asks, "What was the meaning of life to Andy Warhol?"

I let Juniper handle that one. Then the interviewer says, "What's the meaning of life to you, Kai?"

I don't know the meaning of life. The meaning of life is to avoid answering questions about the meaning of life. The meaning of life is to sit next to someone you're sometimes in love with and definitely love. The meaning of life is that we are monstrous to each other, and tender to each other, and that the monstrosity and tenderness are inseparable. The meaning of life is chocolate ice cream. I don't know. So I freeze up and Juniper jumps in.

I feel so stupid in that moment. I hate feeling stupid. It's not unlike the smallness I felt with him, the powerlessness. Maybe the meaning of life is to have enough power that people can't hurt you, can't assert *their* power over you, and I'm thinking all this while Juniper says, "I think to Kai the meaning of life is to be generous toward other people. That's how he acts, at least." I lock back in and say, "Yeah, that's so kind of you,

Juniper. And to Juniper the meaning of life is doing good work with good people," and she looks at me in that way she has, the way that is both genuine and for the camera, that is entirely performed and entirely authentic, and she says, "Gosh, you're a sweet boy."

It isn't even a big deal—Ellen doesn't say anything to me afterward—but I spend the rest of the afternoon hyperaware that I'm in an overlit room with a camera operator, a sound guy, two publicists, Juniper, and a rotating cast of interviewers. It's exhausting. I want to go home. I don't even know precisely what constitutes home at the moment, but I want to go wherever it is. We do another best friend quiz with one of the interviewers, and they ask about our favorite animals, and together we say, "The rhinoceros that escaped the Prague Zoo," and we laugh, but I actually do think it's become my favorite animal.

During a break, Ellen tells me, "They just announced a Paris premiere. Matthew is huge in Europe. This is big, Kai. I've *never* gotten a European premiere before. So on the first you'll be in Paris, then back here on the second for the New York premiere."

"You'll be with me?"

"I should be employed at least until that *New Yorker* profile comes out."

We're back in photo shoots from four until six, and then it's time to go to Matthew's apartment. I realize I don't actually know where he lives, so I text him, and he writes back immediately with an address on the Upper East Side. Juniper and I get in an Uber. When we settle in, she says, "What's the meaning of life to you, Kai?" and I laugh.

Juniper is wearing perfectly distressed jeans and a cozy sweater. I want to reach out and put my arm around her, but I'm not sure if that would be excessive flirting and also I'm not sure I'm allowed to want what I want.

"In my interview with *Vogue* this morning, they asked if you were a good kisser and I said that you were very gentle, and Katie got mad at me because apparently gentle isn't sexy."

"Would Katie prefer me to be an aggressive kisser?"

"I guess so. She said men have to be seen as alphas, and I was like, *not my men.*"

We talk about prep for *Gods of Andromeda*, how we'll have trainers to get us ripped enough to look hot wearing body armor. We leave for Vancouver two weeks after *Andy Warhol Never Gets Old* comes out, and we talk about what we might do during those two weeks. I tell her I might go back to Indianapolis and she says she wants to go with me, see all the corn, and I tell her, *There's no corn in Indianapolis; it's a proper city*, and she laughs.

New York traffic is terrible, and we should've just taken the subway, but I get recognized almost every time I'm on the subway now, and it's a little tiring. The question people ask me most often is why I'm on the subway, as if there's some secret transport system for C-list celebrities. At last we get to Matthew's building, across the street from the park at 85th Street. We tell the doorman our names, and he calls up to Matthew then tells us the apartment is on the fourteenth floor. Instead of the elevator opening into a hallway, it opens right into Matthew's ridiculous apartment, with floor-to-ceiling window views of the Central Park Reservoir and the Upper West Side in the distance. He has minimalist furniture including a black Eames chair, and a huge kitchen where a team of people are working. He's watching TV when we come in but jumps off his immaculate leather couch and envelops both of us in a hug.

"God, I'm a little envious of you two. Just a couple of great young artists bumming around the city, everything still in front of you. I love to see it. What can I get you to drink?"

Juniper asks for a club soda and I order an old-fashioned, and someone in the kitchen gets to work on our drinks. Matthew walks us over to a Warhol painting of a dollar sign—green and blue on a yellow background—and says, "I gave this to myself after we shot our movie. Warhol said once, 'I like money on the wall.' So this is my way of hanging money on the wall."

Juniper tells us that Warhol was beguiled by money, and then she searches on her phone for a quote she remembers from her research. "'American money is very well-designed,'" she reads. "'I like it better than any other kind of money. I've thrown it in the East River down by the Staten Island Ferry just to see it float.'"

"I love that we got to make such a beautiful movie about such a beautiful weirdo," Matthew says. "And the tracking. Have you seen the tracking?"

I don't want to confess that I'm not actually sure what tracking *is*, so I just say no. Matthew ushers us down to the couch, and Juniper sits with her feet tucked underneath her. "We're tracking for twenty million–plus on opening weekend," he says. "With a movie about Andy Warhol. Incredible. How's the press been for y'all?"

"Hard," I say. "But it's fun to be with Juniper."

"He's good at it, too," she says. "You'd never know he hates being famous."

"There's upsides and downsides," Matthew says. "Most careers involve trade-offs. But it's hard to complain when you look down at Central Park."

"And your original Warhol," I say.

"Yes, and that. You'll get here, both of you. You're both so ambitious and smart and *ready* for this."

"Thanks," Juniper says, although I'm not sure it's a compliment.

Over dinner—vegan ravioli with mushroom filling—Matthew regales us with stories of other famous actors, his favorite people to work with, and some of his least favorites. He tells us that when he was young and still did his own stunts, one time he was in a car that flipped over four times and the shot was perfect but he got sick to his stomach while the car was flipping and vomited, and then the car kept rolling, and his own vomit kept flying into his face as the car overturned. He tells us that his team wants him to be the villain in a new *Spider-Man* movie but he only likes villains who can make a strong and straightforward case for their worldview, and Mysterio is what he calls "more of an Iago type."

Juniper asks him to explain, and Matthew gives us an introduction to *Othello*—he says that in the play, the villain Iago acts sinisterly in his own interest, but it's so malevolent and dishonest that it's more repulsive than the villains Matthew likes to portray, the ones who are fighting for a cause greater than themselves but in a deplorable manner. "There needs to be a fatal flaw," he says. "Something noble the villain wants too much."

Matthew shifts back into Hollywood storytelling mode. As if it's an amusing anecdote, he tells us about the time a major Hollywood star pulled a gun on him, and how he thought about pressing charges but didn't want to ruin his costar's reputation.

I think of what my teacher used to say to me, quoting Auden. If we ever got caught, he told me, he'd be "punished under a foreign code of conscience." Weaponizing poetry against me. I think about how everyone knows now, that people see me and think, *That guy got abused as a kid*. Maybe it doesn't matter who leaked it. Maybe it's like one of those Chinese dragons where a lot of people are under the dragon costume, some in the tail and some in the head and some in the middle. Maybe I don't need to know which person inside the dragon told the world, because really, the dragon did it.

7

We're on our way back to the hotel when Juniper's phone rings. "Katie," she tells me.

She answers, and I watch Juniper's face empty of color as Katie is talking. "Yeah," she says. After a long pause, "Yeah." Another long pause. "Got it." Another. "He's actually with me."

She hangs up, and right then, Ellen calls. I send it to voicemail.

"What was that about?" I ask. Juniper looks ashen.

"Apparently there's a Twitter thread. By one of the other kids who got abused. Let's just look."

She opens Twitter and finds it immediately, because my name is trending.

> The truth is, Kai Laramie never said a word about the abuse. If he had, I might have been spared the worst thing that ever happened to me. Instead, I revealed the abuse. I told the principal of our school.
>
> Kai knows this, and he still let the headlines read shit like HERO MOVIE STAR STOPPED HIS ABUSER DEAD IN HIS

TRACKS or whatever. But Kai never said ANYTHING. Obviously he's a victim in this, but claiming he's a hero is a bit much.

Just for the record: I turned him in. Kai testified because I had a weed charge on my record and the prosecutors thought that would hurt my reliability as a witness. I've been through hell with this.

It's fucking humiliating to be put through more hell that makes Kai seem like some kind of superhero and completely ignores what I did. It's typical of the media, of course, but someone fed them these lies and we all know it was Juniper Castillo.

She's so obviously behind all this. She wants to be a star so fucking bad. You go on her Instagram and it's nothing but her and Kai, her sweet and innocent and heroic Kai. But the story is a lot more complicated than the media will tell you.

The truth is, Kai got abused and said nothing and now he's a hero. I got abused and said something and now I'm nobody? Well, I call bullshit. Come out with the truth, Kai. And have your girlfriend apologize for retraumatizing both of us.

The first tweet in the thread had over ten thousand retweets. The first reply, with over five thousand likes, was *Sorry this happened to you, bro. Typical Hollywood bullshit.*

The second reply: *These two are such fucking phonies both of them. He's Mr. Stolen Valor and She's Mrs. Pretend to Love Kai While Hanging All Over Charles Oldham. Probably made up all that bullshit about her poor, dead mother.*

My stomach is in my throat. "Is that true?" I say finally.

"Is what true?"

"Are you hooking up with Charles?"

"One, I am not hooking up with Charles." Juniper's voice is rising. "Two, I am not your girlfriend, so I'm allowed to hook up with whoever the hell I want. Three, how can you ask that right now? This is not about Charles Oldham. This is about someone trying to ruin both our careers, Kai. You understand that? Don't deal with this properly and *poof.* Everything could be gone."

There is something intoxicating to me about the possibility of *poof,* everything being gone, but I don't confess that to Juniper. I just say, "I'll call Ellen."

She picks up before it's even rung. "You will sit down with Jill tomorrow," Ellen says. "You will tell the truth, and this is the truth: You didn't want to talk about your abuse, but it leaked, and now you're going to affirm your fellow victim's victimhood and heroism while also acknowledging that the real villain here is not you but the man who abused you, and the leaker who retraumatized you, who wasn't Juniper. That's all we need to do. We'll let her break the embargo and talk about the movie, which will hopefully minimize the stuff about you. One interview tomorrow morning, before the rest of the junket, and then you don't say another goddamned word about this and we let it blow over."

"Okay," I say.

"I'm sorry."

"Yeah," I say.

"Once you do this interview tomorrow, we can put it in the rearview mirror."

"Okay."

Except it will never be in the rearview mirror. That's what Ellen still can't understand. On some level, even though he's dead, it's still happening. It happens in my mind. It happens when people bring it up. It happens when I dream.

Back at the hotel, I search my name on Reddit and Twitter. Conversations are everywhere about Juniper and me. The big one on the pop culture subreddit already has over a thousand comments. Some people are defending us—especially Juniper, who is seen by many to be "catching strays"—but the most upvoted comments say we're fake and always have been, that you can tell when something is just to promote a movie, and that Juniper probably lies about being abused by her dead mom to get attention and sympathy. The consensus seems to conclude that Matthew Malone is a great guy but these two seem like conniving little starlets.

I'm asleep when the phone rings. I look at the hotel clock: 2:18 a.m. It's Juniper. She's crying uncontrollably. At first I can't even tell what she's saying. "I'll be right there," I say.

I pull on some clothes and race to her room. She's sobbing. "I fucked up and now they're gonna cancel *Andromeda*," she says.

"What makes you say that?"

"I just feel it. I know it."

"Juniper, you're having a panic attack." She's sweating and crying and very clearly in distress, but I am also frustrated with her, because who cares if they cancel *Andromeda*? It's just a movie.

"I have nothing without it," she says.

"That's not true, Juniper."

"I can't not work," she says. "You don't understand. When I'm not working, I'm nothing. I don't matter to anybody."

"That's your mother talking," I tell her.

"I didn't make it up," she says. "I didn't."

"I know," I say, and she relaxes into me as I'm holding her. "I'm sorry, and I'm here." I hold her for a long time, until she calms down and her ragged breaths get deeper.

"You know our Obstacle?" she asks.

"Never have quite figured it out."

"We can't disentangle what we want from what we're supposed to want."

"That's why so many kids our age go to law school," I say, and she laughs. I stroke her forehead, pushing her hair aside, revealing the soft baby hairs above her temple. "I love you," I say. "You're way too into Hollywood, but I love you."

"This is all I've got," she says. "This is everything to me." I want to ask her about me, about her brother, remind her that there is much more to her life than Hollywood, but I don't.

"You didn't leak it, right?" I ask. "It wasn't you."

"Kai, I would never."

"You really want the movie to succeed."

"I do," she confesses. "I do. But no. I would never, ever do that shit. As much as I care about the movie, I care a hell of a lot more about you."

"Will you be there tomorrow?" I ask her. "At the interview?"

"Of course," she says through new tears. "Of course, Kai."

The piece comes out online the same day as the interview:

> Kai Laramie sits with his costar and dear friend Juniper Castillo in a standard hotel chair in a standard, if luxurious, hotel conference room. Despite professional makeup and hair, his eyes are red and he looks like he has been crying. I ask him how he's feeling and he says, "In our business, you have to give up some privacy, but the truth is my abuse is deeply private to me, and I'm sorry that it has been publicized so widely and that as a result, other people were hurt. It's true that my classmate was the one who revealed the abuse to administrators at our school, and I'm very grateful that he did. He saved a lot of people. That I didn't have the courage to say anything is an enduring regret for me."

These words sound rehearsed, like he spent all night thinking of them, but then they also sound earnest. A full profile of Laramie is forthcoming in the magazine, but for now, suffice it to say that Laramie is the type of young person who doesn't seem to know his own innocence, the type you want to protect with a measure of maternal attention. I ask Laramie if he regrets his burgeoning celebrity, and he says, "I don't know if *regret* is the right word. I love acting. I love making stuff with other artists."

When I first interviewed Laramie, we discussed everything from Andy Warhol (the artist at the center of his buzzy new biopic, *Andy Warhol Never Gets Old*) to his childhood in Indianapolis. But now, in our second meeting, there is only one topic: the trending conversation about Laramie's abuse, and his failure to correct the initial reporting that he was the "hero" who turned his abuser in to authorities.

"I didn't want to correct the record because I didn't want to acknowledge the record," he says. (Indeed, at Laramie's publicist's insistence, I agreed not to ask him about the abuse in our first meeting.) "I should've said yes, I was abused, but no, I wasn't a hero except insofar as all who survive abuse do so heroically. I'm sorry I didn't do that."

Laramie is also quick to defend his costar, with whom he has confessed to being "sometimes" in love. "I trust Juniper absolutely and she has no involvement in this whatsoever."

But enough about the scandal. Let's talk about the movie, which succeeds at being what its subject Andy Warhol never was: deep. An astonishingly moving portrait of an artist at the end of his life and two young professionals at the start of theirs, *Andy Warhol Never Gets Old* is the kind of movie that feels at once fresh and classic. Both Laramie and Castillo have survived a lot in their young lives, and somehow this real-life trauma seems to have been carried onto the screen in a way that feels vibrant without ever verging into garish. Castillo, as she detailed in a viral Medium post, "My Mother Loved Me. She Also Abandoned Me," experienced abuse and devastating neglect throughout her childhood. "I don't know what it's like to be loved by an adult who doesn't want something from you," she wrote, and Laramie's sleepless eyes on the morning of this interview are a reminder that, perhaps, Laramie feels the same way.

We romanticize the lives of young and brilliant actors. We think of them as fundamentally different from us. And it's true: Castillo and Laramie are better-looking than I will ever be, their hair just so, their smiles carefully calibrated. But these are just people, people placed into a machine that transforms personal history into media attention, that forges reality into fiction and fiction into reality.

Juniper is reading the story out loud to me as we both lie above the covers on her bed. She pauses and says, "It's really good."

"It's okay," I say. "I seem a little stupid."

"You do not seem stupid, and she called our movie 'at once fresh and classic.' You come off looking mature and self-aware."

"I just hate the idea that for the rest of my life, the first thing people will know about me is that I didn't turn in my abuser."

"You *couldn't* turn your abuser in, Kai. If you could've, you would've."

"Yeah," I say. "I remember when the cops showed up at school and had a warrant to search his office and everything, I remember thinking, *It's over*. But actually it was only beginning. It was the beginning of my parents and brother knowing. The beginning of people at school knowing. Other teachers knowing. The beginning of knowing I was gonna have to testify, and everything else."

"Yeah," she says. "Thanks for staying up with me, by the way. I'm sorry I freaked out. It doesn't matter if they cancel *Andromeda*. I know that. I just panicked. I shouldn't have made it about me."

"It's okay," I tell her, because it is. She can hear her mom's voice the way I can hear his voice, only he wasn't my parent. I ask her to keep reading and she does. I love listening to Juniper read. I've never been able to read out loud with any confidence or fluidity; Juniper reads like a professional narrator, with perfect enunciation and absolute surety. No word surprises her or trips her up. What must it be like, I wonder, to have that relationship with language, where everything flows, where it's no work to decode letters into sounds, and sounds into concepts.

But, of course, it's partly the difference between us that makes it so easy to love her.

8

The next morning is our last day of press in the US. The review embargo breaks that morning, and we're one hundred percent fresh on Rotten Tomatoes until some guy from *Slate* says that Matthew's "hammy, mouth-breathing incarnation of Warhol distracts from what might have otherwise been a pleasant little love story." Still, the reviews are overwhelmingly positive. *The New York Times* says, "Is it Oscar bait? Sure, but this reviewer is hooked." *Variety* calls it, "A lovely, heartrending movie featuring two young actors whose chemistry leaps off the screen." All day long between interviews, Juniper and I are quoting reviews back and forth to each other.

I can't compare it to any other feeling I've known—the world likes our movie, and the love and work we poured into it feel justified. A long time ago, when I lived in the same body but was a different person, my high school yearbook called me "Most Likely to Make It in Hollywood," and now I feel like I have made it, like my life is changing in ways I cannot quite understand.

Bob calls me during an interview and I call him back between setups. "Should've waited for these goddamned reviews before we signed your *Gods of Artessa* deal," he says.

"Andromeda," Zoe interrupts.

"Right, whatever. These reviews, kid. You're a fucking star. You're going to get me invited to the fucking Oscars. Do I even have a tux, Zoe?"

"That's more a question for your wife," she says.

"I'm just so proud of you, kid. I'm just so fucking thrilled. Listen, if I can give you one piece of advice: Make sure there are people in your life who aren't paid to like you. Me and Zoe, we're great. But you need people who don't have a stake in you. Ideally people who knew you from before. A lot of people are gonna want a piece of you."

"And if you're not careful, you run out of pieces," interjects Zoe.

"Thanks, guys," I say.

"All right, kid," Bob tells me. "You're a fucking star. You're a fucking supernova. I'll see you at the premiere Wednesday. Can't fucking wait."

The last afternoon of press is predictable, if still slightly soul-destroying. No one's allowed to ask me about the Twitter thread, and the response to it has started to die down anyway thanks to the *New Yorker* piece. Other abuse victims have spoken up to defend me, saying it's harder to reveal the abuse than one might think, and that there are no villains here except for the dead guy who did all of it.

And so I answer the questions, the same questions I've been answering: It's important for people living with abuse to know that they have no reason to feel ashamed, I say, although I feel ashamed saying it. Matthew Malone is an absolute legend, a paragon of generosity. I love Juniper. Juniper and I share a favorite animal: a rhinoceros that escaped from the Prague Zoo. Working with Juniper is such a dream come true that I can't wait to do it again on *Gods of Andromeda*. Watching Juniper's process is inspiring because she pours her whole self into the role. Her commitment and dedication are unmatched. She is funny, kind, and brilliant. Our favorite thing to do together is watch movies, especially bad movies. I prepared for the role by reading everything I could about Warhol. I love Warhol's work because it is surface-deep, because it is about how a repeated image—whether it's Jackie Onassis or an electric chair—loses its meaning in the repetition. Kathryn is dedicated, passionate, and tireless. I loved the crew on this movie. I am so grateful to them. They're the people who really make the picture. We're just the face of something much larger. I think it's important to acknowledge that victims of abuse have nothing to be ashamed of. Matthew is such a wonderful mentor. He's thoughtful, generous, and openhearted. I love Juniper.

All of this is true, but saying it again and again, it begins to feel like a lie. It begins to feel like a betrayal.

At last, we're done. Ellen and Katie take us to the hotel bar for celebratory drinks, and Kathryn is there, too. Kathryn kisses me on both cheeks and says, "Oh my God, Kai, thank you for suffering through so much press. But I can tell you, the only thing worse than a lot of press is none at all, and so at least we have champagne problems. Speaking of which, do you drink champagne?" I nod. "Perfect, we've got two bottles coming."

Before the champagne arrives, Ellen asks me to go outside with her. She lights a cigarette. There isn't a breath of wind in Manhattan, and even though the skyscrapers around us are blocking the sun, it's warm. It smells, as New York always does to me, vaguely of urine. "I'm really proud of this campaign," she says.

"Me too," I say. "I didn't even fuck up too badly."

"You've done great, Kai. You're a natural. Listen." She starts to say something, then stops, reconsidering. "You remember a long time ago, I said I work for the studio not for you?"

"Yeah," I say.

"Well, I'm about to not work for the studio."

"What happened?"

"I'm done. That's all."

"Because of me?"

"Because of a lot of things. The whole apparatus is obscene. The machine consumes people. There's no humanity left in it, if there ever was. I gotta get out of it. Go private, maybe. Work with a few clients. Spend more time at home."

"Have you told them you're quitting?"

"Not yet. Not till after the premiere. Gotta get you to the finish line." She takes a puff of her cigarette, then exhales. "You know the fucked-up thing? I know it's not that big of a deal, what Todd did to you and Juniper. But the fucked-up thing is that he had to do it. It was the right thing to do for the movie. I told you when all this started that nobody wants to watch a movie with a five-word title about a dead artist. And now it's tracking toward a twenty-two-million-dollar opening weekend. It's gonna be a hit, and that's all thanks to the machine. Todd saw a way to feed the machine, and he fed it. I'm tired of being ruthless. I need a little . . . ruth."

When we get back to the bar, everyone toasts the movie and then splits off into their own conversations. I'm talking with Ellen when Todd shows up. Ellen gulps down her glass of champagne, and then she says, "I've got one for you, Todd."

"A joke?"

"Yeah," she says. "About the farmer and the pig. You know the one?"

"Don't think so," Todd says. I can hear some anger in Ellen's voice.

"A woman from the city goes and visits her brother, who is a farmer, and she sees a pig with three legs walking by. So she asks her brother, 'What's the deal with that pig?' 'Oh,' says the farmer, 'that's Bessie. Bessie's incredible. Once, the barn was on fire and Bessie escaped and banged on the front door with her snout to alert us. She's brilliant.'

"'Okay,' says the woman from the city, 'but what about the three legs?'

"'Another time,' says the farmer, 'Bessie went and corralled all the sheep like she was some kind of sheepdog. She's amazing. Ain't no pig on this farm quite like Bessie.'

"'But why does she only have three legs?' the sister asks again.

"'Oh,' says the farmer. 'Well, a pig like that you don't eat all at once.'"

Todd smiles wanly, then laughs a little. "A pig like that you don't eat all at once," he says. "I'll have to remember that one."

9

We have a half day off, so Juniper texts me in the morning and ends up coming to my room. We sit on the couch and watch a movie—*Spirited Away*, one of Juniper's all-time favorites. I feel like she's looking at me as much as she's looking at the movie, hoping I'll love it the same way she does. Fortunately, I do. We order room service breakfast, but Juniper eats almost nothing—just a couple bites of her eggs—because she's worried about how she'll look at the premiere. We watch the movie in a kind of reverent silence. It's one of those movies where the final scene hits in an unexpected way. I find myself feeling really overwhelmed, thinking of the kid I used to be, and the kid in the movie whose life is restored in a way that real lives can't be. Juniper leans into me as she likes to do, and she says, "I know." I tell her, "Maybe this is the point of movies," and she says, "What?" And I say, "To let people feel things together."

"Art gives form to the formless," she says.

"Kierkegaard?" I ask.

"Original," she says.

"God, I really do love you, Juniper."

"You too, Kai."

As the credits roll, she tells me, "I'm so sorry, Kai. I'm sorry you've had to go through all of it again."

I tell her something I learned in therapy. My dad isn't a big feelings guy, but he paid to put me in therapy immediately after it all came out, and it really helped. "My therapist says that one of the hallmarks of trauma is that you don't know when it's going to end. We can endure almost anything if we know there's an end to it. No matter how much it sucks to run a marathon, you know it'll be over in twenty-six-point-two miles. But when you're going through something really traumatic, you don't know when it will end or how it will end. Or if it will end. And that's what makes it so destructive."

"I probably need to go back to therapy," she says.

"Oh yeah," I say. "Don't take this the wrong way, Juniper, but you need therapy."

Juniper tells me she has to start getting ready for her last photo shoot at one, that's when her hair and makeup people arrive, but she's free until then. It's only eleven. I ask her what we should do, and she tells me she doesn't want to go outside because she doesn't feel like being perceived, which is a very Juniper thing to say. I tell her that we can watch another movie—we have just enough time. So we rent another thirty-two-dollar film on the studio's dime, this time the Barry Jenkins movie *Moonlight*.

It's such a tender film from the start, so earnest without being cheesy, and we watch in rapt silence. I feel very aware of Juniper sitting next to me. I am aware of the unfinished room service atop a white tablecloth. I am aware of how she smells—like her lavender-scented shampoo. I am aware that I want Juniper, that I want her like I have never wanted anyone before. I want to kiss her and see her naked. She is impossibly, phenomenally beautiful to me right now, her smell exhilarating me. She has her feet curled under her body as she likes to, leaning into me so that her shoulder is pressed against my upper arm.

I don't know how to tell her what I want, or if it's okay for me to want it. My therapist says I can't blame him for everything, can't make him the axis mundi around which my life spins, but on this front, he really is. I loved him. Admittedly I'll love anyone, but I loved him. He was so smart, so worldly. He could quote any poet. He understood me, or at least it felt that way for a while. And he used all of that. I'm so fucked up now. Can't even tell a girl who clearly wants me that I want her back, and it's all because I love her. I am terrified of sexualizing love, of ruining it, of making it dirty the way he made my love for him dirty.

It was easier with the social virology scholar because there was never the same bubbling in my belly, the mere thought of her breathing into me like so much pure oxygen. "I like you too much," I finally say, squeezing out the words.

She pauses the movie with the remote. "How's that?"

"When you touch me, when you're touching me, I can hardly breathe."

"I don't have to—"

"I am not sometimes in love with you. I am not *sometimes* anything with you. It is all the time. It is incessant. It has been incessant since I first saw you in that Pittsburgh hotel. But if I tell you that, if I tell you the truth, I put everything at risk. All of me. All of us."

She's just staring at me for a long time, and then she says, "May I kiss you?"

I nod, and we kiss, and it is gentle at first—just like when we filmed—but then it is something more and greater, a devouring, her mouth on mine and then on my neck and ear. I'm kissing her collarbone, her gorgeous collarbone, and she has her hand on my face and I take her hand and kiss her fingers, and then return to her mouth, and she says, "I want to see you," and so I strip off my shirt and feel her hands against my biceps, my chest, tickling along my belly. I kiss her forehead. "I've wanted this for so long," she says, which makes me want her more, and I strip off her shirt and we're still sitting up, so she leans away from me while I stare at her eyes. She unhooks her bra, and I ask if I can look and she says, "That's the idea," and I glance down at her small, perfect breasts and go back to kissing her, our hands discovering each other.

"Stand up," she says, and I stand up, and she asks me if I want to take off my pants, says she'll show me hers if I'll show her mine, and I laugh and strip down. I feel utterly exposed in front of her, my hands at my side, and she asks me to turn around and says I have a cute butt, and I say thanks and she says and also I like when you turn back around. Your turn, I say, and then she wriggles out of her pants and her underwear and turns around for me. I swallow hard and take two steps toward her, and she steps toward me, and he isn't allowed in the room for this. No one is. It's between Juniper and me, the only two people who will ever know the rest of what happened that morning in my hotel room.

My hotel phone rings me awake. She's still naked beside me, one knee draped over my leg under the covers. I roll over. "Hello?"

"Do you know where Juniper is?" It's Ellen.

"Yeah, she's here with me."

"She's late for hair and makeup."

"Ah, right. She'll be up in a moment."

"Are you—Did you—" Ellen starts. "You know what? None of my fucking business. Send her upstairs."

"We were just watching a movie," I say.

"Not my circus, not my monkeys. Send her up to the room, though, will ya?"

Juniper is already pulling her underwear back on, and then hopping into her pants.

"Well," she says. "This is a major development. This is breaking news. Can, uh, can we do this again?"

"I think so," I say.

"Unfortunately I fly to Paris tonight," she says.

"Incredible news: I also fly to Paris tonight."

"Great. I'll make a note of that. The boy I love is flying to Paris with me."

10

That afternoon, I have time scheduled for "fact-checking," which turns out to be a woman from *The New Yorker* devoting two entire hours to asking me everything about my life: Is it true that you went to Greenbriar Elementary School? Were you in a summer stock production of *Annie*? Did you feel, when playing Paul in *You Can't Take It with You*, that you weren't inside your own body? Did you say that you are "sometimes" in love with Juniper Castillo? Your parents both grew up in Evansville, Indiana, correct? Your publicist is named Ellen Kim. Your abuse was widely publicized despite Ms. Kim's attempts to keep it under wraps. You choose not to discuss the abuse with reporters if given the option, but you sometimes aren't given the option. Is it true that when you and Juniper first met, you were drawing an ink portrait of her? You identified as a theater kid, yes, but also played baseball? Is your brother a dentist in Noblesville, Indiana? This is your first feature film? You are five feet and eleven inches tall, of a slight build, and will be starring next in the film adaptation of the bestselling novel *Gods of Andromeda*. You've never made a film without Juniper Castillo. Is it true that you did not know the man who you threw out of a car in Los Angeles?

When she finally finishes, I feel as if my life is some kind of dead butterfly pinned to a wall in a museum somewhere, but it's over, and I realize that Jill can write whatever she wants about my past, but she cannot write about my future. People always say that the present is the only moment that matters, but for me it's the future. When it was happening with him, I would always think about the future, how one day I'd be an adult. Now I think about Vancouver and making a fun fantasy movie with Juniper, and I think about rehearsing and working out all the time to look appropriately jacked. I do not actually have the present, this moment I don't control. What I have, what I will always have, is the perpetual future.

After the fact-checking, I talk to Ellen about how everything went and what I suspect the profile will be (damning of the machine but generous toward me) and then I choose what to bring to Paris among the many things Prada has sent me. I can barely get my suitcase closed, and I know there will be a new outfit for me in Paris, because Prada has told Bob they want me to wear something different at each premiere. By four p.m., I'm down in the lobby, where Ellen and Katie and Kathryn are having a drink at the bar. Kathryn kisses me on both cheeks and says, "Can you believe our little film gets a Parisian premiere?"

Juniper makes her way down in sunglasses and a hat, and then we all drive to the airport, where an elderly man is waiting for us outside who whisks us through check-in and then bypasses the security line, directly to the metal detectors. This causes *more* attention, and I hear someone saying, "Bro, look, Juniper Castillo." After clearing security, some girl comes up to me and asks for a selfie and Ellen says, "As long as you can do it while we're walking, but we can't stop," and the girl holds up her phone and makes a kissy face and I smile while walking. Kathryn says, "This is why I asked them for private; our starlets are becoming proper stars." Juniper keeps her head down and her sunglasses on, and finally we're at the gate. The elderly man from the airport goes up to the counter and the door opens and we board before the babies or the active-duty military or anyone else. We're in business class, with lie-flat seats, and I'm seated directly in front of Juniper, so I kneel on my seat and look back at her as she settles in.

"So it's just gonna be like that for a while," I say, somewhat bewildered by the experience.

A flight attendant brings me champagne, and Kathryn comes from across the aisle to clink glasses with me. Matthew isn't on the plane; I suppose he has one of his own. Soon the flight fills up with civilians, only one of whom asks for a picture with Juniper, which I take. The rest of the business-class cabin either doesn't recognize us or is too cool to say anything about it.

Once we're settled, I watch a movie—*Roman Holiday* with Gregory Peck and Audrey Hepburn—and settle into my little cocoon. I eat some dinner and then lay my seat down to sleep. I wake up once in the night to pee and so walk past Juniper's pod. She's asleep, and I pause for a moment just to look at her, curled on her side.

"Don't watch people sleep. It's creepy," Ellen says from across the aisle, and I turn to her. "Jesus Christ you're smitten," she says.

I give her a look but don't say anything, because they can't quote your looks.

"Oh, don't use my own media training on me, buddy!"

I go to the bathroom, then go back to sleep, thinking about how Juniper is just inches from me.

When we land in Paris, a person is there to greet us and helps us skip to the front of the passport line and then walks us to the exit, where three black Mercedes sedans are waiting for us. Juniper and I get in one with Ellen in the front seat. "Long day today," Ellen says. "We'll give you a minute to freshen up and get dressed and then at eleven we'll start media. Mostly you'll be paired, but Juniper, you've got a photo shoot with French *Vogue* in the afternoon and Kai during that time you'll do a feature interview with a Dutch newspaper called *NRC*. Around three, you'll both go to your rooms for hair and makeup and wardrobe and then we'll be in the cars to go to the premiere by five at the latest. You'll walk the carpet and do some interviews on the carpet and then Matthew will introduce the movie and after the screening, we'll have a panel."

"Great," Juniper says. "Then we get to go back to the hotel?"

"Yes, and in the morning we fly to New York. Light work, as the kids say."

French press junkets are more or less like American ones, except the reporters are better dressed and speak with accents. I tell them that I prepared for the movie by reading everything Warhol wrote. I tell them Juniper is funny, thoughtful, and wise beyond her years. Juniper tells them I am charming, caring, and kind. One time, she even calls me handsome. We exchange anecdotes about the film. Now these stories have lost all their hard edges and have become river rocks we hold in our hands. A different reporter comes in every seven minutes. The set is the same, except the hotel is different and the movie poster behind us advertises the film *Andy Warhol ne Vieillit Jamais*.

Here the reporters are far more comfortable asking us about our personal lives. Perhaps they have less to lose, or maybe the culture's just different, but almost every reporter asks some version of whether I used my own traumatic abuse as a teen to help me understand the challenges in my character's life. I say that of course you bring your full self to a role, but I didn't learn anything from abuse that I couldn't have learned somewhere else, somewhere easier. Whether this answer is true is almost irrelevant to the experience of saying the words; all I know is that the answer, practiced dozens of times now, allows me to feel safe and sane.

The hotel itself apparently provided the setting for an old movie about Paris, and my room has many closets and two bedrooms from back in the day when people would move into hotel rooms for months on end. But I've hardly been in the room—just to change and shower. I'm tired and take a sip of espresso after each interview.

After press, they drive us in the three black Mercedes to the Eiffel Tower, where Juniper and I get out to take some pictures. Matthew shows up just after us, and so we get some trio shots. "My kids," he says joyfully as he gets out of his car and puts his arms around us. At one point he leans his head onto my shoulder, which I can tell will become *the* shot that the publicists blast out to all the European media.

Back at the hotel, the Dutch interviewer—an attractive young man wearing a black suit—meets me for coffee. "You must be tired," he says, and I acknowledge that I am, and then he says, "Warhol was fascinated by consumerism and industrial design. You must also feel like you are commodifying art." I haven't made this connection before, but it's true we're trying to sell something deep through superficial interviews. "Sure," I say. "Warhol loved business. He loved selling things. He said business was the highest form of art. And making a movie . . . it's art. Promoting a movie . . . is business."

"Do you find the commodification of self uncomfortable? Warhol never seemed to."

I stumble through an answer as best I can, saying that I'm not commodifying myself, only talking about my process.

"But your love for Juniper, your openness about abuse, your—how do you say in English—placing this all on the table, this is very un-Warhol. The public never knew Warhol's lovers when he was alive. Never knew Warhol's fears. He was actually very protective of his own privacy, despite having a public life. You're not. Why?"

"I would say I'm just less successful at protecting it, maybe," I tell him. "Or that I live in a different era with different expectations." I think about Matthew—how even he talked about his father's death on TV.

The interviewer keeps asking questions—smart questions—about

Warhol and me, about celebrity and privacy. I'm both impressed and a little scared, but Ellen is with us and doesn't jump in, so I assume I'm doing fine. When, after forty-five minutes, Ellen says, "We're at time so last question please," the young man tells me, "I think the film is extraordinary, and you steal every scene. This is a silly question, but how do you inhabit the character so fully?"

"Instead of making me into him, I made him into me," I say.

"A dangerous game," the interviewer replies. "Thank you for your time."

Ellen and I take a tiny elevator up to my room and she says, "You handled that really well. Some of these Europeans are a bit intellectual for my taste, but I'm sure the piece will come out fine." I reach in my pocket and pull out a stick of gum. "You've got thirty minutes to change, then we're off to the premiere."

I open the door to my room, half hoping that Juniper is there, but of course she isn't. Instead, a hair and makeup person is. I like getting my makeup done; it's rare that a stranger touches your face with kindness, and this stranger with spiky hair and fake lashes is an attractive one, which helps. As I get my hair done, I text Juniper: *Any chance I can see you for three seconds before we do this thing?*

And she responds, *HMU should be done momentarily. I'm in 251.*

Her room is on the same floor as mine, so when they're done with me, I get dressed in a black Prada suit and walk down the hall to her room. I ring the doorbell—there's a doorbell—and she answers. She's wearing a black velvet dress with a plunging neckline. "Holy hell," I say.

"I told you that you'd know when I dressed up for you." I close the door behind her and kiss her immediately. *"Lipstick,"* she whispers into my mouth, and I tell her I don't care and we can fix it later. We kiss for a while, me pressed against the wall and her pressed against me.

Eventually, she pulls away and says, "I like your body when it is with my body. It is so quite new a thing."

"Original?" I ask.

"E. E. Cummings," she says, and I laugh.

"Remember when you told me at the table read that anxiety is the disease of freedom? I think about that a lot."

"Anxiety is the *dizziness* of freedom," she says.

"Oh, I heard it wrong. Well, I like my way better. It's the disease of freedom."

"Whatever it is, we're about to mainline it," she says.

We head down to the hotel lobby together, where Ellen has freshened up into a little black dress and Katie is wearing something similar. Matthew's team is huddled off in a different area until Matthew comes down wearing a tuxedo with a bow tie. "Don't you look dapper?" I say, and Matthew responds, "You're glowing, kid. Glowing."

I can already hear the people outside, but I'm not ready for just how many of them there are surrounding our cars. Juniper starts taking selfies as the crescendo of noise rises, and I take a couple too, grabbing people's phones so I can angle the selfie how I like it. Then Matthew emerges from the hotel and there's a physical shift in the universe as people press past us and toward him. "Matthew, Matthew!" people shout in their French accents, and I can feel myself being pushed until bodyguards emerge and create a path for Matthew to reach his car. Juniper and I sneak into the car behind him with Ellen and Katie crammed in with us, and there are people staring through the window at us, pressing their hands and noses to the car window to see past the tinted glass. The cars have to drive slowly to avoid hitting anyone, but finally we're out on the road and Juniper says, "That was weird," and Ellen says, "The premiere is apparently *packed*, so take a breath while you can."

11

The cheering begins as we drive around the block to the red carpet that's been laid out. Juniper and I emerge, and I can hear people shouting my name, so I try to look and wave at the folks calling to me, but there are so many people. They're pressed against a barricade, and cops are stationed every few feet to make sure the barricades don't fall. Juniper walks over and starts taking selfies with fans, and I do the same for a while, and someone shouts, "I love you Kai Laramie," so I shout back, "I love you too," which I guess I kind of do. Movies need fans, and I'm grateful that we have so many for this one. I've gotten almost accustomed to the sound when Matthew arrives behind us, gets out of the car with his bodyguards, and the cacophony really begins, with people screaming for pictures and autographs. Matthew just waves and shouts, "I love you, Paris! Je t'aime! Je t'aime!"

I make my way to the red carpet with the step-and-repeat behind me featuring the movie's logo. I stand there in my suit as a dozen photographers shout at me to look this way and now here and chin down please. I don't know what to do with my hands. After a minute, Juniper shows up and we take some pictures together, and then I make way for her to do her solo shots. Ellen brings me back to the carpet when Matthew arrives, and he's got his arm around both Juniper and me and without breaking his smile says, "Just let 'em turn you into an object."

Farther down the carpet, cameras are set up to do interviews. It's hard to tell what anyone is saying to me in the interviews because of their accents and the noise behind us, but I struggle through. Ellen's behind me, just off camera. I think about how Ellen's dress is meant to make her disappear into the background, while my suit is made to pop. An interviewer asks me how I'm finding Paris and I say, "It's lovely. I want to move here," even though all I've seen is the Eiffel Tower and the insides of hotel rooms. I take a step down the carpet and another interviewer is there and asks, "Juniper just said she loves you. Do you also love her?"

Juniper jumps in then, her arms around me, and says, "Yeah, Kai, *do you*?" I'm surprised by her presence on my back. Touch without warning always makes me anxious. I'm looking at the interviewer, and then at the camera lens, and then back at the interviewer. "I am a little overwhelmed right now."

Ellen grabs me. "You're starting to look panicked," and I say, "Yeah," and she says, "You know what, let's skip the rest of the interviews and get you inside."

Inside the theater: Red carpet on the floor. Arches above. Painted ceiling. This is a classy movie palace, probably from the early twentieth century. I tell myself all the things I'm supposed to when I get scared: Come into your body. Notice whatever there is to notice. Your feet are on the floor, in Prada shoes that are a bit too tight. You can hear the noise outside, but it's at least a little deadened. Smell the popcorn. How is the air on your skin? Stale, slightly warm. Where are you? Paris. Are you with someone you love? Yes. Okay. Breathe. In through the nose, out through the mouth.

I can't stop sweating. Hate sweating. It reminds me that my body is mammalian. There's a concession counter up ahead with prepackaged containers of popcorn. Ellen grabs one, asks me if I want a drink, and I say *Do they have whiskey*, and she says *For the star of the movie they do*, and a minute later she appears with a plastic glass full of whiskey and ice. I'm calming down. I know I shouldn't use alcohol this way, but it does the job. The thing about alcohol is it quells my anxiety in the short run and worsens my anxiety in the long run. This is also the thing about weed, and the thing about Instagram. I take a long drink. It burns my throat going down. "We can go to our seats," she says.

I find the seat marked KAI LARAMIE, next to the one marked JUNIPER CASTILLO. Juniper shows up a few minutes later and sits down next to me, and just the smell of her calms me down. "You're stunning," I tell her, and she blushes.

The theater fills with people—hundreds of them. We're in the sixth row, and so almost everyone is behind us, but people keep coming up and congratulating us, wanting to shake our hands.

Matthew stands at the front of the theater, his shadow double his size, crawling up the screen. He thanks everyone for coming. "I was in Portugal last year," he says, "and I visited an old ossuary—a place where the bones of the dead are stored. They were stacked high, room after room full of our ancestors. And in one room an inscription on a small tablet read, 'These are the bones that wait for your bones.' Warhol's bones wait for ours, but he is also with us, now, more than ever, in an image-saturated world. I'm so proud of this film, and especially of the brilliant young people at its heart—Kai Laramie and Juniper Castillo. I love them, and after watching this film, I know you will, too."

The applause begins as the credits start to roll. There's especially loud clapping for Matthew, of course, but both Juniper and I get some as well when our names flash up on the screen.

I'm not so much watching the movie as I am listening to hundreds of people watch it; the way the energy shifts in the room during the nightclub scene where Juniper's bleeding all over me, the way people laugh at Andy's dry humor, and especially the weeping as Warhol dies and the news reaches us. When the Lou Reed song that Juniper hates plays, the whole place is crying, including me, and then the movie ends and everyone immediately stands up and starts applauding. Juniper is still holding my hand even though it's sweaty, and she pulls me up with her to wave at the crowd, and then we go up to the front and sit between Kathryn and Matthew and answer some British reality TV star's questions about the movie, and then I take a shot of whiskey backstage from a flask that Matthew's handing around because my brain is flooded with all kinds of chemicals I've never felt before, and then Juniper and I are in a hotel room, taking very nice clothes off each other.

Juniper and I end the night by closing down the hotel's rooftop bar. It's warm in Paris, and we've got a hell of a view of the city. She tells me about being a kid, about the little pool in her LA apartment complex, and how there would always be other kids swimming in the pool who were also in town for pilot season. She tells me that her mom would get so drunk at the pool that Juniper worried she would drown, and I tell her that she really didn't get a chance to be a kid at all, and she says that we're still just kids. I tell her about growing up in Indianapolis, how I did summer stock at Butler University and only felt like I was myself onstage or on the field. Had to be playing.

Talking to Juniper is the opposite of talking to a reporter.

On the plane the next morning I can't sleep. I don't know exactly what I'm feeling, but I'm feeling a lot of it. I'm trying to watch *Crouching Tiger, Hidden Dragon* on the little screen. The flight attendant keeps filling my wineglass with cabernet, and I keep drinking it. Across the aisle from me, I can see Juniper sleeping. I want to sleep with her again, but I also don't. The thought of having sex again kind of submerges me. Sex is so physical, so organism-y, so base. I think about how she told me once that after men have you, they don't want you anymore. I don't want to be that kind of man, but I'm terrified I'm going to be. I always recoil in the face of actual intimacy. It is so easy to say *I love you*, and so hard to let myself feel it.

Finally I fall asleep. I wake up vaguely hungover as we're descending.

"You'll have two hours at the hotel." Ellen is talking at me on the drive to the Mandarin Oriental. "Hair and makeup will come at two p.m., then you are in the car by four, then we walk the carpet. Screening starts at six and then the panel will be at 8:05. Then there's the party, and you can leave that whenever you want and then, my friend, you are free. You have one night at the hotel to do with as you please, and then you are no longer my ward and we just wait to see if anyone actually shows up to see this movie."

Ellen's always talking logistics, and it occurs to me that I haven't really had freedom of movement since that week between the audition and the junket, that I've been on someone else's schedule the whole time. But it's crazy to complain about my job. Shameful, even.

Anyway, all that's going through my head when we arrive at the Mandarin Oriental and Juniper texts me *my place or yours*, and I go to her room and we have sex and then call for room service.

"You okay?" Juniper asks while her head is against my fast-beating chest.

"Yeah," I say, although during the sex I'd been stuck in my head.

"Our movie is premiering tonight," she says. "People will see it starting Friday. We fucking did it."

12

The screaming starts even before we get out of the car. I'm in another Prada suit, this one slightly navy I think? Juniper is sitting next to me in another Dior. An indigo gown wrapping her delicate shoulders and plating the rest of her body like armor. She looks uncomfortable; the dress isn't made for sitting. As our car rounds a corner, I see people lined up on either side of the street, five-deep behind barricades. They are yelling, and it is a little hard for my brain to differentiate between excited yelling and terrified yelling.

Strange to think this is my life. I feel very aware that I'm living *the* dream even if I'm maybe not living *my* dream. But what is my dream anyway? Juniper reaches over, grabs my hand. She's wearing a diamond ring on her right ring finger, on loan from her jewelry sponsor. I'm wearing a Tag Heuer watch, even though I'm not a watch guy. She looks so pretty, a bit too made-up for real life, but perfect for the cameras.

When we get out, the screams crescendo. "KAAAAIIIIIII," I hear from behind me, and I turn around, but then the people in front of me are saying, "KAI!!!!" too, so I turn toward them. I don't know where to look. Juniper starts walking up and down the barricades, taking selfies with everyone, but I feel so overwhelmed by the noise I don't know what to do until I feel Ellen's hand on the small of my back moving me toward the barricades. I come into my body, wave at the crowd, and then make my way to the red carpet, where Kathryn is standing in a lovely gold fitted suit. I get in line for the carpet. Ahead of me is a small child wearing a tux. "That's the winner of the National Spelling Bee," Ellen explains, "and ahead of him is the guy who won the Indy 500, with his wife. Premieres always bring out an odd assortment."

Finally it's my turn and I stand before the wall of cameras with everyone shouting my name. If there were a dozen cameras in Paris, there must be over fifty here—clicking and flashing as the photographers shout over each other to try to get my attention. Even though Ellen has told me just to stare straight ahead and not listen to any of their requests, they're all shouting my name and I want to be a good celebrity who looks at each of them and gives everyone their shot. I see my parents and brother and hug them and my mom says, "I'm proud of you, Kai." My dad is excited to meet the IndyCar driver, so I introduce them, and then I have to go back to the photographers to take pictures with Juniper. I put my hand on her waist and feel the surge of her body entangled with mine. She looks up at me, gives me half a smile and a wink, and then turns to the cameras.

We stop for interviews—*Time* and *E!* and *Teen Vogue*, and when I'm talking to *Entertainment Weekly*, a wall of noise erupts from behind me, and I realize that Matthew has arrived. At the end of the carpet, Juniper introduces me to a friend of hers who turns out to be Very Famous, and I say, "It must be overwhelming to be you," and she says, "That's empathetic of you to say," but actually I'm just multiplying the amount that I feel overwhelmed by the amount of her celebrity. Juniper asks if I'm okay, and I nod. I should ask her if she's okay, but I don't. Too overwhelmed to think about anything or anyone else except the cacophony in my brain.

The director Ryan Arnold and his wife come up to me. He's making Matthew's next thing—a big musical—and he says I hear you're fantastic in this movie, and I say thanks, and he says I'd love to meet up for lunch sometime if you're ever in LA, and I say *Yeah yeah of course.*

I see Bob and Zoe. He hugs me and Zoe asks how I'm doing and I say, "A little overstimulated," and she says, "Don't worry, Kai. It'll all be over soon."

Before we can get inside the theater, Ellen walks me back to the photographers one last time to take a big group photo with the producers and Studio Todd and Juniper and me and Matthew. Matthew has his arm around me, and we walk together. He's telling me how proud he is, and at the end of the carpet, he gestures to the cameras and the fans behind them lined up along the barricades. "You really were Most Likely to Make It in Hollywood, kid."

"Wait, from my yearbook? How do you know that?"

Matthew shrugs ever so slightly. "Always good to do a bit of advance research. Sent my guy to poke around your school."

Something cracks inside my chest. All at once, I understand. "*You* leaked it," I say. "It was you." I look up at him. He's still smiling at his assembled admirers.

"Look how great it all turned out. You see why I had to do it. You get it." I don't get it, but I'm quiet. I'm always quiet in the face of betrayal. Always scared dumb. "Look at all these people," Matthew Malone tells me, "for a movie about Andy Warhol? I know it's been rough on you, kid, but we fucking did it."

He doesn't define the it. He's looking at me now, and seems to be waiting for some absolution or something. After a moment, he says, "You don't get to be Matthew Malone without wanting it, kid. You've gotta want it really fucking badly. Like Junie does." Again, I'm not sure what the it is. Success? Fame? A life in entertainment? Andy Warhol paintings on your wall? I can't say anything. My throat is strangled shut. "If you need me to be your villain, I'm happy to play the role," Matthew says calmly. "But ten years from now, you'll have me to thank for your career."

Juniper's already in her seat at the theater. I sit down next to her, lean close, and say, "It was Matthew. He just told me."

"He leaked it?"

"He didn't even say he was sorry. He just said he had to do it."

"What a fuckface," she says, and then after a second, "But, I mean, we have to work with him."

"We do?"

"It doesn't end today," she says with a measure of pity in her voice. Again, that terrible pronoun. "Hopefully there will be an awards push. Lots of screenings. A whole *campaign*. And he'll be there for everything. What are we gonna do?"

She's not asking *Are you okay?* or *Do you want to get out of here?* She's asking what we're gonna do. I feel the panic rising up in me again, the old dread. Somebody's got me in their clutches, and there's no good way out. If I run up to the front of the theater and shout that Matthew Malone is a fucking monster who will screw anyone to get ahead, I hurt the movie and myself and Juniper. So what can I do? All I want is not to feel the way I'm feeling right now—cornered, helpless. The movie starts. I'm sweating again. I can't think, can't even feel the comfort of Juniper's hand in mine.

After the screening, I'm up at the front of the theater with Matthew and Juniper and Kathryn, and Juniper's Very Famous friend is interviewing us. I say that Matthew is so kind and generous and funny. I elaborate on his generosity with a story I've told a dozen times before about how he gave the whole crew cash bonuses. I hate myself as I tell this story, but I would hate myself more if I didn't tell it.

Matthew tells the audience that he loves working with us because "there's a purity in their acting that you can lose along the way, a willingness to be fully open and vulnerable with each other, which is essential to great films." The audience applauds that, as they applaud every Matthew applause line, and laugh at every Matthew joke. I realize the audience is also playing along, that they're also part of the show. Everybody feeds the machine.

How to describe the feeling? In high school, we'd have two dances every year. I am a good dancer—I understand my body in space; I've taken classes; etc.—and I'd always be out there during the upbeat songs. Maybe on the slow songs I'd dance with a girl.

But he was always there. He was always a chaperone, always lurking, often in literal shadows. He was there to prevent kids from hooking up on the dance floor or spiking the punch or whatever kids weren't supposed to do. I would always feel him there, even when I was dancing and trying not to be self-conscious, trying to give my body over to the music, I would sense him, and it would make me feel like I wasn't actually in my body but was instead observing it from somewhere else. Like I was hovering up by the ceiling of the gym, looking down at everyone, including me. And I feel like that again. I feel like my soul is not in my body but instead somewhere up in the balcony, looking down on these tiny figures in their fancy form-fit clothes. Nothing has changed. He's still in the room with me. I'm still dressed up. And I'm still really scared.

I'm not sure exactly when I decide to do it. Maybe it's during the movie. Maybe it's at the afterparty, as I'm dancing with Juniper, flipping her upside down as she gasps and laughs. "Kai," she says, "you can *move*." Maybe it's when Matthew puts his arm around me while the DJ plays The Killers' "Mr. Brightside" and shouts the chorus, expecting me to shout it along with him, which I find myself doing because I don't want to make a scene. Maybe I don't decide to do it until I'm outside, sweaty, my bow tie untied. Maybe I don't decide until I see a cab and flag it down. Maybe I don't really make the decision until I'm in the back of the cab, saying, "Can you take me to the Mandarin Oriental, please? And then on to JFK."

"What airline?"

"Not sure yet."

At the hotel, I grab my passport but leave my suitcase. They've got clothes wherever I'm going.

I wonder sometimes if I enjoy fucking up my life, if there's something way down deep within me that wants to see everything torn to rags, that wants to walk away calmly from the explosion of my self. I don't drink too much (or at least didn't before the junket); I don't do hard drugs; I don't cut myself. But I still need that jolt, and I get it by sabotaging my own life. Which is why I'm not entirely surprised to find myself plotting against my own best interests as I sit in a cab on my way to the airport and book a flight on my phone to somewhere warm and far away.

I've cleared security and printed out my boarding pass. I'm walking to the gate when I get a text from Juniper: *Where'd you go? There's an after-party at Matthew's.*

I look at my phone for a second, dump it in a nearby trash can, and keep moving.

PART 4

THE COMEDOWN

JUNIPER

DAY 1

There's a phenomenon I've experienced after a film comes out that I call The Comedown. It happens with good movies and bad ones, and even with TV shows that run on Nickelodeon for six years. One day you're working, rolling some ball of art ceaselessly uphill, and then you wake up the next day and it's just . . . over.

After Kai fails to show up to the premiere's afterparty or respond to my late-night my-place-or-yours text, I call him that next morning, but it goes straight to voicemail. I figure he's still asleep. "Good morning. Call me when you charge your phone and get this. I love you." Then I call my agent, Jamie.

"Juniper, my love, how are you?"

"How's the movie tracking?"

"We're still hoping for a twenty-plus opening weekend. We'll know more tomorrow night once we get some actual butts in actual seats. You feeling good?"

"Sure," I say. "What should I be doing today? Posting? I've got a carousel I could post of Kai and me, or I could do a live, or—"

"Definitely post stuff from the premiere, Junie, but you need to chill a little. You did it. Take a week off."

"I don't need a week off. I need the movie to be a hit."

"It already is; have you read these reviews? There's gonna be plenty to do. A whole awards push probably. But for now, the train has left the station. Work on *Andromeda* if you need to work."

"Got it," I tell her.

"I'll call you tomorrow with more."

"Sure. Thanks, Jamie."

I don't start worrying about Kai until around ten thirty a.m. I call him again. Straight to voicemail. I don't want to be That Girl, so I tell myself he's fine and just sleeping in. I go for a run in the hotel's gym. I prefer running around Central Park, and we're right around the corner from it, but I don't want to get recognized, especially when exercising, because I have a goofy running gait. So I put on a hat and some workout clothes and run on the treadmill, and then Katie calls me and tells me my flight to LA leaves at eight p.m. but she has gotten me a late checkout so no rush.

I ask her what I need to do to promote the movie, and she says, "Christ, Juniper. You did it. Once the movie is in the present tense for the audience, it's in the past tense for us. Now it's all about advertising and the studio's marketing team. You junketed the living hell out of that movie. Take a nap."

I call Kai again, and then finally I check in with Ellen.

"Hey," I say.

"Hey, is Kai with you?" Ellen asks.

"No, I was hoping he was with you."

"He's not answering his phone."

"Straight to voicemail."

"Okay, I'm officially Slightly Concerned," Ellen says. "Let me have the hotel check on him. Probably just a bad hangover combined with low battery."

While I wait for her to call back, I post that carousel of Kai and me on Instagram—pictures of us throughout the junket, culminating with us together on the red carpet, me laughing with his arm around me. Caption: *I love you, Kai Laramie. And I can't wait for the world to see why.*

Ellen calls back as I'm reading the first comments. "So all his stuff is still there. Doesn't look like he slept there last night; the bed is still made. I'm officially Moderately Concerned."

"Fuck," I say.

"I'll call the studio," she says.

Kai disappearing feels precisely like when my mom would disappear. The same all-over bodily fear. The same resentment and frustration. The same awareness that however much they love you, they love whatever they abandon you for more. I've had that enough from a mother not to want it from a boyfriend.

As a kid, I yearned for a normal life, one where your mom wakes up before you do and makes you breakfast and takes you to school. Instead, I was always chasing her around. She'd go out one night and just not come home, and then I'd call and call until eventually she'd answer and I'd figure out how to get her home, even when I was eleven or twelve. She'd come back smelling like whiskey and cigarettes and tell me she'd met a producer who was going to make us a star or whatever.

But, of course, every time there was a possibility that something worse had happened. Something dangerous. Something fatal. That was always a worry with my mother, and now that is a worry with Kai.

To distract myself, I keep scrolling through Instagram, searching for Kai's name, hoping he'll post or someone will post about him, that he'll show up hungover in some paparazzi picture. I've been doing that for a while when I get a call from a 310 number I don't recognize.

"Hello?"

"Hey, it's Todd, with the studio," he says. "I need you to come to the New York office if you don't mind. There's a car waiting for you outside."

"Is everything okay?"

"We'll talk about it shortly." He hangs up.

As the car fights its way down Seventh Avenue, I can't get air into my lungs. I think about how Kai seemed yesterday. He was out of it, but that's to be expected at a premiere, where everything is happening all at once. He was shy around my friends. He was pissed about Matthew's betrayal, but not so much that he abandoned the premiere.

I imagine him hurt. I imagine him dead. I imagine how I will hug him when I see him. If I see him.

I'm dropped off at a skyscraper in lower Manhattan, where a security guard personally escorts me up to the seventeenth floor and into Todd's corner office with a view of the Statue of Liberty.

I sit down on a plush couch and resist the urge to speak first. Todd stands up and walks to a little bar atop a side table. "Drink?" he asks.

I shake my head.

"Well, I'm having one." He pours a scotch and toasts in my direction. "So we tracked Kai's phone to JFK, where he dumped it in a trash can. But we can tell from his credit card charges that he took an early morning flight to Jamaica and booked a beach hut at a resort called GoldenEye. That's all my guys know."

"Your guys?"

"This sort of thing happens more than you might expect with actors," he says. "Not everyone is a pro like you, Juniper. Some of them are . . . well, *artistes*. I'm afraid Kai may be an *artiste*. Problem is, he's also a damn good actor and we need him to be in Vancouver in two weeks prepping for *Gods of Andromeda*."

"Right, of course," I say.

"I think we'll have to recast the movie if he bows out."

"Yes, I understand he'd have to be replaced."

"The two of you are a package, Juniper. The story is, two talented kids stick together for a big tentpole movie. Without both of you, that story falls apart. You're brilliant, but I think realistically we'd have to recast both roles."

"You're telling me that if Kai doesn't come back, you're firing me from *Gods of Andromeda*?"

"*Firing* is a strong word, kid. Recasting."

"You're gonna fire *me* because some boy skittered off to Jamaica?" I am not only mad at Todd. I am also mad at Kai.

He pauses for a moment, sits down, and puts his feet up on his desk. He's wearing black lace-up boots. "Yeah," he says. "I'd have to. But I think we can still save this thing."

"And how do you propose we do that?"

"I've got you on a flight to Jamaica first thing tomorrow," he says. "You'll be swimming in the ocean by noon. All expenses paid."

"Because you think I'm the only one who can bring him home."

Todd takes a long breath. "Yeah," he says. "Because I think you're the only one who can bring him home."

When we started *Andy Warhol Never Gets Old*, I was the star. I mean, Matthew was the star, but I was the starlet, the one with boundless potential, the one who might just be the Next New Thing. But instead, Kai has taken on that role—in part because of his inexperience, his lack of polish. Of course, that's also part of why I fell in love with him. He is so goddamned charming, and so dreamily unaware of his charm.

"So I show up for every shoot on time. Every interview on time. I'm the consummate professional. And you fire me because *he* isn't professional. Have you ever noticed, Todd, that it's always the men who get to be, as you call them, *artistes*? Have you ever noticed that women don't get that luxury?" I'm staring at Todd's boot soles, which are closer to me than any other part of him.

"I know you think I make the rules," Todd replies. "But I got into this business to make great movies, and now I'm stuck being The Man. I don't make the rules any more than you do. There's a Man behind me, and one behind him, like Russian nesting dolls only they get bigger and bigger until you get to the shareholders, and all that matters to them is the stock going up. It's the market you're mad at."

"Nobody wants to own up to their own power, Todd. It's inconvenient. I'll go to Jamaica. I'll bring Kai back. And you'll remember that I went on an errand for you the next time I need a favor. You'll remember that I—unlike most people in this fucking industry—can be counted upon."

"I like your spark, kid."

"Yeah," I say.

I call Jamie and tell her she better keep me in the movie regardless of whether Kai is in it. I call Katie and bring her up to date. Then Ellen, who tells me, "He's just scared, Juniper. He's panicking. He'll come home with you." But I have spent my life chasing after irresponsible people who have excuses for being irresponsible, and one does rather tire of the labor. In fact, one begins to feel just the tiniest bit enraged.

DAY 2

The next morning a car is waiting for me at five a.m. I take the car to the airport, and then a plane to Montego Bay, and then a car along the northern coast to Oracabessa, the little town where Ian Fleming lived while writing the James Bond novels. My driver keeps pointing things out to me along the way—here's the beach where they filmed *The Blue Lagoon*; here's where you can swim with dolphins; here's the haunted Rose Hall Great House.

When I arrive at the resort, a young woman named Hazel tells me they've reserved the Fleming Villa for me, the house where Fleming actually lived. The villa—with a private pool, a private beach, three separate living quarters, an outdoor bathtub, and an expansive view of the ocean below—seems a bit much for a single person, but I don't turn it down.

I know I need to look for Kai, but I don't really want to, so I spend the morning journaling as Agrippah, trying to inhabit her voice. When I'm working on a character, it's hard to say if her voice becomes mine or mine becomes hers, but there's a moment past which I feel comfortable as that new person, and I'm not there yet.

The hard thing for me isn't Agrippah's power or need to cling to it. I understand that. What I need to get closer to is Agrippah's vulnerability, the way Gavinth both exposes and exploits her compassion. Compassion is often mistaken for weakness, but it is vastly stronger and more courageous than apathy, and I want to express that through Agrippah. I've packed a book of nineteenth-century women writers, and I read the preface while thinking about how much Agrippah knows of her husband's betrayal, and when she knows it.

The truth is, I want Kai to find me. I want him to rush toward me and apologize for abandoning me, for reading my text asking where he'd gone and then literally throwing his phone in a trash can rather than responding to me.

I decide to go swimming. After a long period in the abstract time of junketing and promoting, it feels strange and lovely to walk into the eerily calm water, my skin prickling until I get used to the temperature. I swim out into the ocean a little and turn onto my back to float and stare up at the cloudless sky. Feels good to use my body. If you're not careful, you can forget that you have a body—that, on some level, you *are* a body.

I swim around to a lagoon where smaller villas dot the shore. A lifeguard offers me a mask and a snorkel, and then I can see thousands of little fish wending their way through the seagrass below me. Halfway around the lagoon, I notice a sea turtle swimming calmly a few feet away from me. I track the turtle for a long time, watching it come up for air every so often, its grace and size an absolute astonishment. The thing is, sea turtles know exactly how to be sea turtles, whereas I do not know very much about how to be a human. So much of what is within baffles me. I feel to myself mostly like an abstraction, like that Joan Mitchell painting in Pittsburgh.

I make it back to my private beach, tired from the long swim. I towel off, put on a cover-up, and set out in search of some food. And that's when I finally catch up with Kai, who is daydrinking at an outdoor bar on the ocean's edge. The bar is plastered with photographs of reggae stars, and Kai is saddled up next to it, drinking a Red Stripe beer while staring out at the ocean. There's a well-fed tabby cat curled beneath his chair. He puts the beer down and hunches over his sketchbook. He's drawing the view.

"Kai," I say.

"Juniper," he answers. If he is surprised to see me, his face doesn't betray it.

"You can't just make me fall in love with you and then disappear," I tell him. "It's inconsiderate."

He smiles unabashedly. "I just couldn't take it."

"Then call me and say you can't take it."

"I didn't want to ruin your night."

"Instead, you've ruined much more than my night."

"Sorry," he says without the faintest hint of actually being sorry.

"You didn't even respond to my text. You read it, and then you threw your phone in the garbage. How is that supposed to make me feel?"

"You said—when I told you it was Matthew—you said, 'What are we gonna do?' You didn't say you were sorry. Or that you were angry. Or that Matthew is despicable. You said, *What are we gonna do?* Like everything that happened is just some minor inconvenience to your career goals."

"You can't just disappear on people because you don't like how they reacted to something. We can talk about it; we can fight about it, even. But you can't just disappear. Can you imagine how it felt to me? To wake up and you're nowhere? I thought you were *dead*."

"We have nothing in common," he says. "People go through these experiences together and they think they're in love because you have this huge thing in common, which is the movie, which is the junket, and then it ends and they realize that's the *only* thing they had in common." He takes a sip of his beer. "I guess we do have one thing in common: We're both trainwrecks. I just want to blow up my life, and you're still chasing your dead mother's dream."

"That's really hurtful," I say. I can feel the tears behind my eyes and I try to stop them but I can't.

There is such coldness in his voice. "Who sent you, anyway? The studio?"

"The studio told me where you were, but I wanted to come."

"How'd they find me?"

"They had people trace your credit cards."

"That's so fucked up," he says. "Even without my phone they can track me. They think they own me."

"But I wanted to see you. To make sure you're alive."

"I'm magnificent," he says. "I am living the dream."

"Will you come home with me?"

"Absolutely fucking not."

"Kai," I say.

"You wanted to see if I'm okay. I'm okay. Mission accomplished."

I walk away, hoping he'll call after me and apologize. But he lets me go. I walk back to my villa and let myself cry a little. He is right about the premiere, of course. I shouldn't have said, *What are we gonna do?* But what *are* we gonna do? How can you respond to betrayal when all the responses make your life worse?

I wonder if Kai is right about me, that I am still just chasing my mom's dream. After *Star Catcher* wrapped, Mom told me I would probably never work again on anything of significance. She told me this while hammered, of course, but still, she said it, and now I have vanquished her, finally proving her wrong. I've never had a movie get near these reviews, near this buzz, and I *do* feel like I have something to prove to her even though she is dead. Maybe especially because she is dead.

I walk down to my little private beach and lie in the sun and call Jamie.

"It's still early, but we're slightly overperforming expectations," she says.

"Slightly?"

"I think we're looking closer to a twenty-five million opening than twenty, which is amazing. I won't lie, with our momentum I was imagining we might even get to thirty, but twenty-five is miraculous. And that's just domestic. Almost double the budget without a significant ad spend. We're gonna win the weekend. And the CinemaScore is good: A-minus."

"Minus?"

"Juniper, you are hard to please."

"But the test scores were so high."

"This is a win. Twenty-five is a massive win. This project is mostly a stepping stone, anyway. And now you step to *Gods of Andromeda*."

Every project is about the next one. Real success is right out there, just past the horizon line.

"This movie isn't about the first week. It's about the first decade. It's whether it's in the awards conversation. We've got a long way to go. Just get that kid's head straight and we'll be fine. But we need him for a campaign. You can't win shit in this town without a good campaign."

I stay down at the beach for a long time. I want Kai to come and find me, but I know he won't. I read for a while, and discover an Emily Dickinson poem I really like. I'm not even sure what the poem is about, but I like how it ends:

So We must meet apart –
You there – I – here –
With just the Door ajar
That Oceans are – and Prayer –
And that White Sustenance –
Despair –

You there, I here, with just the door ajar. It makes me think of Kai, the unsolvable distance between us, the way I can't get into his head and he can't get into mine even if we're both pretty good at getting into other people's heads. There's always a distance between you and I, a chasm that cannot be bridged, and even though we are both at the same resort on the same island, I am here and he is there, with just the door ajar.

I call Matthew Malone that afternoon.

"Kid," he says, "our movie is gonna be number one at the box office this weekend."

"Yeah," I say. "Looking like twenty-five."

"Twenty-seven the last time I heard, and that's just US. Might have to get myself another Warhol. You feeling good?"

"Matthew, you need to call this resort, GoldenEye, ask for Kai, and apologize."

"Apologize for what, the abuse thing?"

"Yeah. *For the abuse thing.*" I feel the frustration in my voice.

"No worries, I'll give him a call. He had a rough go of it, huh?"

"Yes, Matthew. You revealed something intensely private to the world."

"I figured he might not understand."

"I also do not understand."

"We trade in our frailties, Juniper," he says. "Even the everyday person on Facebook, they get more attention when they reveal their dog just died, or they've gotten cancer, or whatever. The world runs on attention. Who gets it, and who doesn't get it. Your life is better if you get it. And I got plenty of it for Kai, and our movie. Someday he'll thank me."

"I doubt that."

"Well, someday at least he'll understand," Matthew says confidently. "I'll give him a call. We need to be copacetic for the awards campaign."

At dinner, a guy—graying dreadlocks, dressed in shorts and a tank top—sings reggae songs accompanied by a single-string guitar. He tells us between songs about performing with Ziggy Marley, then sings a haunting, harrowing version of "Redemption Song," and I wonder how it must feel, having played for thousands, to now play for a few dozen tourists, most of whom aren't even paying attention. I think about how even the best female actors with the best careers are often retired by the Industry before fifty.

But it's still a gig. You're still getting paid to do what you love. Kai is wrong about me there. I'm not just trying to live my mother's dream. I am also trying to figure out my own dream for myself. I pull out my notebook and write a little.

> *The point is to do what you love as long as you can do it as well as you can do it. That's what art demands of us. But isn't that also what your mother told you? That everything must be sacrificed in the name of the great god Art? Maybe*

I've been choosing wrong the whole time. Kai was an asshole when he said I was chasing my mom's dream, but he wasn't wrong, just like I wouldn't be wrong if I said he's running not because it's the noble or heroic thing to do, but because it's the thing he couldn't do when he was in high school. How can we escape being products of the past?

Back at my villa, I take a shower and then yet again reread the *Andromeda* script. I can hear the waves lapping against the beach just upwind. When I walk outside to see the stars, there's Kai in a beach chair, looking out at the ocean, chewing a piece of gum.

"Nothing like a nighttime hangover," he says. "Why'd you have Matthew call me?"

"Because he needed to apologize."

"Well, he did. He said he was sorry if he hurt me. I love an apology with an *if*."

The distance between us feels unbridgeable. I here—you there. I walk over and sit down on the chair next to him and look up at the star-drenched sky.

"I'm really fucking mad at you," I say at last. "You can't abandon people like that."

"Well, then we *do* have something in common, because I am really fucking mad at you," he answers.

I don't want to lie to him, or hide anything from him, so I just tell him. "They're gonna fire me from *Gods of Andromeda* if you don't come home. Todd says we're a package deal. Both of us or neither of us."

"Your priorities are so fucked up," he says. "There will be other movies for you."

"There will be," I say, "but I don't want to make other movies. I want to make this one. With you."

"I am so sorry to inconvenience you," he says, "but I'm not going home. I'm not making *Gods of Andromeda*. I'm done. I'll find something else to do. Maybe I'll become a server here."

"You're being ridiculous. You're acting insane."

"There is nothing ridiculous about aspiring to be a server. I was a server eight months ago."

"I came all the way down here to get you, and you're being—"

"I didn't ask you to come here."

"You said you loved me."

"I do love you."

"Then fucking act like it?"

"By going back into the meat grinder? No thanks. I don't love you that much."

"You're being a child."

"Fuck off." He stands up. "I don't need to be lectured by you." He looks down at me, something new and scary in his eyes. "Are you here because you care about me, or are you here because you need me to do *Gods of Andromeda*? Because if you actually cared about me, would you be asking me to go back to that world?"

With that, he leaves. It feels like he is a stranger, like I have been tasked with bringing somebody I've never met back from the Caribbean. His eyes, usually so warm and attentive, are distant now. I want to scream at him that we are supposed to be in love, but I just let him go. I go back to staring at the stars and end up falling asleep beneath them.

DAY 3

The next morning, I don't know what else to do with myself, so I read the user reviews of our movie as they come in. I read every single review on Rotten Tomatoes—from "Juniper Castillo's reach exceeds her grasp" to "It's a great movie, starring two good actors and one woman with tiny tits." I read and read, even though it makes me feel a little sick. I also read lots about Kai—mostly in praise of his performance and some in praise of his looks but also people keep using the phrase "stolen valor." I hope he's not reading these reviews.

When I was on *Star Catcher*, I knew that my castmates found me annoying. I was always trying too hard in class and on set, always raising my hand or asking for another take. They just wanted to get on with the job. Sometimes I'd obsess over the idea of putting a recording device in my costar's trailer, where they all hung out, so I could know what they said about me. Being able to read reviews from critics and users alike is like listening to the live thoughts of the world about me and my work, and I simply cannot resist it.

By lunchtime, I feel overwhelmed by the task of being Juniper Castillo, of a literal million people getting to have opinions about me. But isn't that precisely what I want, what I've been seeking this whole time? I haven't had a real hit since *Star Catcher*, and now I have one. Plus it's seen as Proper Art, as a movie worth your time.

We've made something special, and I want to celebrate that. But the only person I want to celebrate with is getting drunk at the resort bar while staring at the ocean as if conversing with it.

I see him at dinner, and ask if I can sit with him. He is drinking Red Stripe again, and nods at a seat next to his. The restaurant is crowded, and I can feel eyes on us.

"How was your afternoon?" I start.

"Living the dream. There's a good coral reef just outside the lagoon. Lots of fish."

Silence.

"This is the part where you ask me how my day was."

"How was your day?"

"A little stressful to be honest. I have this movie that came out yesterday and I want to celebrate with this boy I love, but he's mad at me."

"That sounds stressful."

"I'm also mad at him. He is sort of ruining what should be a fun weekend."

"Sounds like an asshole."

"If only it were that simple," I say. After another silence, I try again. "Kai, four days ago we were in bed together; can we at least be cordial? I shouldn't have responded the way I did at the premiere. I was stressed. I fucked up. I'm sorry. But also, I *am* practical. I *am* ambitious. I *do* want you to win all the awards for your extraordinary performance, okay? I want to win them, too. I want to get dressed up with you and go to very nice parties and then get undressed with you. I can't apologize for wanting that, and wanting to be smart and tactical in how we pursue it."

"It was hot, you knowing exactly what you wanted. It was intoxicating."

"Past tense?"

"I'm just really fucked up right now, Juniper. I don't know my tenses, okay?"

"Okay," I tell him, and he gets up from the table, leaving me to pay the check.

That night, he shows up at my villa again, looking up at the stars. He clearly wants to be near me, and I want to be near him, but we don't know how to deal with the Obstacle.

"How's the movie doing?" he asks.

"Beating expectations. Should come in around twenty-seven for the weekend."

"Which is good."

"Very good."

"How's the stolen valor narrative?" he asks.

"It's present. But it doesn't matter, Kai. People love you in the movie, and that's what matters. It's the work that matters, not the . . . everything else."

"We are literally in a business where we are defined entirely by what people think of us."

"Yeah," I say. "You always say you're not smart, but the reason it's so exhausting to argue with you is that you are in fact very smart."

I ask Kai to come inside the villa and watch a movie—I even tell him he can pick the movie—but he declines and says he'll see me in the morning. So I get a soda called Ting out of the fridge and walk down to the ocean to watch the waves lit by moonlight, breaking and receding across my little strip of beach. I can't make out any of the constellations, but I still find myself drawing lines in my mind between the stars. This was one of our first forms of art as a species: We looked up at the randomish dots in the sky and made patterns from them, and then told stories about those patterns. Maybe telling stories is what we do the way swimming in the ocean is what sea turtles do.

I don't know what it's like to be Kai, but I know something about having my life scrutinized instead of just my acting. Just before my last movie came out, I published an article about my mother's neglect. She was dead by then. It's a strange thing to disparage the name of a dead person. They can't fight back, but also, it's not like I was lying. She did drink. She did leave my brother and me for days on end. She did tell me that I'd never be anything, that I didn't want it badly enough. The post went viral, especially a part at the end I wrote about how hard it is to love others when you didn't grow up feeling loved. *I played so many roles, but the only one I ever wanted was to be her beloved daughter,* I wrote. *I realized too late that I am not a burden on those who love me, but a gift in their lives. I deeply wish my mother could have seen me as a gift. I am determined to see myself as one anyway.*

But I published that essay during a quiet movie push, a failed movie push. Kai has been strapped to a rocket ship and told by Matthew Malone, "Now go talk about this thing that you don't yet know how to talk about."

I respond to some celebratory texts from friends, including Jaya's text congratulating me on winning the weekend box office. But I can't stop thinking about Kai. You don't have to be an actor for the world to pound away at you, to render you two-dimensional, to villainize or heroize, or do both at once. But if you're an actor, everyone gets a ticket to the show.

I start wondering how much Kai's trauma will really make us at the box office. Surely there is a number. Three million? Twelve? What number is worth forcing him to sit in front of camera after camera and relive it?

Katie calls. "Hey," I say.

"Hey, I know you're in Jamaica, but the awards campaign is starting to take shape. The studio's behind it. They've got our first lunch with Academy voters scheduled for next Wednesday. You ever do this before?"

"No," I say.

"Well, it's just lunch with old people. Some guy who costarred in something forty years ago is in the Academy and gets a vote, so he shows up to this lunch and you charm him. The campaign will center around Matthew, of course, but they're going to push Kai hard, too. And you. I think getting you nominations will be a bit tougher, because it's such a strong year for women and you'll be up against more established actors, but it's good just to get you in the conversation. Matthew's going all out for this. He's not even taking a movie through the beginning of next year to focus on it. I know you've got *Gods of Andromeda* starting in two weeks, but until then I'd like to squeeze as much juice as we can; sound good?"

"Sounds good," I say.

"Okay, Junie, you're the best. Get that boy home. I'll talk to you soon."

I fucking hate being called Junie.

I watch the waves roll in and draw out. I pull up the *Andromeda* screenplay and run some lines, shouting into the ocean about the future of the Realm, and then I head up toward bed.

As I lie beneath a mosquito net looking at the screenplay on my phone, I can't shake thoughts about the campaign. Something wells up in me, and I decide to call Katie.

"I won't do a campaign with Matthew Malone," I say. "I will not go to lunches with him. I will not go to screenings with him. I will not say nice things about him. I have no interest in helping Matthew Malone in any way at any time, and I will never work with him again."

Katie fights back, as any normal publicist would, saying that it's business and there's no room for feelings in business, and that I need to think about my career and what's good for me. And then she says, "Honestly, Junie, if I'd known about Kai's abuse, I would've leaked it too. It's gold."

"You're fired," I say.

"Junie, you're being irrational. I get it. You're in love. I've been in love. It makes you crazy. What Matthew did sucked, but it's over. Kai needs to grow up a little, to be honest with you. He's still young. But you? You know how it works."

"What part of 'you're fired' was confusing?"

"Junie."

I hang up.

It takes a long time to fall asleep that night. When I finally do, I dream of Kai. I dream of his mouth on my neck, and then my cheek against his chest, feeling his breaths rise and fall beneath me.

DAY 4

Part of me wants to fly to LA and find the next thing. Let Kai recoil. Let him live his life, even if it's the end for our movie and for us. But also: I know something of what Kai is running from, and I know you can't outrun it.

I'm getting ready for the day—in pajamas, applying all the necessary serums to the face and brushing my teeth and whatnot—when I hear a voice shout, "Juniper!" I walk out to the pool, where Kai is standing, wearing board shorts and a long-sleeve T-shirt. The air is warm on my skin, a light breeze blowing. I walk up to him and hug him and feel him collapse into me. His breath smells like beer and when the hug ends, he holds on to my shoulders, just looking at me. His face is so symmetrical, his mouth so full, his nose so straight that it's easy to forget he is real, except for those eyes. The bloodshot veins around his deep green irises remind me: This is just a person, and to be a person is to be vulnerable and frail and temporary.

"Can we just watch a movie in total silence?" he asks. "Don't ask me anything and I won't ask you anything and we just watch a movie?"

"Hell yeah," I tell him.

I walk him over to the veranda, which opens up to a small patch of grass and the sea below. I show him the villa's little collection of DVDs and he chooses one, appropriately a Bond movie from the 1980s called *A View to a Kill*. If Bond has teetered between campy and earnest over the last sixty years, this is the campiest one I've seen—silly and overblown and featuring loads of anti-communist propaganda that feels, to put it charitably, dated. I lean against Kai like we always do, and he has his arm across the top of the couch, floating just above me. Throughout the movie, I keep glancing over at him.

He doesn't speak, and neither do I. This is part of what movies can be, a shared experience for people who don't know how to share experiences. Movies are something we watch together when we can't look at each other, when we don't know what to say to each other. They are a site of shared enchantment. At last, just as the action is reaching its peak absurdity, Kai says, "Well, this is not very good."

"How did people in the 1980s survive with such entertainments?" I ask.

"I'm mostly watching for the costumes," he says.

"I'm watching for the deeply developed female characters," I say.

He laughs. "I love movies. In spite of it all, I fucking love them."

After the movie, we walk over to the restaurant for some lunch. The waiter asks if he wants a Red Stripe, but he just orders a Diet Coke. He is a little more talkative now. "There are probably ways to just act," he says. "Regional theater or whatever."

"You would absolutely *crush* a local production of *Hamlet*," I tell him, and then he starts in on some *Hamlet*.

But that the dread of something after death,
The undiscovered country from whose bourn
No traveler returns, puzzles the will,

And makes us rather bear those ills we have
Than fly to others that we know not of?
Thus conscience does make cowards of us all . . .

"Wow," I say. "How much *Hamlet* do you know? Do you know more than that? Keep it coming."

"'What is a man, / If his chief good and market of his time / Be but to sleep and feed? A beast, no more.'"

"Kai, I'm not gonna lie. That's sexy as hell."

"An indecisive hero who can't quite pull the trigger on his possibly self-destructive dreams? If you like that, well, I'm your man."

"I'm sorry I didn't walk up to the front of the theater and tell everyone that Matthew Malone sucks and will do anything for a little statue that he wrongly believes will finally make him enough in the eyes of whoever didn't love him," I tell him.

"Nah, I get it. To be honest, I don't really want people to hate Matthew. People get too much from loving him. I don't need the public to think Matthew Malone sucks."

"But you need me to think he sucks," I say, realizing it as the words come out.

"Yeah," he says.

Back at the villa, we watch another movie, this one a nineties action movie called *Rush Hour*. Then I tell him I need to work out, and he offers to exercise with me, so we go to the little indoor/outdoor gym at the resort and I lift weights and do push-ups and crunches. Kai runs on a treadmill for a while. I like the way he looks sweaty and tired when he finishes, drinking a little paper cup of water as he sits on a weight bench and works his breath back into his body.

That night, Kai and I start our third film of the day, *The Pursuit of Happyness*, an old Will Smith movie about fatherhood. As we watch it, I feel Kai starting to lean toward me, wanting to be closer to me. I'm watching him watch the movie more than I'm watching the actual movie, feeling his body almost touching mine, his head close enough to me that I can smell the dried salt water on his skin. I keep glancing over at him, trying not to move my head so he won't sense me, and at some point I notice he is crying. As an actor, Kai could cry with his whole face contorting into sobs, but as a person, he cries silently, wiping away tear after tear without any fuss.

I think back to when Kai asked me what even makes a movie good. To be honest, I don't love the movie; it's a bit overwrought and melodramatic for my taste. But I find myself crying, too. Maybe a movie is good if it lets us feel things that are otherwise hard to feel. As cheesy as the movie is, it reminds me that love really does have power—maybe never as much power as it should, but enough to help us survive what we must survive. Movies can give us a window into a deeper self, that way-down place that hurts so bad we can only glimpse it in fragments.

"He fucked me up," Kai says. I look up at him. "That's what you must understand. I'd never even kissed anyone before. I had my first blow job before I had my first kiss. It strangles me. Even trying to tell you that now . . . strangles me."

I put my arm across his chest and tell him the only true thing I can think to say, the thing he told me once when I needed to hear it. "I'm sorry, and I'm here."

"I never got to figure out what I wanted, you know? Sexually, obviously, but even in other ways. I never got to develop my own desires because he defined them for me too early, too soon."

"Right."

"I'm so scared, Juniper. I'm. So. Fucking. Scared."

We cuddle on the couch until he falls asleep in my arms.

DAY 5

I wake up before him, make coffee, and then sit on the veranda to drink it. I have a splendid view of the ocean, but I keep looking over at Kai sleeping, his body hidden by a comforter, his head on a throw pillow. He looks beautiful there, and I remember reading a comment saying that his interview with *The New Yorker* came across as "thin-skinned." But really, isn't that the truth of skin?

I want Kai to be an actor because I want *Gods of Andromeda* to happen, but I also want Kai to be an actor because he is brilliant at it, because he has natural gifts. You hear some singers and think, *Well, she's just* got *it*, and Kai just has it.

But none of this is what Kai wants. It occurs to me I've never really asked Kai what he wants. For that matter, I haven't spent much time in my life thinking about what *I* want, because I've always been so busy wanting what the world wants me to want.

When he finally wakes up, I tell him, "You don't have to do *Gods of Andromeda*."

"I know," he says.

"I don't care if you run from the Industry, but I care a lot if you run from me."

"Yeah," he says. "Yeah, that part I'm really sorry for."

"Like, being abandoned by people who say they love me is . . . it's kind of, as the kids would say, *triggering*."

"Right," he says. "I know. I'm sorry. I panicked."

We walk down to the ocean together and haul a two-person kayak into the water. We kayak through the lagoon. We see another sea turtle, and Kai keeps saying, "Wow," as it swims beneath us in the transparent water.

We talk about acting, about how it felt on set and how it felt in the audition for *Andromeda*, and we talk about junketing, how it felt to be asked over and over how you survived something you haven't yet survived. When we make it back to the beach, I tell him, "You should call Ellen." I hand him my phone and he says, "Yeah. Right. Good shout."

I can't overhear most of their conversation as he paces along the beach, but he sounds meek. He keeps saying, "Yeah," and "No, right, I get it," and "I know." I do hear how the conversation ends, though. "I love you, Ellen. I'm sorry . . . I know. I know."

He walks back and sits next to me on the beach. "Did you fire Katie?"

"I did."

"Why?"

"She said what Matthew did was smart and that she would've done it if she'd known, so I fired her."

"And you told her you don't want to do a campaign with Matthew."

"Yeah."

"Even though it might cost you an Oscar nomination."

I shrug. "I'm a long shot."

"You really love me," he says. He seems surprised by it.

"I really do."

"It's very easy to say 'I love you,' but very hard to hear it, to *really* hear it."

"Kai, look at me," I say as I stand up. He's staring at me, his searching green eyes nervous and hopeful and above all *real.* "I love you, Kai. I loved you in Pittsburgh, and in LA, and in New York, and I love you in Jamaica, and I love you wherever you're headed."

"I don't want them to fire you," he says.

"There will be other movies."

"But none where you can play Agrippah, Queen of the Realm."

"True."

"And none where I can play Gavinth, your occasionally cuckolded husband."

"Also true."

"You wanna run lines?" he asks.

"I do."

At the villa, we're standing together in the hardwood-floored living room, sparring again as Agrippah and Gavinth. "You dare disturb the lawful trial of Medivh?"

"I fear I must, for—"

"Strike this woman!" he shouts. He scares me when he says it. So much anger, verging on disgust, in his voice.

"The orcs," I say. I'm more scared than I expected to be in the saying of it. "The orcs, my lord. They have laid waste to Calenbath. What is not fire is ash. Our allies are gone. Our enemies are at the gate. The future is in doubt and the past is buried in the ground, my lord. There is only time, and that time is now."

"Can it be—" He sounds so shocked, so scared.

"The time for questions has passed, Gavinth. The time of speaking has passed. We fight now, all of us. No trials. No tribes. No guilds. Only human and orc. We fight for the Realm that was." I pause, letting the emotion well up in me. "And we fight for the Realm that shall be!"

It takes a moment for the spell to break, for Gavinth to be Kai again, and for me to be Juniper.

"That was good," he says. "That's so fucking fun."

"And I don't even have to get coked up and bleed all over my shirt in this one," I point out.

"And I don't have to be heavily traumatized, just ravenous for power."

We watch a movie, one of the newer Bond films. Slicker, less corny, propulsive in its action sequences. He doesn't say much until it's over. The credits are rolling over an Adele song when he leans across the couch and closes the distance between us, kissing me first softly—inquiringly—and then with real passion. For the next little while, we make out like a couple of kids, which I guess we still sort of are.

Later, down at the beach, we're both reading when he says, "I think I want to go home."

"Where is that exactly?"

"I'm not sure," he says.

DAY 6

At breakfast the next morning, I tell Kai again that I don't care about doing *Andromeda*, because I really don't.

"Maybe you'll move to Indianapolis with me. There's a good theater company there. Better than you'd expect."

"I love you, but I don't know that I Move-to-Indianapolis-Love-You." I smile as he laughs.

"I like real theater," he says. "I like the spontaneity of it, the one-chanceness of it."

I tell him I've never done much proper theater, that I've always acted for screens, because that's what my mother wanted me to do. "I can't believe it's been more than a year," I say. "I've had two movies come out since she died."

"She'd be really proud of you."

"Yeah, a little too proud. I wish she'd loved me for being a good friend or a good sister or whatever, but it was only ever for being a good actor."

Suddenly I notice a teenage boy standing over our table. "Has anyone ever told you that you look just like Juniper Castillo?"

I tell him that I am, in fact, Juniper Castillo, and then I take a picture with him. When I sit back down, Kai asks, "That doesn't bother you? I mean, in the middle of a serious conversation."

"Without fans, there's no job."

"But you could've just told him *I'm sorry, I'm eating breakfast* or something."

"That kid is going to meet me one time in his life. I want him to have a good memory. Doesn't cost me much, and gives him a little something hopefully."

"I'm not sure it doesn't cost much," Kai answers. "But I love that about you, you always having time like that."

We eat for a while, and then I say, "You know, I realized something last night. I was thinking about how pissed I was about you leaving, and how pissed I was that Todd planned to recast the movie if you wouldn't do it and I'd lose *Gods of Andromeda*. And I just reflexively wanted it, because I am supposed to want it, because it's the studio's next tent-pole or whatever. But what I realized last night is that if you're not in *Andromeda*, I *want* them to recast it. I don't want to be in it with Charles Fucking Oldham. I don't want to be opposite some other actor. I want to be opposite you, playing with and against you. That's the movie I want to make. I spend so little time thinking about what I actually want."

"It's not like we can just take roles together for the rest of our lives. We'll work on different stuff."

"Yeah, I know, but we could take *this* together. My point is just, they tried to threaten me by saying I can't do it without you. But I don't *want* to do it without you. Without you, it's just a movie."

He looks at me. One of the nice things about Kai is you can tell when he's processing information, but you can't actually tell what he's thinking. He's too good of an actor to get an easy read on. I like that.

After working out, we make our way down to the beach. Jamie has sent me an advance readers copy of the second *Andromeda* book, so I'm reading that while Kai swims in the ocean. For an Indiana boy, he's comfortable in the water, periodically diving under the surface before reappearing again a few yards away.

As I read, I'm also thinking about what I actually want, and how to even figure out what I want. I know I want to act. I love and crave the feeling of becoming someone else, of playing with others in the hopes that our make-believe can bring forth something real. I miss being on set—not just because they tell me when to wake up and what to say, but also because I miss being part of a team creating something bigger than any individual on that team could ever make. I open my journal.

> *Someone told me just after it happened that when a parent dies, you are released from their care, for better or for worse. But I still don't feel released and expect I never will. I miss my mom. I miss when I was little, when I called her mama. I miss when I was scared and cuddled into her. I miss when I would book a commercial and she'd take me out for pizza. I miss being loved by her. She did love me in some fucked-up way, and that's the worst part of it. Not that I was abandoned by my mother, but that I was loved by her AND abandoned by her.*

Kai's shadow appears over my journal and I look up at him, dripping wet from the ocean. "God, you're gorgeous," I say.

"Can I borrow your phone?" he asks.

I unlock it and give it to him. He sits down on the beach recliner next to me and stares at me as he holds the phone to his ear. "Todd Simons, please," he says.

"Hey."

". . ."

"Todd, let me tell you what's going to happen. I'm gonna do *Andromeda*, but I will not participate in an awards campaign for *Warhol* and neither will Juniper. Also, you will pay for Juniper and me to stay here in Jamaica until we fly to Vancouver in ten days. In exchange, I will not make an Instagram video telling the world that Matthew Malone is a conniving little bitch."

". . ."

"You don't understand, Todd. We're not negotiating. I'm informing you of what's going to happen. You don't own us. The truth is, Matthew owns *you*. You need him for the next Matthew Malone joint, and the one after that, and the one after that. And me, I just realized I own Matthew."

". . ."

"*We*—and I can speak for Juniper here—don't give a flying fuck if you recast *Gods of Andromeda*."

". . ."

"Good doing business with you."

Kai hangs up. "We're making *Andromeda* together," he says.

I laugh and hug him. "I don't care if we make the movie. I care if we're together."

"I know," he says. "That's what I need. I need you to want *me*, not Gavinth."

"Oh, I want you," I tell him. I kiss him, then walk him up to the villa, where we have sex, which Kai—somewhat charmingly and somewhat cringingly—calls *making love*.

I don't feel self-conscious or even self-aware; I'm just in my body, entangled with his, in rhythm with each other such that neither of us needs to speak, only to feel each other. Afterward, I convince him to stay in bed. I turn on the TV and find a movie playing. I don't recall the film, but I remember just how it felt to watch it with Kai.

EPILOGUE

In the end, Kai and I both squeak out nominations for Independent Spirit Awards, but we get shut out of the big prizes, not least because we don't play the game. Ellen is our publicist by then, not the studio's anymore, and she revels in telling the studio, *No. No, they meant it when they said no campaign.*

Andy Warhol Never Gets Old keeps chugging along, eventually making over one hundred million in global box office. The trades call it the most profitable movie of the year, and even though most of that profit goes to the producers and Matthew, a bit of it trickles down to us, enough that with the *Star Catcher* money Mom didn't spend, I can get a little bungalow in West Hollywood.

Matthew doesn't win many awards, but he gets nominated for all of them. On one late-night show after his Oscar nod, he says, "I always wanted to make stuff that people would actually watch, but it turns out you can make films people watch *and* films where nothing blows up." He is always careful to extend credit to us, to say what geniuses we are, and even once mentions how much we sacrificed in the process, without acknowledging who made us the sacrifice.

We ride out the success of *Andy Warhol Never Gets Old* mostly in Vancouver, where we prep for *Gods of Andromeda* by eating lots of grilled chicken and working out for 150 minutes each day. We keep separate apartments for the movie, because we don't want the world to know. We want a secret, Kai especially—a truth that belongs only to us.

In Vancouver, I start going to therapy and eventually Kai and I do some therapy together. In one of our first sessions, Kai cries while telling me all about the stuff that actually happened with him and the teacher and the testimony he had to give, and he throws up in the middle of it, and the therapist says, "You don't have to say anything that makes you feel unsafe," and Kai says, "You don't understand. There's no going back. You don't get to feel safe again."

And that's the truth of being an adult, I guess, insofar as we are adults. We've both had the kind of childhood where you learn too soon that you aren't safe, that you never were, that the people tasked with protecting you can't, or won't, because they want something more from you than mere love, which is all children really have to offer.

I start clashing with Brian Arawas almost the moment we begin rehearsing—he wants an Agrippah vastly more dismissive of Gavinth than I think the script calls for—but I make his movie anyway, because that's the job, and in spite of it all, I enjoy the job. Acting against Kai is thrilling, although we are now part of a bigger cast, a proper ensemble, which dilutes the experience a little bit. There is quite a lot of acting in front of a green screen, with markers attached to our faces to trace facial expressions so that we can be CGI'ed into other worlds, and to some extent other bodies. I like the work, though. I always like to work. It's still too much of how I measure my worth, but at least now I know that when I conflate my career with my self, I'm doing both a disservice.

Then comes March of 2020, and the movie gets shut down. The world changes, and Hollywood changes.

When they send us home from the movie, Kai and I initially stay in my little bungalow, but we get cabin fever, so we drive halfway across the country and rent a place in Indianapolis, just a few blocks away from his parents. The house backs up to a paved trail, so we can run every morning together and be outside, and it's close to this huge cemetery called Crown Hill, where you can walk for miles with plenty of social distance. Some mornings while I drink my coffee, deer show up in our backyard. I sort of fall in love with Indianapolis despite myself.

I like Kai's parents a lot—more than he does, really—and they love me, too. His mother starts calling me her third kid, and I don't mind it. By the time the movie starts up again with daily Covid tests, I'm sad to leave Indianapolis, but in the end home is as much who you're with as where you are, and I'm with him.

On our *Andromeda* junket, we stick together. Kai politely says, "Next question" whenever asked about his abuse, and I answer questions about my mom with a boilerplate that's true, but not especially intimate. The junket is even longer than the *Warhol* one—three continents—but we survive it.

That's the wonder of it all. You survive. It's a dirty lie that what doesn't kill you makes you stronger, or that everything happens for a reason, but this much is true: You survive.

The miracle of love is that Kai loved the Juniper he met in that Pittsburgh hotel, and he also loves this me. The miracle of love is that yes, I am here and you are there, but the door is ajar. We get through that door with empathy, with imagining, with acting. We play our way through it with music and dance and art. We break down the door with love. We love others until they can love themselves, until we can love ourselves.

And all along the way, the future remains yours, ineluctably and irrevocably. You can cling to that future, as long as you need to, until with work and with time the future becomes present and the present past. You survive, and you survive, until one day, you survived.

ACKNOWLEDGMENTS

Most people who end up with any modicum of fame choose a public life. They may regret that choice, or experience negative impacts from that choice, but still: The choice was made. That's often not the case for their families, so I'd like to begin by thanking my wife, Sarah, and my children, Henry and Alice, for their love and forbearance. The adventure of being here with the three of you is the greatest joy in my life. Sarah, thank you for being my first and most cherished reader, and for all our collaborations down through the years. I should note, also, that Sarah is a Warhol scholar, and I simply could never have written this (or any) book without her. *Andy Warhol Enterprises*, a book she co-edited, was an essential source for me, but also every time I had a question about Andy, I had the good fortune of being able to shout it down the hall.

I'm also grateful to my brother and sister-in-law, Hank and Katherine, and my parents, Mike and Sydney, for loving me up into and through this world. Our best friends, Chris and Marina Waters, have also been steadfast companions through some very strange days since we first met back in 2007.

On the publishing front, I have been exceptionally lucky to publish with Julie Strauss-Gabel at Dutton for my entire career. It's been nine years since I last wrote a novel, and in that time, Julie never asked when the next book was coming, or why the next book was a history of tuberculosis, or anything like that. Instead, she has nurtured my writing and indulged my creative wanderings for now more than twenty years. My agent, Jodi Reamer, has supported me with acumen and passion. My longtime producing partner, Rosianna Halse Rojas, read every draft of this book with a copyeditor's eye and a great reader's generosity of spirit.

At Penguin Random House, Anna Booth, Cassie Vu, Ilana Jacobs, Rob Farren, Natalie Melius, Vanessa Robles, Kaitlin Kneafsey, Abby Synnes, Kim Ryan, Helen Boomer, Emily Romero, Christina Colangelo, Bri Lockhart, Alex Garber, Carmela Iaria, Trevor Ingerson, Maggie Searcy, Kelsey Fehlberg, Jen Loja, Jocelyn Schmidt, and Stephanie Sabol all made essential contributions to the book you're reading.

I've been so much luckier in Hollywood than almost all authors, and for that I am deeply indebted to Wyck Godfrey, Marty Bowen, Isaac Klausner, and Laura Quicksilver. They've paddled my stories through some tough rapids, and also provided essential feedback on the Hollywood aspects of this novel, as did my longtime film agent, Kassie Evashevski. Thanks also to Erin Siminoff and Elizabeth Gabler for their support. I'm also so grateful to all the actors, directors, and crew who have worked on adaptations of my books, and I'm so appreciative for all they've taught me about their craft. I want to thank Nat Wolff especially, who always seems to call me when I most need to hear from a friend.

Among early readers, I must thank Stuart and Ann-Marie Hyatt, Laura Sandahl, Paige Lewis, and Kaveh Akbar. The wonderful Ed Coleman introduced me to that Dickinson poem. Ilene Cooper and Bill Ott made everything possible.

On some of the hardest days of my life, Elyse Marshall Pfeiffer has been there for and with me. This book is dedicated to her because with her friendship and guidance over the last sixteen years, many of those hard days have also been lovely ones.

I have tried here to write about the machine that turns private experience into public expression and then commodifies that expression. Much is lost in that process, and many are hurt. Still, I love books. I love movies. I love art. They help me to feel what there is to feel while I am yet here. To everyone who makes art, in spite and because of it all: Thanks.